AMY
CHELSEA
STACIE
DEE

A MESSAGE FROM CHICKEN HOUSE

Amy Chelsea Stacie Dee is the rivetingly scary story of a kidnapping, a captivity and – worst of all – the dark secret kept by one of its victims. Mary G. Thompson takes you beyond the nightmare to its consequences, and keeps you questioning: what really did happen to Amy and Dee? But despite the horror and suspense, this is also a tale about the awesome power of friendship and family to survive anything, and to brave everything. Stories like this are why we read novels.

BARRY CUNNINGHAM
Publisher
Chicken House

AMY
CHELSEA
STACIE
DEE

MARY G. THOMPSON

Chicken House

2 Palmer Street, Frome, Somerset BA11 1DS
chickenhousebooks.com

Text © Mary G. Thompson 2016

First published in the United States by G. P. Putnam's Sons,
an imprint of Penguin Random House LLC, New York.

First published in Great Britain in 2017
Chicken House
2 Palmer Street
Frome, Somerset BA11 1DS
United Kingdom
www.chickenhousebooks.com

Mary G. Thompson has asserted her right under the Copyright, Designs
and Patents Act 1988 to be identified as the author of this work.

Cover and interior design by Helen Crawford-White
Cover photograph © Emma Delves-Broughton / Trevillion Images
Typeset by Dorchester Typesetting Group Ltd
Printed and bound in Great Britain by CPI Group (UK) Ltd, Croydon CR0 4YY

The paper used in this Chicken House book is made from
wood grown in sustainable forests.

1 3 5 7 9 10 8 6 4 2

British Library Cataloguing in Publication data available.

PB ISBN 978-1-910655-81-8
eISBN 978-1-911077-31-2

For Linda Heurgué

1.

I am the last one off the bus. It was only half-full to begin with, of shaggy-looking young men and older ladies and one mother with two rowdy kids. The mother is the last to go before me. She yells at the older boy in Spanish and then turns around and rolls her eyes at me. I smile back without even thinking about it, sharing a moment with this woman who I've never seen before, sharing something just because we're women. Because she saw something kindred in me. My smile fades, and the kids race away from their mother towards the gas station/convenience store that serves as a bus stop in this tiny town.

I watch the drizzling rain roll down my window. This is it. I've been on the bus for hours, and I haven't had a chance to pee, and I'm starving. And if I don't get off in the next ten minutes, the bus will start going again, and it will take me away from Grey Wood, Oregon, and on to the next town. And maybe that's where I should go, anywhere but here. Anywhere but Amy's home.

'Isn't this your stop?' says the bus driver, a burly man with a gut spilling over his eighties jeans. He wears big plastic glasses and smells like cigarettes even from back where I am, in the middle.

'Yeah,' I say.

He stands, raises his arms, and stretches, making a yowling sound like you make when you've just woken up. 'Wish we'd finally get some sun,' he says. 'It's frickin' June, right?'

I don't answer. I stand up and grab my cloth Safeway shopping bag, which contains everything I own in this world. *Come on, Chelsea*, I think. *Move.* If I stay on the bus, where will I end up? How will I live? I have no money and no identification, and I'm only sixteen years old. There's no way I could pass for older, with my mismatched old clothes and the haircut I did myself.

An old lady climbs back on the bus. The driver has to sit down in his seat to let her pass, and I know I can't wait any longer. I walk straight, past the driver, and down the steps.

'Good luck,' he says from behind me.

'Thanks,' I say. I'm shivering, and not because I'm suddenly being pelted with good old-fashioned Oregon drizzle. I walk towards the convenience store. I remember this as a 7-Eleven, but now it's something else, a 'Publik Mart'. Amy used to come here to buy candy on the days

2

when she went with her mom to work. As I look past the store, I can see the cross street where the post office was, where Mom worked. I wonder if she still works there, if she's there right now. But today is Sunday, so no, she wouldn't be there. She'd be at home. Assuming home is in the same place.

'Getting back on?' a voice says.

I jump. It's the lady with the two kids, who are already running up the bus stairs.

'No,' I say. 'This is my stop.'

'Ah, happy landings, then.' She smiles at me.

'Safe travels.' I try to smile back, but I'm not used to talking to people, and I'm afraid it looks more like a grimace.

'*Gracias.*' She gets on the bus.

I take a few steps away, and I watch as the doors close and the bus turns on and exhaust spits out the back. The bus driver waves at me, and then the bus huffs and puffs and pulls out of the parking lot. I'm standing here, right where Amy used to stand, and there's no going on or going back.

2.

The jacket that I'm wearing isn't mine. It's too big, and I'm drowning in it as I trudge down the sidewalkless side of River Road. It probably makes me look even younger than my homemade haircut. Also, it's pink, because pink is Stacie's colour. Purple is my colour, and that's why I'm wearing a purple T-shirt, and my jeans have little purple patches on the pockets. My shoes are a dark red, because I guess Kyle couldn't find any purple shoes at Walmart or wherever he went the last time he bought us clothes. That bothered me at first, but I've been wearing them a while now. Maybe red is kind of my colour, too. Is it OK to have more than one colour? Amy had lots of colours, I remember. Amy used to go down to the river, right there where I'm passing, and she used to wear khaki shorts, just like her

4

dad's shorts, and she loved blue. Blue shirt and khaki shorts and white sneakers. That's what she was wearing that last day, when she and Dee went to wade in the river.

Did I just happen to walk by here, or did I come here on purpose? This is the way home, so I must have known it was coming. There's a little path from the street down to the creek, and there are people down there. I can see them through the trees, which are so thin. I don't remember them being thin. I remember them being large and green and hiding us when we wanted to pretend we were in another world, a world with just us and the ducks and the crayfish. And aliens. I dreamt up aliens that landed on that rock in the middle of the water. Without letting myself think about it, I walk down the little path. I stand at the end of it, watching the man and the boy on the left who are trying to fish, even though my dad used to say this spot was terrible for fishing. There are also two girls feeding the ducks to the right.

I stare at the rock, and my hand goes into my Safeway bag, and I pull out the doll. She has blonde hair, and she's wearing a pink skirt and a pink shirt. She's been beat up over the years, so there are scratches on her face, and her hair sticks out from her head at a weird angle. But she still has her blue eyes, larger than life, staring at me. I hold her against my chest, feel her hard plastic press into my breastbone.

I remember Amy and Dee sitting on that rock together. It was a struggle to fit them both, but they did it. Whenever there was only room for one, whatever it was, they always made it work for two.

One of the girls sees me. She holds out a piece of bread. 'Want to feed the ducks?' she asks. And as she looks straight at me, I see that she has big blue eyes. My chest seizes, and I shove the doll back into the bag and push it down beneath the clothes.

'No. Thanks anyway,' I say. I turn and push my way back down the path. I'm not looking where I'm going, and I get scraped by a big blackberry vine. As I make it back to the street, a car whizzes past, and I almost scream. I'm not used to nearly stepping into cars. Because nobody used to come where we lived. There didn't used to be anyone but us.

Always *us*, never me. I'm not supposed to be here without her, anywhere without her. But I can't stay here on the edge of the street, so close to the river, with nothing but my Safeway bag. I can't stay, so I keep moving.

I run my hand through my hair, which is getting soggy with the drizzle, and adjust the bag on my shoulder. I keep as far to the left of the road as possible and walk in the mud of the shoulder, listening to the creek flow beside me. It's weird walking down here, because we used to always ride our bikes. So it feels like it takes forever to get to the turn in the road, where it curves away from the creek and heads to the right, and then it seems to take even longer, like hours and hours, to walk two more blocks, to where River Road crosses with Oak Street. But once I turn the corner on to Oak, it takes no time at all. I'm in the driveway, and it has the same mailbox, the one shaped like a tiny house, and it's tilted a little on its post just like it always was, and it has the name across the bottom in carved wooden letters: MacArthur. Amy drew little toenails on the *A*'s feet, and the outlines of them are still there.

There's a car in the driveway, but I don't recognize it. It isn't new, just different. It's white like our old one, but it's smaller. Like it wasn't meant for a family of two parents and two kids. *Maybe they're not here,* I think. But if they moved away, why would the mailbox still say MacArthur? I stand in the driveway, staring at the house. It's painted light blue, a fading blue that hasn't been redone in a while. I don't remember it looking that shabby before, but I can't be sure what I remember. It seems smaller to me now, too. I picture the insides, the living room, the hallway with all the bedrooms: first Jay's, then Amy's, then Mom and Dad's. I picture the cream-coloured carpet that Mom just put in, that she was so excited about. That she saved up for. That she argued with Dad about over the cost. Only she didn't just put it in, did she? She might have changed it again by now, and inside, the house might not be anything like I remember.

The living room curtains flutter, and a face peers out.

My heart leaps. Suddenly it's beating fast, a million times a minute. Sweat soaks my T-shirt. Is it her? I can't tell if it's her from here. I have to move closer. *I could still run away*, I think. I could get on another bus. Except that I have six dollars left, and six dollars won't buy me dinner. My stomach twists, and I'm glad I haven't eaten all day, because I don't know if I could hold it in. I walk forward, and the face leaves the window, and it's as if the driveway is a magic

7

portal, because suddenly I'm standing in front of the door, and I hold up my fist as if I'm going to knock, but I don't. I stand there with my fist in the air and my stomach twisting into knots.

The door opens, and she's standing there. She's cut her hair, too, and it's part grey now. But it's her. She has dark brown eyes, just like mine.

'Yes?' she says.

I open my mouth, but nothing comes out.

She stares at me. She folds her hand around the door-knob, as if she's about to close it.

'Mom,' I choke out, 'it's me. It's . . .' Her name is on the tip of my tongue, but I can't say it. It's like the name has been erased from the world, like it's gone.

She stares at me, and her hand leaves the doorknob. Both her hands hang in the air. Her fingers twitch as if she's grabbing on to something that isn't there.

'It's . . .' I choke on the name. It won't come out.

'Amy,' Mom says. 'Amy. Amy! Amy! Amy!' She grabs me, pulls me into a hug, hangs on to my back. 'Amy! Amy! Amy! Amy!' She can't stop saying it. She's sobbing. She holds on to me. She's squeezing me so hard that I can't breathe, but there's nothing I can do about it. My arms are around her back, too, but I don't squeeze; I let them lie there. I can feel the bones of her back beneath my fingers. The bones of my mother's back.

'Amy, Amy, Amy,' she sobs.

'Mom,' I say. Because that's one name that's easy. That's one name that was never gone.

3.

Mom spits out the questions as she cooks. She's making Amy's favourite meal, macaroni and cheese. Her hands shake as she grates the cheese, and I'm afraid she's going to cut herself. I want to help her, but I don't know if I can move. I sit at the table, my Safeway bag on the seat next to me. The same dining room table, the same chairs. And even though she's older, the same mom. She stands in front of the stove, with her head tilted to the right and that tiny gap where her hair parts. Freckles dot the arm that holds the wooden spoon. I want to reach out and touch them.

'What happened?' she asks. 'Where have you been? Where's Dee? Who was it? How did it happen? How did you get away? Why now? Do you want to take a shower? There's a desk in your room now, but we can move the air bed in until we get you a real bed. Are you tired?'

I don't answer any of the questions. I can't answer any questions. I *am* tired, so tired I want to collapse and never get up again. But my mind spins; my heart beats.

'It's too soon, isn't it? Never mind. We'll eat. You can talk about it when you're ready. Your dad. We have to call your dad.' She turns around. Her shaking hand knocks the wooden spoon against the edge of the pot. 'He . . . he moved to Colorado. Boulder.'

'Oh,' I say.

'But he'll come back,' she says. 'He'll be on the next plane.'

'OK.' The last time I saw my dad was another Sunday. *Watch out for cars,* he said. And we did. We watched out for them. I thought he would be here. There was never a time when there was Mom without Dad, Dad without Mom.

'We have to call Aunt Hannah,' Mom says. She puts the dish in the oven, and she pushes it so hard that it slides all the way to the back. 'Do you want to take a shower?'

'I'll wait,' I say.

Mom pulls a phone out of her pocket. 'What am I going to tell her?'

I shake my head.

'I have to tell her something,' Mom says.

I look down at my bag. I want to pull out the doll, to run my fingers over her hair, to look into her eyes, which are blue just like Stacie's. Only they're not *just* like hers; they're darker, a true, pure blue. I run my hand over my neck, across my face. I cover my eyes with my hand and will the room away. But Mom is still there, and so are her questions. So is her voice, talking to Aunt Hannah on the phone.

Mom tells Aunt Hannah that I'm back. She repeats Amy's name over and over again, just like before. And then she says Dee. Dee Dee Dee Dee. The name floats in the air, and I cover my left ear with my left hand, but if I want to cover both ears, I'll have to take my hand off of my face. So I hear it with one ear, Mom saying she doesn't know, no police yet, Amy won't talk, she needs time.

'Amy, honey?' Mom says. She puts a hand on my shoulder. I let it sit there, but I don't move. I hear the word Lon, my dad's name, and Amy, and yes I'm sure. She's my daughter. And she doesn't know, and Dee, and not yet, no police, and *I don't know, Lon,* and then there's silence.

The kitchen timer dings, and I let my hands fall to my lap, and I watch my mom take the macaroni and cheese out of the oven. She spoons it on to a plate for me and pours ketchup so that it makes a little round pool, and she knocks the salt and pepper shakers together as she sets them on the table.

I take one bite, and my stomach untwists, and I take another bite and another, and pretty soon I've eaten almost the whole dish.

Mom is watching me with her eyes wide and sad. She looks at my raw, scraped-up hands. My fingers hurt as I curl them to hold the fork, but I pretend I can't feel it.

'Nobody starved me,' I say. 'I just haven't eaten all day.'

'Oh. Good.' I can see the questions on her face, more who and where and when and why. But she doesn't ask them. Because she loves Amy. She would do anything for Amy, like any mom. If Mom thinks it's best for Amy if she gives her space and doesn't ask all the things she wants to ask, then that's what she'll do. That's what any mom would do.

'Where's Jay?' I ask. He was eight years old then, and I remember his round face and his big brown eyes, and the way he ran and ran, and how much he wanted to come with us, and how we wouldn't let him. Because he was a pain in our butts, the way he was always underfoot. He said he just wanted some blackberries, so Dee said we'd bring some back, and Amy rolled her eyes, and Dee glared at Amy, and Amy promised. *We'll bring you some stupid blackberries, OK?*

'He's with his friends,' Mom says. 'But he's supposed to be back by six for dinner. I . . . I could call him, too.'

'No,' I say. 'I'll wait.'

There's a pounding on the door, and then the door bursts open, and Aunt Hannah runs into the room, and she looks at me, and just like Mom, she doesn't recognize me at first, but then she does. She takes a step towards me as if she's going to grab me and hug me like Mom did, but she's looking behind me, to either side of me, around the room, as if she's looking for someone, and she keeps looking, even though it's obvious that there's no one else here.

'Where is she?' she asks. She looks from me to Mom.

Neither of us says anything. I look at the ground.

'Where is she?' she yells.

Mom stands. 'Hannah, she needs time.'

12

'*Where is she?*' my aunt cries. Tears stream down her face. '*Where is she?*'

I cover my face with my hand. I can't look at her, so desperate. I know how she feels, what she wants, what she's lost.

'*Where is she?*' Her voice echoes in my head, and so does the answer. The words I can't say, the images I can't see, the truth I can't even let myself think.

And then the cops come.

I'm in Amy's old room, sitting in the desk chair.

A woman in a black uniform asks me questions in a soft voice.

What is your name?

'Amy MacArthur.'

How old are you?

'Sixteen.'

Is Dee Springfield alive?

. . .

Amy, I don't want to hurt you. I don't need to know the whole story right now. I just need to know if Dee is alive. I need to know so that we can help her.

. . .

If you don't want to say it, you can nod. You can nod yes or no. Can you do that?

I keep myself still. I don't move my head at all. I stare at the lady's stomach. I watch her uniform shirt flutter as she breathes in and out.

Just a yes or no, honey.

. . .

Where is the person who did this?

Was it a man?

Was it more than one person?

Amy, I want to help you. I want to make sure you're safe.

'I'm safe,' I say.

Is he dead? Is that why you're safe?

Did he promise not to find you?

Did he make you promise not to tell?

I stare at her stomach until she takes her stomach away, and then I'm staring at the wall. There's a framed picture of Amy and Jay when Amy was ten, the studio kind of picture with a weird coloured background, and their faces are frozen into awkward smiles. Amy has long hair, and it's a lighter brown with tinges of blonde still running through it. I remember when we took that picture. It was the last summer Amy was here.

Mom comes into the room. She puts her arm around my shoulders and brushes the greasy hair out of my face. 'The police want you to talk to someone,' she says. 'This person can help you tell them what they need to know so they can find Dee.' She gets down on her knees and looks up at me, just like she used to do when I was little. 'And if they can't help her, then they need to know that, too. Aunt Hannah needs to know that. And Lee. They both need to know what happened to her.'

I stay where I am, and another woman comes in. She's wearing jeans and she looks a little frazzled, like someone who just got called somewhere on a Sunday and doesn't know what she's getting into. She sits on the floor, because there's nowhere else in this room to sit. And then she tells me she's a psychologist, and she works with victims of abuse and sexual assault and kidnapping and all kinds of things. And everything I'm feeling is normal.

I stare over her head.

She talks, and she asks. And she talks.

'I'm tired,' I say. And it's true, but it's also a lie, because my heart is still pounding. Sweat pours from my skin, and sitting still is the hardest thing I've ever done. Sitting still and being quiet, when there's so much inside I want to say.

She leaves, and the cops leave, and Mom comes into the room with Jay trailing behind her, fourteen-year-old Jay, who looks nothing like the version I remember. He has a thin face now. He's beanpole skinny, with a buzz haircut and a baggy T-shirt, and he's about six feet tall if he's an inch.

He has the same eyes, though. Huge and brown and staring from his new face.

'I'm sorry I never brought the blackberries,' I blurt.

He stares. His jaw clenches, and his whole body tenses as if he's about to run.

'I'm sorry,' I say. I don't know why I say that, except that I can see he's hurt. I can see that it was more than blackberries I took from him, more that's changed than his height.

'Honey . . .' Mom says. I don't know if she's talking to him or me, but I know she wants to close the space between us. Always, even before, she wanted us to be close, to not fight, to take care of each other. But the three feet between Jay and me is a chasm.

'You were OK,' he says. His eyes are filling up with tears, and I see the little boy that I remember. I want to step forward and hug him, but he's leaning away.

'I'm OK,' I say.

'All this time. We thought you were dead, and you were *fine*.'

I stare at him, searching for something I can say.

Tears spill from his eyes, and he almost bumps into Mom as he speeds back through the bedroom door. Down the hall, another door slams.

'He needs time,' Mom says.

'It's OK,' I say, but it isn't. I imagined seeing him again. I would give him those blackberries. I would take him into my arms and hug him. I would tell him how sorry I was for all the times I snapped at him or ignored him. I would tell him I loved him. But he thinks I didn't try to come home, didn't care that they all thought I was dead. I can't blame him, because he doesn't know. But he's wrong. He's so totally and completely wrong.

'He'll be OK,' Mom says. 'Now that you're back, we all will.' She wraps her arms around me again.

I close my eyes. I wish I could erase all the hurt I just saw in Jay. I wish my dad was here and not in Colorado. But at the same time, I don't know if I could handle them here, loving me, either. My mom's love is already so much, it's overwhelming. It radiates from her body, almost explosive. I love her, but it's too much. I'm not ready for all this love for Amy, who I haven't been in so long.

Sweat still pours from my skin, and I need space. I need

time to let this all in, to figure out where I am and what my name is and how to live here. I want to lie down in the dark and the silence and let Amy go, and be Chelsea again. Or be neither – no name and no thoughts and no one I have to love or who loves me. I want out of this, but I can't get out. I chose to come home, and I'm staying here.

4.

ONE KIDNAPPED GIRL RETURNS
Fate of second girl unclear

JUNE 13

AMY MACARTHUR has returned. In a case that rocked the county and made national headlines, the girl, now 16, and her cousin Dee Springfield, who would now be 18, were seen being forced into a vehicle by an unidentified man six years ago. According to Grey Wood police, MacArthur appeared at her mother's door Sunday afternoon with no warning and no explanation. Police are now reopening the investigation into the girls' disappearance.

'Miss MacArthur was unable to explain her whereabouts for the past six years,' said a police spokesman. 'This makes it even more important that anyone with information about the kidnapping comes forward.' The spokesman did not provide any information about MacArthur's mental or physical health, except to say that she is not being treated at a hospital at this time. Anyone with information about the case is asked to call 1-800-555-9192.

The next morning, I'm wrapped in a towel in Amy's bedroom. My hair smells like apples. Mom offers me her clothes, jeans and a T-shirt. She stares at the scar on my left arm that goes halfway from my elbow to my shoulder, the one from when Kyle threw me into the kitchen counter. Her mouth moves like she wants to ask, like she's already asking, even though she can't say the words.

'It looks worse than it is,' I say.

She keeps staring, holding the clothes.

'I have clothes,' I say.

Mom takes a breath, then holds up my jeans. 'These need to be washed,' she says.

'I only wear purple,' I say. I take the jeans out of her hand.

'Let me wash them,' she says. She takes them back. She puts them in a pile with the rest of my clothes, which I've already worn several days in a row. I guess she still washes her clothes after just one wearing. She doesn't realize what a waste it is, how you wear out your clothes faster that way.

'Do you have anything purple?' I ask.

She hesitates, but doesn't question me. 'Sure. I think so. Let me check.' I wait, and she comes back with a pair of purple jogging shorts and a ratty old sweatshirt, which isn't purple, but it's white with purple letters. I'm not comfortable, but I know she's going to wash my clothes. At least the purple letters are big. They say 'Grey Otters'. The Otters were the Grey Wood High School mascot back when Mom went there, but it changed to the Grey Wood Turkeys when I was a kid. Mom used to say otters were a lot better than turkeys. She used to strut around town wearing this sweatshirt, like she was making a huge statement, defying the oppressive overlords of the school board.

'Thanks,' I say. I take it from her. 'You sure? What if I spill something on it? You can't get a classic like this anywhere.'

She bursts into tears.

'I'm sorry,' I say.

She grabs me and hugs me. My towel starts to fall, and I grab it, dropping the clothes.

'You remember,' she says.

'The big Otters versus Turkeys battle? Of course I remember,' I say.

'I wasn't sure,' she says, pulling away from me again.

I'm not even sure. I remember, but it wasn't me who listened to Mom and Dad talk about the glory days of the Mighty Otters and how they defeated the Pleasant Valley Lions in the big game. It was Amy. Amy saw Mom walking around town in that sweatshirt, not me. And it wasn't Amy who came back. But no mom wants to hear that. She wants to hear that her Amy is back and she's all right.

'I never forgot,' I say.

The story I used to tell pops into my head. *Once upon a time, there was an otter and a turkey. An otter is an animal that lives in the water. It has slick brown hair and whiskers, and it slides around faster than water going down the drain. A turkey is a big bird with lots of feathers and a wattle hanging down from its neck. A wattle is like a lot of skin, right here. Well, even though the turkey had wings, he couldn't fly. So when he saw the otter whizzing down the river, he thought, I want to be just like that.* I can't think about that now. I shouldn't think about that ever.

'I'll let you get dressed,' Mom says. She stops at the door and turns around. 'We kept all your things. We can get them out of storage if you want. Your dad and I, we just couldn't . . .' She closes her eyes, and it's like when I put my hand over my face yesterday. It's like she wishes she could go away. Tears are still leaking out, and I can see her struggle, how she wants to stop them.

'I can get them later,' I say. 'I don't care about that stuff.' And I don't. I just want her to stop crying, because she hates that. When she cried, she'd always say she was sorry, like it embarrassed her. She never told me I shouldn't cry, but I learnt it, too. I learnt to be strong, and I know it helped me. I know I'm here partly because of that.

Mom opens her eyes and takes a breath. 'We kept your room the same for a while. Almost a year. But it was

21

haunting me. It was like you were in there, needing me, and I couldn't help.'

'Mom . . .' I don't know what to say. I tried not to think about what she must be feeling. I tried, but I *did* think about it. Every day, I thought about it and pushed it back. I couldn't let it through, or I would never have got out of bed. I would never have eaten and worked and put one foot in front of another. And there are more days to get through. Today and tomorrow and the next day.

'It was a long time before I stopped hoping.' She wipes a tear away, and I can see it all in her face, how she's thinking like I am. *Keep it inside. Keep upright.* 'I kept the key in my purse – to the storage unit – for years. I still know where it is. Any time you want, we can go.'

'It's OK, Mom.' I want to step forward and hug her again, but I don't. I can't handle it.

'It's not OK,' she says. 'I should have *known* you were alive. I should have found you.'

'I'm home now.'

She steps through the door. 'I should let you get dressed. I'll be right out here.'

'I'm OK.' She needs to hear that. I need to make sure she believes it. I need to learn how to smile and pretend, how to make it true again.

'I love you so much, Amy.' She gives me a last look and closes the door behind her, and that's when I remember the right response. The thing I haven't been allowed to say for so long.

'I love you, too,' I whisper. I stand there for a long time

holding my towel up, feeling the breath that makes the words. 'I love you, Mom,' I say, louder. She isn't there to hear me, but I'll tell her. Before it becomes too late again.

5.

My dad is an old man. His hair has gone almost completely grey, and he's gained so much weight that his belly spills over his slacks. He used to be skinny. He used to pull his pants up and tighten his belt. He's six feet tall and now it seems like he's three feet wide. He walks slowly, with a hesitation I don't remember.

I stand when he comes through the door, and we stare at each other. We examine each other's changes. He's thinking that I used to be a little girl, a ten-year-old kid with long brown-mixed-with-blonde hair, and now I have breasts and a teenage face and short brown hair that looks like I cut it myself with kitchen scissors. I'm five feet and five point five inches tall, and I'm thin but I'll never be as skinny as that little girl with no breasts. I'm more person all over than I used to be, but the way he looks at me like he doesn't know me, like he's not sure if I'm me at all, it's like I'm also less.

And I'm wondering what happened. Because the last thing I remember, Mom and Dad were happy together. Dad owned his own construction business and Mom worked part-time at the post office, and we were a perfect family.

Dad hugs me, and he cries, but not loudly like Mom cried. He doesn't say Amy's name. He just lets the tears roll down his cheeks. I wrap my arms around his back, and it's nothing like it was before. He's soft, and my arms don't connect, and he has come from outside our house with a suitcase.

But who am I to complain? I'm the one who left. Even though I didn't want to leave, I did. And I only tried to come home once. It comes rushing back, that day only six days after Kyle took us, and I suck in a breath, try to push it away. I was going to try again. If it had worked out, I wouldn't have come home alone. I should have tried harder. If I'd tried harder, Dad would never have left Mom and Jay.

'I guess we've both changed a lot,' he says.

I nod. I want to say how sorry I am, but that would only bring more questions.

'I don't do the hard work myself now. I guess you can see that.' He laughs, and the corners of his mouth turn up, and he shows his teeth, including the chipped one in front. I remember that, and I watch it. You couldn't fake that, if you were trying to fool me. So it's my dad, sitting here on the love seat next to me.

'Why Colorado?' I ask.

He can't look straight at me. 'It was hard,' he says. He closes his mouth.

'It's all right,' I say. 'You can say it. You broke up because I was gone.'

'When you love someone that much,' he says, 'it's not the same without them.'

I think about Jay, who is still in his room and hasn't come out since yesterday. When Mom knocked on his door to tell him that Dad was here, he didn't answer. This is why he hates me. I destroyed everything. And I should have tried harder.

I rub my left arm over my T-shirt, where the scar is. That was just for saying *someone will find us*.

'We searched for months,' he says. 'Everyone in town searched. And when the cops gave up, we kept searching. We never wanted to believe we wouldn't find you. We never meant to give up.' He bursts into tears now.

But I did. I meant to give up. I made the decision not to try again.

'I'm so sorry,' he says. 'I'm so sorry.' He wipes his face with both hands.

'It's all right,' I say. My eyes are filling with tears, too. I don't remember ever seeing my dad cry, and it's my fault he's crying. Not Kyle's. Mine.

'I want to know what happened,' he says. 'Your mom didn't want me to ask. She said you need to see the shrink but . . .'

'I can't tell you,' I say. This is the first time I've said anything in response to that question. There's something about my dad crying. It's like, moms are supposed to cry, but not dads. I owe my dad something.

'The police will help,' he says. 'They'll find him. Whatever he threatened you with, it won't happen.'

I say nothing.

'Please.'

I put my hand over my face.

When I was Amy, my best friend was my cousin Dee. She was two years older than me, but she didn't act like it. Between her and her sister, Lee, who was my age, she was the most fun. Lee was already into make-up and fixing her hair, and she was afraid to get dirty, but even though Dee liked dressing up, too, she still liked to ride her bike around town and go hiking through the woods and wading in the creek looking for crayfish. That summer when I was ten and she was twelve, we spent almost every day together. We loved being outside, and we loved the water, so we spent a lot of time at the creek. There was one spot that we liked the best because it had a cool sandbar, and from there you could walk up and down the river, and it was like we were in our own little separate world.

Dee was really bubbly and friendly most of the time. If someone else was down at the river, she would always talk to them. She talked so much that some people thought she was annoying, which was probably why I was her best friend – the girls at school kind of shunned her. It made her sad, and she'd cry about it, but then five minutes later, she'd be her old bubbly self. That was how Dee was. She never held a grudge, never remembered why she was mad.

So that day in June, I knew something was wrong. She was quiet the whole ride to the river. Usually she'd be yelling at me over the wind, chattering away about anything and everything, but that day we just rode, and it wasn't until we were down on the sandbar, trailing our bare feet in the water, that she burst into tears.

'Dee! What's wrong?'

'I . . . oh my god, Amy, it's so gross.'

I couldn't imagine what she was talking about. But I knew Dee just needed to talk it out, and then she'd be herself again. 'What?' I asked.

'I got . . .'

I stared at her and waited.

'You know . . .' She made a face and wriggled her shoulders. And then I got it.

'You got your period!' I screeched. I thought this was a good thing. In my grade, everyone wanted to get theirs. A couple of girls had already, and everyone was jealous. It was this weird, special, mysterious thing. And Dee already had boobs. They weren't big boobs, but they were something. I had absolutely nothing.

'Shut up!' She waved her arms and looked around, but there was nobody else there.

'Isn't that good?' I asked.

'It's disgusting, Amy. I'm bleeding all over the place. I have to wear pads, and they stink, and it's going to happen every single month. It's not fair!' She burst into tears again.

I was confused. I wouldn't have been crying. I would have been happy. 'It's just a few days, right?'

'I guess.' She kicked her feet in the water. 'You're lucky you're only ten.'

And all of a sudden, there was this big space between us, even though we were sitting so close that we were almost touching. She was twelve, and I was ten. She was a woman, and I was a kid.

6.

Mom bars Aunt Hannah from the house, but two days after my dad comes home, Lee visits. I stand in my room with my ears pressed against the crack in the door, listening to her try to talk my mom into letting her see me.

'I'm not gonna lose it, Aunt Patty,' Lee says. I don't recognize her voice, but I heard my mom greet her, and who else would call my mom Aunt Patty? 'I won't ask her anything, I swear,' she says. 'I just want to give her a big hug.'

'She's hurting, Lee,' my mom says. 'She isn't the same person. You have to understand that.'

My heart leaps. I knew that my mom had noticed, but I hadn't heard her say it yet. When she's talking to me, she acts like I'm Amy. Amy who only wears purple and likes to put her hand over her face.

'I know,' Lee says. 'But she's back, right? She's not going to live in that bedroom alone.'

I'm not? I take a step back from the door, then two steps. I don't know if I'm ready to see Lee, whoever she is now. I picture her at ten, her blonde hair perfectly set, wearing little kiddie high-heeled shoes. She was always nice to me, even though we were different. She was one of my best friends. But Aunt Hannah hates me for not talking. What if Lee hates me, too?

Mom peeks her head in. 'Lee's here,' she says. 'Do you want to see her?'

'OK,' I say. Because I do want to see her. I missed her, too, and I thought about her and wondered what her life was like. I remembered her the same way I remembered Jay. I just hope she doesn't hate me.

Mom moves away from the door, and a girl appears. She still has blonde hair, and it still looks perfect. It flows down her back in soft curls. She's wearing jean shorts and a white tank top with a brown leather jacket over it, and she's flaw-lessly tanned. But what strikes me the most, what tears the breath out of my chest, is that she looks a lot like Stacie. She has the same nose, the same forehead, the same eyes. I stare at her, frozen.

She smiles big. 'Oh my god, Amy!' She rushes towards me and throws her arms around me. She squeezes and then pulls back to look at me. But she's not crying like my parents did. She's still smiling, the smile Stacie rarely showed. 'Amy, I can't believe it! I'm so glad you're back.'

Like I was never kidnapped, like her sister isn't gone. Like I'm her friend.

'Thanks,' I say.

'Wow, you turned out pretty.' She tilts her head like a bird, examining me. Her face is like Stacie's, but it isn't. Lee's face is thinner. Her features are more refined, more perfect. 'You might need to get your hair trimmed,' she continues, 'but that's easy.'

I just shake my head. I don't know what to say to that.

'Don't you think so? Look.' She grabs my shoulders and turns me towards the full-length mirror that hangs over the closet door. 'You have a perfect complexion. I don't think you have a single zit.'

I see my face, my dark brown eyes and my eyebrows and my cheeks. It's just a face. It isn't pretty or ugly or anything. But she's right – I've never had zits. Stacie always used to say I was lucky because of that. Also, because I didn't get my period until I was thirteen.

'You look pretty, too,' I say. The appropriate response. I think it must be true. People always said so, before. They said it about both her and . . . Dee. The name spills through my brain, threatening to pour out of my mouth.

'Thanks. I have to work at it!' She smiles and continues examining me in the mirror. 'I bet you need some new clothes. Want to go shopping? I already asked your mom, and she said she'd give you the money if you're up for it. We can drive to Portland and go to the mall.'

I try to think of something to say, to decide whether I want to do that, but she keeps talking.

'Aunt Patty told me that you like purple, and that's great. We can find you lots of purple stuff. She doesn't know if you should leave the house, but you can't spend all your time in a psychiatrist's office or something. You didn't come back to be locked up somewhere, right? You're free to do whatever you want.'

'I'm . . .' *Dee Dee Dee Dee.* The name bounces around between my ears. Not Stacie, Dee. And her face fills my head, too. Her blue eyes, her blonde hair.

'And I won't ask you any questions, I promise. You don't have to tell me anything. I don't even want to know. If you told me, then I'd have to tell my mom, and she can't handle it. She's better off not knowing.' Lee's eyes well up and she stops talking. We're both staring into the mirror. I'm staring at her face and she looks at mine. And both of us, in our own ways, are seeing Dee.

Tears spring from Lee's eyes, but she stands perfectly still, and long seconds go by. 'I want to think of Dee like she was,' she says. 'Like, she's alive in my memory. And she could be alive. So don't tell me, OK?'

I'm still frozen. There's nothing I can say to that. How can I even move without giving something away?

'So what do you say?' she asks, wiping the tears away. 'Shopping trip?'

It seems like Lee's really trying, like she wants to help me, and I didn't expect that, not after how Aunt Hannah acted. And I feel terrible for thinking Lee might act the same way, because I remember how she used to be. How she was always offering to share her Barbies, showing me

33

their house and their car and their clothes, handing me the ones she liked best. She'd even offer to let me wear those ridiculous high-heeled shoes. Lee didn't understand why I liked to read books sometimes instead of hanging out, or liked to roller-skate or ride bikes with Dee instead of playing dress-up. But she was always my friend, whether we understood each other or not.

I have to learn to be normal again, to be Amy. I can't do that if I never leave this house, and who else will help me? What other friends do I have? I can't believe she *is* my friend, still, but she's here. Promising not to be like Aunt Hannah, not to ask.

'OK,' I say. My pulse races, and I'm about to take it back again. I never got to go anywhere, not for six years, and God knows I wanted to. But the mall seems impossibly far away, in a world that I can't believe even exists.

'Great!' She smiles big again, and I think she's going to leave, but she doesn't. She sits down at the end of my bed, which is now a real twin bed that my dad bought for me. He's been sleeping in Jay's room on the air bed for the last two nights, even though Jay will barely speak to him. 'So . . . how does it feel to be back?' She's ignoring the fact that she was just crying, that she believes that Dee is dead. She's trying to pretend that things are normal, and I need it. I need to pretend and pretend and pretend.

'Um . . . it's good to see my mom,' I say. 'And my dad and Jay.' I sit down on the other end of the bed. We're silent for a second. 'What's been going on with you?'

She latches on to my question and begins to talk. She

tells me about her boyfriend, Marco, and how he plays basketball and he's trying to make varsity next year and how she tried out for cheerleading but twisted her ankle during tryouts, so she didn't make it, and her best friend is Kara and her other best friend is Christina and Kara and Christina are in a fight, and when she's done talking about her friends, she starts talking about school and how her math teacher was really easy but her Spanish teacher was really hard, and how she got a C and her mom was mad and grounded her for a week and now she might not get to go with Kara's family on vacation, and I wonder if she's going to stop talking, but she doesn't. She tells me about how she and her mom yell at each other and then make up and where people our age hang out when they go to Portland and what music she likes and how she'll show me what's cool. 'Do you have any music?' she asks.

I look around the room. Amy used to have some, but I don't see it. I barely remember what music sounds like.

'Well, I've got tons of new stuff for you! There's a lot we need to catch you up on!' She stands. 'So, tomorrow? I'll pick you up at ten?'

'I have to see the psychologist then,' I say.

'So noon? How about one? That will give you time for lunch.'

'OK,' I say.

'Great!' She reaches down and hugs me again. 'I'll see you tomorrow.' And then she leaves. I hear her saying goodbye to my mom and telling her it went fine and that we're going to the mall tomorrow.

35

'I don't know,' my mom says. 'If you don't leave until one, then—'

'It'll be fine,' Lee says. 'Plus, you already agreed. You'd better give her a lot of money. She needs a whole new wardrobe!' And then I hear the door close behind her.

So I guess I'm going shopping. I know I'm not ready, but I also know I need this. I need to see something outside these walls so I can figure out what the world is like now. If I can act normal, then maybe they'll stop asking questions. Maybe they'll realize that I'm not crazy, that I know what's best for me, for all of us. A picture jumps into my head, of the cabin, of *them*, and I have to sit down, have to force the picture from my brain. But I need to be able to stand up. I need to be able to act like none of the last six years ever happened.

When we were kids, Lee was the cool one, the one who always knew how to act. She's the one person who could help me figure out how to be the Amy I was supposed to be. I try to picture that Amy, but what I see is a blur. I have no idea who I would have become. Lee can't really change me into the Amy who was never kidnapped, but she can help me pretend. She is throwing me a rope, and I'm going to take it. I'm going to learn how to be Amy, and I am going to be strong.

7.

After Dee told me about getting her period, she brightened up again. It was only a couple of minutes before she was in the water.

'Let's make it all the way to the big bend this time,' she said. The big bend was this place where the creek made a turn, right before it merged with another branch and became a full-on river. Our parents had forbidden us to ever wade as far as the river because they were afraid we'd get swept away, so the big bend was the furthest we were allowed to go.

I didn't feel like wading any more. I was still thinking about how I wanted to have my period, too, and how I wanted to have breasts, and how Dee would probably forget about me soon to be with her middle school friends.

'Come on!' She started moving.

I slid into the water, which was up to the middle of my legs. It was cold, the kind of cold that feels good at first on a hot day but then chills you from the inside out. I followed Dee as she waded slowly, taking care not to slip on the wet rocks or gouge her feet on the snails and sticks and occasional beer bottles on the creek bed. There were days when the creek was full of people, and since it was Sunday, I expected people to show up any minute, but they didn't. I could hear the cars going by on the street above us, and the sound of a dog barking somewhere, but in the creek, it was just Dee and me. Her wispy blonde hair bounced as she walked, flying everywhere in the breeze.

'. . . so I said she could have the shoes if I could have her red bag with the feather, and Lee said it wasn't fair because they don't even fit me any more, but why should I just give her something? I mean, I could sell them. Or I could give them to charity. Or I could just sit there and look at them if I want to because they're mine, right? But then *Mom* came in and she said I had to give them to Lee because they don't fit me. And because Lee is my sister and we're a family and families share. But they're *my* shoes. And she never gave me anything for them!'

'Uh-huh,' I said. Sometimes Dee's stories about the fights she had with Lee baffled me. Having a little brother, I didn't have to worry about sharing my clothes, and I didn't imagine that if I had to share them, I would care.

'And this morning she was wearing them, dancing around, rubbing it in my face!'

38

'That's mean,' I said.

'I know!' Dee splashed the water with her hands as she walked. 'Oh look, a trout!' She pointed at the fish that darted away from us, its silvery skin flickering under the water. 'And I know she's *still* going to be wearing them when I get home. She'll wear them out just to make me mad, and I should just ignore her and, like, turn the other cheek, but I can't! She's doing it on purpose!' Dee kept talking about it as the water got deeper, and I tried to listen, but my mind was going in different directions. Why did Dee have to change? With all this talk about shoes and clothes, it was like she was becoming more like Lee every day, but I wasn't changing. I wanted to change, but I also didn't want to. I wanted all of us to stay the same.

We weren't anywhere near the big bend yet, but I was cold to the bone. Today I couldn't ignore it the way I usually did. I wanted to sit in the sun and dry out, and maybe go home early.

'I'm cold,' I said. 'I don't know if I can go all the way.'

'Oh,' she said. She looked down the river like she really wanted to keep going, but then she shrugged. 'OK.' Before I'd even started moving, she was splashing her way to the bank. We'd stopped at a place where there wasn't much of a beach, just a row of rocks and pebbles that led to a steep bank. There was a super-skinny path, though, just a strip of dirt through the undergrowth. Dee stopped at the rocks and turned back. 'Should we head a little further?' She pointed upstream to where the rocks turned into dirt that was easier to walk on. But there wasn't a path there, and I had decided I wanted to go back to the street.

'No, this is fine,' I said. I brushed past her, sat down on the little strip of rocks, and started putting my shoes on.

She sat down next to me. 'Are you mad at me?'

'No, I just don't feel good.' My feet were soggy inside my now-wet socks and shoes, but I didn't care. I just wanted to get back to my bike. I honestly was starting to feel a little sick. I was wet and freezing, and the sun was starting to cloud over, and there was something going on with my stomach. If we had gone back on the bank it would have been slow-going, and it would have taken us longer to get to our bikes. So when Dee started hiking up the little path, it seemed right.

'I'm sorry,' I said as I followed her.

'It's OK,' she said. 'Maybe we can just hang out at your house.'

I kind of wanted to be alone, but I couldn't say that. Dee couldn't stand being alone. She had to have someone to talk to all the time, but when she was at home with Lee, who also loved to talk, she never felt like anyone heard her. It wasn't her fault she got her period, I thought. I told myself I was being stupid. She didn't even want it. She wanted to hang out with me and go wading in the river, so why couldn't I just do that?

'We can go back if you want to,' I said. 'I'm feeling better.' Even though I really wasn't. But then again, I never really felt that sick.

'No, it's OK,' she said. She pushed her way through some shrubs and ended up on the gravel shoulder of River

40

Road. There was a car parked there, a four-door Subaru that had seen better days. The rear window facing us was broken and covered in duct tape.

The first thing Amy noticed about Kyle was his head. It was really small. He was a big man. To her he was huge. He must have been at least six feet four, and he had broad shoulders and a thick neck, the kind you expect to see on athletes. But his head was made for someone like Amy's dad, someone tall but thin. It was narrow, and the way his shaggy hair fell over his face made it seem even smaller. But he had a big smile, bigger than the face should have allowed. It was kind of like a clown's smile, and the way he walked was kind of clowny, too, kind of buffoonish. The way he smiled, the way he walked, he didn't seem like that big of a man. He seemed more like a child.

8.

'How are you feeling today?'

I'm here with Dr Kayla, the same therapist who came to see me on Sunday, four days ago. She doesn't look frazzled any more. Now she's immaculately dressed, with long, straight dark hair and a kind, in-control look. I think she's been told not to ask me directly. There's some plot going on behind the scenes, between the cops and my parents and Aunt Hannah, to get me to tell them, to trick me into letting it slip. The cops are ready to run if I say something, ready to burst in and save Dee.

There was a time when I would have liked that.

Dr Kayla waits. I'm already learning that she's calm. I can't wear her down by my silence.

'I feel good,' I say.

'How has your sleep been?'

'Fine.' It's been two years since I've had trouble sleeping. And when I dream, it's bizarre. I don't dream about things that happened, or things I worry about. There are dolls in my dreams, though. Blonde, blue-eyed dolls. They appear randomly in places they shouldn't be. I don't remember much of last night's dream, only the dolls. A Lola, waving her chubby baby arms. A Barbie in a pink tutu, dancing.

She asks more mundane questions. Am I eating? Am I getting along with my mom? How does it feel to see my dad? And then: how do I feel about the news coverage? Have I seen what they're saying on TV?

I know I've been on the news, but my parents won't even turn the TV on, so I haven't seen exactly what they're saying. There was a news truck parked outside the house this morning, though. I think they stayed away at first out of respect for what they think I've been through, but now my grace period is over. It's been four whole days. How much time to recover could I need? And how much money can they make off me?

'I'm trying not to see any of it,' I say. I'm sure they're showing Dee's picture, and mine, from six years ago. They're talking about the day Kyle took us, rehashing how some man saw him forcing us into the car, but by the time the cops came, we were long gone. I saw that in the newspaper on Monday, before Mom cancelled our subscription. I don't need to see those pictures or hear that story. How if the cops had come faster, they might have found us. If the man had been closer. If if if.

'One of the most difficult things for people to deal with is all the attention,' she says.

'I don't want to think about it,' I say.

'What don't you want to think about?'

I'm not going to be trapped. I will only tell her what she already knows. 'The day I was kidnapped. How someone saw us.'

She won't ask the next question, about who kidnapped me. She's trained in how to manipulate people. How to get them to talk even if they don't want to. So she changes direction.

'It looks like you like the colour purple.'

I say nothing.

She waits.

I say nothing and I say nothing, and I say nothing.

The time ticks by.

Lee picks me up at one o'clock sharp. I've barely said a word to my mom since I got home from therapy, and she's even more worried about me going to Portland now.

'Are you sure you want to go?' she asks. 'Lee will understand if you don't want to.'

'I want to go,' I say. The truth is I don't feel anything about it right now. I don't want to go and I don't want to stay home. I want nothing. I sit as still as I can, as if my stillness will stop the questions, maybe the world.

Lee doesn't knock. She bursts in, and she's smiling from the first second.

'Hello, cousin! Are you ready for a whole new wardrobe?'

'Lee, I'm not sure—' my mom begins.

'Fork over the cash, mama!' Lee interrupts.

Mom glances at me.

I stand up. I smile, even though the smile is plastic. I'm going to walk through this. Every day I have to walk and talk and smile like I'm Amy, and I'm back, and I'm fine. And the last six years were nothing. They never happened, and Kyle is not a real person. He never pulled Dee into the car, and I never went in after her, and we didn't drive away, and there was nothing after.

Dee never became Stacie, never began to change and crack. And the cracks never spread and widened, never tore her apart until nothing was left.

Lee is smiling Dee's smile, talking fast the way Dee did. I realize that when they used to fight, it was because they were so alike, more than we ever realized. As I watch her talking to my mom, cajoling her credit card off of her, assuring her that she'll take care of me, that it will be good for me to get out, that I deserve to be free, I realize there is something I want, and it even fits with being Amy. I want to be back down by the river, and see Dee's face when she got to the top of the path, the way she smiled that always-forgiving smile. I want to see that smile again.

Lee turns it to me. She waves my mom's credit card in the air. 'Let's go!'

I nod. The shape of her face is a little wrong. It's a little too narrow when it should be round. Her hair is too curly.

Her chin is too small. But I'll take it. I pick up my Safeway bag, which is the closest thing I have to a purse. At the bottom, I still have the Stacie doll. I don't like leaving the house without her.

As we're about to leave, Jay comes out of his bedroom. He sees us and turns back down the hall.

'Jay!' Lee calls. 'Want to come to the mall with us?'

'No thanks,' he calls back.

'He'll come around,' she says, unlocking her car with the press of a button.

'I know,' I say, even though I really don't. He has every reason to be mad, and I don't know where to start with him. He's more like a stranger than the Jay I remember. I'm in a world full of strange new people, and one of them is driving me away, wearing Dee's eyes and Dee's smile. We're heading into a world I tried not to remember, a place I'm sure will feel new and strange too.

9.

It was how she didn't scream.

How one night, she was silent.

How the darkness was almost peaceful in that one room.

Where I was allowed to sleep, but couldn't.

But she was never allowed.

That's how I knew she was Stacie, and I was Chelsea, and it was for ever.

Lee makes me get a haircut first. She leads me towards a salon, a devious light in her eyes. 'You didn't think I'd let you keep looking like that, did you?' She pushes me down in the seat, and I don't resist. She starts giving the lady directions. 'Bring out her cheekbones. Doesn't she have beautiful cheekbones? You should be an actress, Amy. You'd look great on camera.'

'Is that what you want?' the lady asks.

'Whatever she says,' I say.

'This will look great,' she says. 'Your friend is right. We'll just even this up here . . . a few layers . . .' Snip, snip, snip. The haircut I gave myself with kitchen scissors disappears, replaced by something that looks like it was done on purpose. The face that was just a face looks totally different. I don't know whose brown eyes are staring back. This isn't my face, and it isn't Amy's either. I don't know if my cheekbones are beautiful, or what I'm supposed to be seeing as the lady hands me a mirror and turns my chair this way and that. It's like I'm watching a girl in a movie, and there's no connection between her and the person inside me at all.

Lee hands over my mom's credit card, and before I know it, we're walking through the mall again. She drags me into one store and then another, throws clothes at me. I try them on, and I let her buy what she thinks I should want. Only some of it is purple.

'Get this,' she says, tossing a bracelet made of purple beads on top of a pile of clothes at the register. 'That way you'll always have something.'

'Do they have a pink one?' I ask.

She stops, a sudden silence in the stream of words. She fingers something I can't see. 'Not a bracelet, but they have a necklace. Do you want this one instead?' She holds it up, a chain of pink plastic. Even I can tell it's ugly. But I want it.

48

'I'll take them both,' I say.

Lee sets the pink beads on top of the pile softly, as if it's important that they not break. She pulls out my mom's credit card, and in silence, we both watch as the clerk swipes it and bags the clothes.

I pull out the jewellery and rip the tags off. I put the bracelet on my wrist and the necklace around my neck. I haven't said a word about what these things mean, but as we trudge through the mall, weighed down by all the stuff we've bought, Lee is still silent.

We sit down on a bench and watch the people. A woman walks by with two kids, a baby in a stroller and a toddler she holds by the hand. As she passes us, she smiles at me. Not at Lee, at me. I'm sure of it.

'Amy?'

I watch the woman as she walks away. Where do they live? I wonder. Do they live in a house, with a lot of rooms, and a big yard, and does she have a husband who loves her? Do the kids have a dad who takes care of them? Will they grow up to be happy?

'Amy.' Lee pokes me in the arm.

'Oh,' I say. 'What?'

'I said your name three times,' she says.

'My name is Chelsea,' I say.

'Oh,' she says. 'Do you want me to call you that?'

I can't believe I said that. The truth just popped out. I can't let that happen.

'No,' I say. 'Call me Amy. I have to remember.' It's a lot of work to be Amy, though. That's why I slipped, I tell

49

myself. This day has been exhausting. First, I had to be silent. And then I had to talk as if I were normal. I don't know which one is harder.

'OK, well, I promised your mom I'd get you home by nine, and it'll take an hour and a half at least, so we should probably go.'

'OK,' I say.

'But we can stop at the food court for some ice cream!'

We used to do that together, all four of us, me and Dee and Lee and Jay. We'd make a big extended family trip here every August before school started.

'That would be great,' I say.

Will they ever go to a mall for ice cream? I wonder which flavours they would like. I remember what Dee liked, though. Peppermint. And Amy always liked chocolate. She always wondered how Dee could get peppermint when there was chocolate in the world.

'I bet you want chocolate, right?' Lee asks as we get in line.

I want peppermint. I want peppermint more than anything.

'Yes,' I say. 'And you want vanilla.'

'You remember!' She knocks against me with her shoulder. 'Some things never change, huh?'

'Yes,' I say. I haven't had chocolate ice cream in six years. I wonder if I'll still like it. I wonder if when my name changed, the whole world shifted, so that nothing is what it was before. So I decide not to have chocolate, because I don't want to know. And I definitely can't have peppermint, because I will never be able to keep it together if I do that. 'One scoop of vanilla,' I say when I get up to the front.

Lee stares at me.

'I can have chocolate next time,' I say.

'I'll have chocolate,' she says to the kid scooping it up. 'We can taste each other's.' She smiles, but it's not just a smile; it's a smile with a little bit of the corner of the mouth turned down, and I wonder if she knows what I'm thinking, why I didn't want chocolate. And then she says something that makes me know she does. 'It'll be just as good,' she says. 'Trust me.' She winks as she takes her chocolate, and I notice that she got two scoops instead of one.

And it turns out it is good. It's everything I remembered.

I used to daydream about chocolate ice cream. The smooth bitter and sweet flavour rolling over my tongue. I would close my eyes and picture a cone and myself licking it, and the rasp of my tongue against the checkerboard sides of the wafer. I would picture one of my mom's white bowls, the small ones she used to trick us into thinking we were getting more. I would run my spoon around the outsides of the scoop and capture the liquid. I would slurp it down and then I would take a big, solid bite out of the middle of the ice cream. I would feel the ice cream headache and the relief when it passed, and I would take another bite and another.

Once I was sitting with my eyes closed on the edge of

the bed, and Lola grabbed on to my leg. 'Chel! Chel!' she said.

I opened my eyes.

'What are you seeing?'

'There's this food called chocolate ice cream,' I said. I rolled my tongue around my mouth, trying to think of some way to explain it, but I was drawing a blank. 'It's really good.'

'Can I have some?'

'Well, we don't have any.'

'Ask Daddy,' she said.

'It has sugar,' I said. 'Daddy thinks sugar is bad. He wants us to be healthy.'

'Why?'

'Healthy is good,' I said. I was afraid she was going to latch on to it and start begging for chocolate ice cream, but she didn't. She knew from when she could first talk that if Daddy thought something was bad, we didn't ask for it. That was just the way life was. So there was no ice cream in our house. And I wonder if she remembers, if she imagines herself eating whatever it is she thinks ice cream might be. I hope she does.

10.

The morning Lola was born, I was a little girl.

That night, I was a mother.

No, I didn't give birth to her. I didn't carry her for nine months. I didn't endure the pain that made her life possible.

But I was her mother, because Stacie was fractured. Stacie was a little girl then, and she would be for ever.

'If you don't get in the car, I'll kill her,' said the big man with the little head. He held a knife to Dee's throat. It was the largest blade on a big fat Swiss army knife that he held in his fist. Even I could have cut Dee's throat with that. He had his arm around her, too, an arm big enough to squeeze out her last breath.

Dee was making sounds like a balloon losing air fast. *Zee*

zee zee. Tears were rolling down her face, but her eyes were closed.

Never get in the car. That's what they tell you. Once you get in the car, you're dead. They used to teach us that at school. How you shouldn't talk to strangers. How if a car drives up alongside you, you turn and walk in the other direction. But whoever taught us that never had someone threatening their best friend with a knife.

I could have run away.

And then my mom would never have gone through this. And my parents would still be together. And Jay would only hate me the normal way a brother hates a sister, and he would secretly love me.

But if I got away, and Kyle thought someone would find them, he would have killed her. He had followed her around Grey Wood for weeks, even sitting outside her house and peeking through her bedroom window. He was obsessed with her, and in his own way, he loved Dee more than anything in the world. He loved her so much that no one else could ever have her. He only took me so I wouldn't tell, so nothing could get in the way of the life they were supposed to have together.

I thought about the things they'd taught us in school. It all went through my head in a second, and my legs tensed as if to sprint away. My eyes latched on to the road behind the car. I calculated how long it would take the man to turn the car around. I could get away, I was sure of it.

Zee zee zee.

'Now!' the man yelled.

I took the three steps towards the car. I fumbled with the door handle.

'Get in!' he shouted.

I jumped in, and I pulled the door shut behind me. It locked with a loud click, like the pop of a cap gun.

He leant over Dee and pulled the passenger door shut. There was another click. It hit my heart like I'd been shot. I gasped, and the car started, and we were driving. We were driving fast, faster than normal, faster than any car I'd ever been in.

Dee burst into full-on tears, her little breaths changing to gulping sobs.

I froze. It was like I wasn't breathing at all.

'It's all right,' the man said to Dee. 'I'm not going to hurt you.' He slowed down until he was going a normal speed. He turned his head towards her and smiled that big clown smile. 'Everything's all right.'

Dee kept sobbing.

'My name's Kyle,' he said.

I watched the road through the window, trying to figure out where we were. But we were already somewhere I didn't recognize. We were out of Grey Wood, heading away from our old lives.

Once you get in the car, you're dead. I gasped again, only my second sound.

'Everything's going to be fine,' he said. He turned back to me and smiled. His eyes were a light brown, like a deer's eyes.

55

*

By the time we got to the cabin, it was dark. Dee had stopped sobbing. I guess you can only cry so much, no matter what's wrong. She had gone completely silent, like me.

'I bet you're hungry,' Kyle said as he stopped the car in the dark driveway.

I was, but really, I had to pee. We'd just bounced up a long, winding gravel road after hours in the car.

'We're going to get out of the car now,' he said. 'There's no point in screaming because this is the only place around for a while. And if you run, you won't get anywhere.' His voice was matter-of-fact. And from what I could see, it was true. There wasn't any light anywhere except what came from the car's headlights. We might as well have been on another planet. He unlocked the doors, and I got out, stepping on to the dirt.

Dee stayed in the car.

I walked over to her door and pulled it open. 'You have to get out, Dee,' I said.

'Why?' Her face was in a bright spot of light reflecting off the cabin wall. It was blotchy and distorted.

'Because I know you have to pee as bad as I do. And we have to eat.'

Suddenly, Kyle was behind me. He pushed me aside with one hand, grabbed Dee's arm, and pulled her out of the front seat.

'Stop it!' Dee yelled. She twisted and writhed, but she was no match for him. He held her close from the back and lifted her so that her toes left the ground. 'Stop! Stop!' she kept yelling, but he didn't pay any attention. She might as well have been a pile of firewood he was carrying inside the house to burn.

11.

There is one question nobody asks me. At first they asked about Dee, and about who took us, and about what happened to me. Now they're dancing around those questions, just waiting for the right time to ask them again. But the question they won't ask is: why didn't you run?

There was a road.

There was a phone. Kyle kept it on him, but there was one. I could have got it if I'd tried.

I could have run in the middle of the night, down the road until I found someone. We were isolated, but we were in America. I could have walked far enough to find someone.

Dr Kayla, my therapist, doesn't seem to think it's a question.

'It's normal to feel like you can't escape, even to feel a bond with the person who has kidnapped you. Many kidnapping victims don't make a meaningful attempt to escape.'

I say nothing.

'It's not your fault, Amy.'

'I know.'

'But if you feel like it was your fault, it's OK to talk about it. It's OK to feel that way.'

'I know.'

'It's even OK to worry about what will happen to the kidnapper. Many victims worry, especially after many years.'

I'm not worried about Kyle. I hate Kyle. If it were only Kyle, I would have told the truth in a heartbeat.

There was only one time I tried to run.

Six days had gone by, but it felt like each moment was a year.

There were tears and more tears.

Bruises and a cut all down my left arm.

Screams.

A key on a lanyard around Kyle's neck.

A pair of scissors in the kitchen.

I made it to the door before he woke up. My hands shook, but I got the lock open.

I thought Dee was behind me.

She was behind me, but so was Kyle. He was standing in the doorway holding her, his big arms wrapped around her neck and shoulders.

'I'll kill her,' he said. He didn't even have to yell it. I had only got as far as the Subaru.

'Go!' Dee yelled. Tears streamed down her face. 'Go go go go!'

Kyle clamped a hand over her mouth. 'She's my Stacie,' he said. 'No one can take her.' He was crying, too. He clung to her. 'I'll kill her if you ever tell. She's mine.'

Dee's eyes were still saying *go*. She wanted me to save myself, even if he would have done it. And I thought about it. For three impossibly long seconds, my legs braced themselves to run.

'I hate him,' I say, and my voice cracks. I grip the sides of my chair and try to hold the emotion back. I'm not supposed to show emotion here. I have to hold it in for them. Because he thinks they're his, too, and he'll never let anyone take them. My arms shake as I release my hands from the chair, let them fall back into my lap.

'That's also OK,' she says.

'My mom used to tell me that I couldn't hate,' I say. 'She said I didn't have to like everyone, but I did have to love them.' I think that was something she got from church. We haven't done any praying before dinner since I've been back, I realize. I wonder if she would still tell me that.

'There's no way you have to feel,' says Dr Kayla. 'Hate is a natural emotion. I want you to feel whatever you feel. Recognizing those feelings is the first step in letting yourself heal.' She wants to ask why I hate him. I can tell. But she's afraid I'll shut down again. She thinks that I'm close to breaking.

'I hate him,' I say again. I'm recognizing that feeling. It doesn't hurt anyone for me to recognize it. 'I hate him.' I stand up. 'I hate him.' I pace around the room.

Dr Kayla watches me and says nothing. She's waiting for me to snap.

'It must have taken a lot of courage to leave,' she says. 'You need to give yourself credit for that.'

I stop pacing and turn back to her. This is her way of asking. *How did you get away, Amy? Where are they?*

'It's hard to come back into the world,' she says. 'And look at you. You aren't wearing purple today.'

'There weren't that many purple clothes at the mall,' I say.

Why do you like purple so much, Amy? Well, that one I can tell her. It won't give anything away.

'My name is Chelsea, you know, like the doll? And he had one that was wearing this purple dress.' *And he had a Stacie doll that wore pink.* 'Chelsea had brown hair like me, and so she was me, and I had to look like her.' *And the Stacie doll had blonde hair like Dee. So Dee was Stacie.*

'How did you feel about that?'

'I didn't care what colour I wore.'

'How did you feel about getting a different name?'

'I didn't like it,' I say. I start pacing again. 'I told him my name was Amy.'

'What happened when you did that?'

'He hit me.' He knocked me across the room. I wasn't really hurt that time, but he could have hurt me. He could have killed me with a single kick.

'Were you hurt?' Her expression is neutral. She's lying in wait. Hoping I'll give up a name, a place.

'No.'

And that's it for the session. I walk out.

Kyle had a lot of dolls. Not a lot of dolls like a toy store. Not a lot by the standards of some ten-year-old girls. Lee, for example, had more dolls than Kyle. But Kyle had more dolls than a man should have. A man shouldn't have any dolls unless they're action figures and their purpose is so boys can pretend to fight each other. Is that sexist? I don't care. Because Kyle never should have had dolls.

He had several Barbies and their friends, including Chelsea and Stacie. He had ballerina Barbie, wearing pink. He had doctor Barbie and mermaid Barbie and bride Barbie. He had baby dolls – one called Lola and one called Dream and one called Brianna. They were all sitting on the bed in that one room, staring at us as we walked in.

'Well, hello ladies,' Kyle said. He smiled at them.

I ran to the bathroom. At that moment, I didn't care about the dolls. All I cared about was emptying my bladder. It had been so long that it hurt to pee. And while the pee was flowing, all I could think was that Dee was out there with him, and I had to get back out there.

He had let her go, but he was standing between her and the door. 'I told you there's no place to run to,' he said. 'Why don't you sit down with the ladies, and I'll make us some dinner?'

Dee ran to the bathroom. I stood outside the door and listened while she went, and once she was done, she didn't come out. She started crying again, deep, guttural sobs. She wouldn't come out for dinner, but I couldn't help myself. Kyle had made spaghetti – wholewheat spaghetti, I later learnt, because Kyle thought white pasta was bad. I ate it, but I ate it slowly, because my stomach was so tight that it felt like there was a belt around my middle. I wasn't sure I was breathing except when I opened my mouth to take a bite.

He sat across the tiny table from me. 'Your friend will be all right,' he said. 'She's just in a little funk.'

'Are you going to kill us?' I asked. 'They tell you if you get in the car with somebody, then you're dead.'

He laughed. It filled his whole narrow face, that big mouth smiling. His shoulders jiggled. 'That's a silly rule. What's so special about cars?'

I didn't answer, but a tear rolled down my face. The hand holding my fork shook.

'I can tell you're a good girl,' he said. 'All you have to do is be good. Better finish that.' He pointed to my half-full plate of pasta.

'Someone will find us,' I said.

He picked up my plate and with a single motion, dumped the whole thing in the sink.

I could still hear Dee crying, and I started to stand up, hoping she would let me in the bathroom, and then we could at least be together.

'Nope,' he said. 'Sit.'

63

I sat.

Dee didn't come out of the bathroom all night. Kyle locked the cabin door from the inside and put the key around his neck. This was before I saw the scissors, before I thought I had a chance to escape.

I went to the bathroom and sat down outside it. 'Dee,' I whispered. 'Dee.'

The door opened a crack, and I crawled in. She wrapped her arms around me, and she was still crying. Maybe there isn't a limit, I thought. Maybe she can cry for ever. And that was when I started, not just the few scared tears that had been coming and going, but full-on sobs. In a cabin that small, I'm sure Kyle must have heard us.

Kyle made us stand in the middle of the single room, next to the little kitchen table. I tried to hold Dee's hand, but he pushed me away from her, leaving a couple feet between us. He looked from one of us to the other, eyes lit, as if this were a huge, momentous occasion. He held up the brown-haired doll. She smiled at me in her purple dress with hearts on it. 'You'll be Chelsea,' he said. He put the doll down on the kitchen chair and picked up the blonde one, the one in the pink skirt and the pink blouse. 'And you'll be Stacie.' He grinned at Dee. 'Stacie is my favourite.' He ran a single large finger over the doll's hair.

I didn't say anything then because I was hungry. I hadn't eaten since the night before, when he'd thrown half my meal out. Now there were three boxes of cereal sitting on the little table, waiting for Kyle to finish talking.

He put the Stacie doll down next to the Chelsea doll. They were in a row of Barbie and her friends, all sitting facing forwards on the chair, all smiling.

'What's your name?' he asked Dee. He leant over her.

She burst into tears. I didn't know how there could physically be tears left.

'What's your name?' he said again.

'Stacie,' she whispered.

'That's wonderful, Stacie,' he said, and he put his arms around her. He pressed her face to his chest, and she stood there, shaking. He patted her head. 'My little Stacie. We're going to be happy,' he said. 'Aren't you going to be happy?'

'Yes,' she whispered.

Not letting go, he turned to me. 'And what's your name?'

'Chelsea,' I said. I wanted the food.

'Good.' He smiled. 'Which cereal does Chelsea like?' He pointed to the table. The three cereals were a generic brand, each one bland and boring and healthy.

I walked to the table and poured myself a bowl of dry wheat sticks.

'All right, what about you, Stacie?'

Dee was shaking, wiping tears from her eyes. Kyle's hand on her shoulder couldn't hold her still. She didn't answer.

Kyle guided her over to the table and pushed her down into a chair. He poured her a bowl of the same cereal I had.

She sat there and stared at it.

'Dee—' I started.

Kyle grabbed my bowl from the table and tossed the cereal in the sink. He glared down at me. 'What's her name?'

'Stacie.'

'What's her name?'

'Stacie.'

'What's her name?'

'Stacie.'

Dee shook in her seat.

'Stacie,' I said. 'You have to eat.' *We're going to get out of this,* I thought. I tried to tell her with my eyes.

'Stacie, honey,' said Kyle. He knelt down next to her and took one of her hands. 'You're my precious little girl. You have to be strong. Now why don't you take a bite?'

Dee picked up the spoon in her other hand. She scooped up some cereal, but her hand was shaking so much that by the time she got it to her mouth, most of it had fallen out.

'Try again, honey,' Kyle said.

She tried again, and again almost all the cereal fell out. She stared at me, and she was saying something with her eyes, but I couldn't tell what it was. I didn't think it was, *Yes, we're going to get out of here.* I thought maybe it was, *He's going to kill us,* or *We're going to die,* or maybe nothing that coherent.

Just play along, I tried to say. *We'll think of a way out.*

She closed her eyes and took a bite, but it only took a few seconds. She threw up right there on the table.

That night, I was on a pile of blankets on the floor, and

Kyle lifted Dee up and dropped her on the double bed. Dee screamed, and Kyle told her it would be all right. He told her she was his precious little girl. She screamed and cried, and she said the word *stop* over and over. But he said *It's all right*, and *Shhhh*, and *It's all right. Stacie, it's all right.*

The next day, I told him my name was Amy, and he kicked me. I told him someone would find us, and he threw me against the kitchen counter. He didn't try to patch my cut, and he didn't give me any food.

The day after that, I agreed my name was Chelsea.

Three days later, I made it as far as Kyle's car.

And then Stacie stopped screaming.

12.

The safest thing to do would be to stay in my room with the door closed. The more I talk to the people around me, the more chances there are that I'll slip up.

In the week since my dad came home, he's looking like my dad again. Under the grey hair, behind the extra padding, there's the man who used to take me fishing on the real river, the part where the fish really liked to bite. There's the man who taught me how to ride my bike, and pooh-poohed the training wheels my mom wanted me to use. There's the man who took Jay and me on camping trips in the mountains. And also the man who cracked jokes at dinner and made my mom crazy by tracking mud through the house, and who listened to hip-hop music in the garage.

He left before we woke up in the morning.

He was always home for dinner.

He helped me with my homework.

He read to me.

He always listened when I talked.

He smiled a lot.

He was a real father. The kind every kid deserves to have. The kind who doesn't have moods, doesn't lash out, doesn't punish them by tossing their food. Doesn't hit them. The kind who loves his kids' mother for all the right reasons, who loves her because of who she really is.

There's another kind of love. It's the way you love the things you own, like your sports car or your favourite outfit – or your dolls. Some people would say it's not really love at all. But they never saw the way Kyle looked at Stacie. They never saw the way he held Lola in his arms and smiled, the way his eyes lit up as he told her what a precious little doll she was. How angry he became when we didn't act like dolls were supposed to. There's a kind of love that's just like hate, that won't let go, that doesn't give but only takes.

That wasn't the way my dad loved me, or the way my dad loved my mom, once.

They tiptoe around each other, as if they don't know what to say.

There are six years of history, unspoken. Rips and tears and cracks and mountains between them.

The safest thing would be to stay in my room, but with them here, I can't do that. I can't do that because even though they're as broken as I am, they still love me and each other. I can feel it in the way my mom's hand cups the carrots she's chopping for the stew she's making, which was one of my dad's favourite dinners. I can feel it in the way my dad stands in the kitchen door, nervously fingering the broken trim. I remember that he used to do that while Mom cooked, and he'd be talking about his day at work. He didn't talk in a steady stream like Lee – and Dee. For him it was burst of information punctuated by quiet. A complaint about a client, followed by a joke, followed by Mom's soft laughter, followed by Dad rubbing his hand along the trim. Then Dad would say something else, and Mom would reply. There was always laughter.

Now Dad stands in the doorway silently. Jay, who used to be a bundle of energy, always running around, sometimes racing through the kitchen between Mom and Dad, sits on the couch, also silent. He sits with his arms crossed, and when he sees me coming from the hallway, he looks away. It's not supposed to be like this. He's supposed to call me a stupid name, ask me what I'm doing, ask me to play a game with him. But I'd settle for him to say anything to me at all.

I sit down on the other end of the couch. 'Hey.'

He still won't look at me.

'What's going on?' I think that's what you say to people when you're trying to just say hello, but it sounds strange coming from my mouth. In the last six years, I don't think I ever said it.

Jay picks up the TV remote, then puts it down again.

'I'm sorry you can't watch TV,' I say. It's still banned in our house because of all the news about me.

'Did you have a TV?' he asks.

'No.'

'That sucks.' He fiddles with the remote.

But that wasn't what sucked. I did miss it sometimes. I wanted something to pass the time, to give me a moment of escape. Because I had something to escape *from*, while he was here, safe and sound. Free. And he can't appreciate it. I want to tell him that at least it wasn't him, at least he got to grow up with a home and parents and school and, yes, TV.

'That's not what I missed.' I hear the tone in my voice, the annoyed snap. I used that tone so much with him when I was ten. And afterwards, I wished I hadn't. *We'll bring you some stupid blackberries, OK?* Those were the last words I ever said to him, and I still can't find something nice to say. It's not his fault he was safe. I'm *glad* he was safe.

Jay doesn't reply, just keeps fiddling with the remote. I think that I should go back to my room and wait until Mom calls me for dinner, but then Dad comes over and sits between us.

Go back, I think. *Talk to Mom the way you used to.* But I like the fact that he's here, that I don't have to miss him any more. I don't have to miss any of them, but we don't talk. We sit on the couch in silence until Mom comes out of the kitchen.

She sits in a chair near the living room window.

I suddenly want to be here so much it almost knocks me

over. I want to be here and to have always been here and for all of us to be together. I want to be the girl who grew up as a big sister, who snapped at her brother and never thought a thing of it. I don't know what I would have done today if I was that girl. Maybe Dee and I would still be best friends, and we would have gone to the lake together, or the library, or ridden our bikes around town. Maybe we'd have grown apart, and I'd have gone to the movies, or watched TV, or played soccer. Maybe I'd have lain in bed all day here at home and never talked to anyone, or surfed the internet for celebrity news. But whatever I would have done, I want to have done it, and I want to be sitting here now watching TV, listening to Mom and Dad talk, telling Jay to stop annoying me.

But.

Lola and Barbie need me.

I never meant to leave them. Not ever. Not for anyone. Even Jay. Even Dad. Even Mom.

The thing that you have to understand is, being a mom sucks. Changing diapers is disgusting, and I know that people say it gets less disgusting, but it doesn't. It's disgusting a whole bunch of times a day. Babies have to be fed, and little kids have to be entertained, and they always want your attention, and you would think that with three people to give them attention, it would have been easier. But that's not true when you're the only one in the room who's sane.

I know I don't seem sane right now. And the truth is, I'm a mess. There's so much on my mind that it weighs my whole body down, and it makes me silent, and it makes me cry, and it makes me hide behind my hand as if I could really brush the past away. But trust me, I was sane. I was the one who got up to feed them, and held them and rocked them until they slept. I changed their diapers, and I told them stories, and I played with them and taught them.

All I wanted to do was sleep, and let that little room and the big man with the little head and even Stacie fade away into nothing. But I got up every morning and fed them. I kept going. And it sucked.

But also, it didn't suck. Also, I never knew what life was for before I had them.

If I didn't have them, I would have only had that little room, and the big man with the little head who raped Stacie and treated me like I was nothing, and a cousin who was no longer my cousin, who had disappeared into darkness.

Lola and Barbie never knew that their lives were supposed to be different. They were born whole. They were born for me to love them, and to love me in a way I thought I'd lost for ever. So I would go back to changing diapers, to losing sleep, to bathing and feeding and playing and protecting. I would go back in a heartbeat.

13.

When dinner is ready, we all go sit at the table. We sit in the same spots as we used to – the spots that no one ever assigned but that we just fell into because they were ours. Even after so much time, it feels right to be in the chair facing the refrigerator. It would feel wrong to be anywhere else. There's nothing on it now, though. No pictures. No calendars. No list of chores we're supposed to do. It's an empty white space, and I wonder if that's what we are – if we should at least try to be something new instead of what we should have been.

'How's Beth?' my mom asks.

My dad is putting his phone away. He just stepped outside to talk to her – Beth – his new wife. I think he was trying to hide it from me, but in this small house, it's impossible.

He glances at me.

'It's OK, Dad,' I say. 'I know you're married.'

He clears his throat. 'She's fine.' He pauses. 'Kids are fine.' He turns to me. 'Beth's kids. Liam is five and Beatrice is three.'

Just like Lola and Barbie.

'He acts like they're his,' Jay says. 'New wife, new kids, new life. Forget about you, forget about us.' He picks up his plate and heads for his bedroom.

'It's not . . .' Dad shakes his head and can't finish his sentence. Because really, it is like that. I can see it all over his face, in the way his shoulders hunch and he stabs the meat with his fork instead of shovelling it in. *Best dinner ever, Patty*, he used to say. 'They need me, too.'

'I know, Lon,' Mom says. She's on the verge of tears, but she takes a bite.

'What are they like?' I ask.

'Beth is a teacher,' he says. 'High school math. Special-needs kids. Liam . . . typical boy, rambunctious. Bea is always asking questions. Always wants to learn everything. She reminds me of you, Amy. A lot.' He spins the fork, and I can see that it hurts him. Even after he ran away, he still thought about me. Of course he did. He's a parent. Just because he's a dad and not a mom doesn't make it any different.

'They're good people,' Mom says. She chews her hurt and her anger with her food, swallowing it. She's not happy he's gone, but she's accepted it. Just like she accepted that I was dead.

Did that make you feel better? she used to ask me when I was little. She'd ask it after I had a tantrum or said something mean. I'd have to admit that it didn't feel better to get angry, but only made me feel worse. So I know why she accepts things.

'I'd like to meet them,' I say.

'They'd like to meet you, too. After your mom called, we told them they had another sister. They were really happy. Bea wanted to know all about you.'

'She sounds great.' I eat and watch my parents eat, and we all try to pretend that Jay's chair isn't empty. This may not be the normal we wanted, but it's a lot closer to normal than what I had. This is my family. They're broken, and I'm the reason, but they're still Mom, Dad and Jay.

I look at the plain white refrigerator, the metal sink with the two halves, the curtains with the yellow flowers over the kitchen window. The cookie jar that used to be my grandma's that has the word *home* written in white ceramic letters. Mom's beat-up Betty Crocker cookbook. The line in the table where the leaf goes in. My dad's red knuckles curled around his fork and the clip holding back my mom's now partly grey hair. My mom's nose, narrow and sharp, and her long eyelashes. The glass of milk Jay left on the table.

And the taste of my mom's stew, something I never thought I'd eat again. I hold a bite in my mouth, the savoury gravy floating over my tongue. *This* is food.

It's dinnertime, but we're having cereal.

It's about a month after he took us, and I'm never sure if

I'll be allowed to eat. Some days we get three meals, but others we get one, even if we do every single thing he asks. If we screw up, we get nothing. I've been careful all day not to do anything to set him off. I've answered to the name Chelsea, and I've called Dee Stacie.

I've sat quietly unless he tells me to do something.

I've comforted Stacie, but not too much. Never reminded her of home, never said a word about the world outside. It's better if I say nothing at all.

Kyle pours cereal for both of us, and I'm so hungry, it's all I can do to wait until he's done pouring. We haven't eaten anything all day, but he has. He had canned soup that he heated on the stove, right in front of us, just a few feet away. We smelt it, and Stacie gripped my hand, and we stayed quiet.

The cereal is dry and bland, but we eat it. Taste means nothing when you're hungry. There isn't much that means anything then.

As I savour my mom's stew, I think about the food we had later, what Kyle bought when he finally went to town for groceries. Eggs, milk, wholewheat pasta, cheap meat. I cooked it well enough so we could eat it and keep going another day. After the girls were born, it started to taste better, even though I didn't do anything different.

Lee calls, but I tell Mom to say I'll call her back. I like her, and I missed her, too, and I know she's trying to help me, but I'm not ready to see her again. I want to go to the mall again and to other places with people, but not yet. For now, I need to be with these three people, these people who cared so much about me that they broke apart.

Jay goes out during the day. He grabs his bike and rides off the first chance he gets. Mom has taken leave from the post office, where it turns out she works full-time now, so the three of us are at home together.

Dad drives me to the lake, and we go to the far side, away from the area where there are a lot of people, and sit at the edge of the water in the summer sun. He knows he shouldn't take me to the river where Kyle found us, but he also knows I like the water, that I need it. I don't know how he knows this. Maybe it's because I got that from him. We sit at the edge of the lake and talk about things that wouldn't mean much, if you were normal. But to me, they mean everything.

He took over a friend's business in Boulder, and they have twenty-five employees.

Beth needed her kitchen renovated, and when she came into his office, Liam ran away from her and jumped into Dad's lap.

They live in a two-storey house with a garage and a basement and a backyard shed.

Bea drew with crayons all over the family room wall, and they couldn't bear to paint over it, so now it's the wall everyone's allowed to draw on.

Dad has to watch his sugar because he's prediabetic.

There are sailboats on the lake, and I watch them float around the water as I listen. There isn't much I can tell him

78

in return, but he lets me be silent. The best parts are when we're silent together, when a burst of talking is over and we look out at the sailboats.

I think about the times we used to come here as a whole extended family, Mom, Dad, me, Jay, Aunt Hannah, Dee, and Lee. We'd go to the other side of the lake, where there was parking and a roped-off swimming area and bathrooms and a concession stand. Dee and I were the first to jump in, but even Lee liked to swim. She'd be wearing her sparkly pink tankini while she raced us to the buoys. And then Jay would come through and splash us all, and we girls would gang up on him. Lee and Dee actually went in together on one of those tankinis for me on our last Christmas. It was just like Lee's, except blue.

I stare at the sparkly swimsuit wrapped in tissue paper. It's so not me that I can't think of a thing to say, so I just keep staring.

Lee and Dee giggle. Dee thinks my reaction is so funny that she has to hide her face in Lee's shoulder.

'Come on, Amy, try it on!' Lee says.

'Oh my god,' I say.

'Amy, you'll look great in it,' Dee says.

'Of course she will – that's why I had the idea,' says Lee.

'Guys, I mean, thank you, but . . .' I stumble over my words, and I can see Mom raising her eyebrows at me from Aunt Hannah's couch. I doubt she wants me wearing this kind of swimsuit, but I doubt more that she wants me to be rude about the gift. 'Thank you.'

'Come on!' Lee grabs one arm, Dee grabs the other, and they pull me past the Christmas tree, up the stairs, and into Lee's

room. *A picture of a ballerina in a pink tutu hangs above her twin bed. 'Dee, turn around.' They huddle together while I change out of my jeans and T-shirt into the suit. I feel ridiculous, but when they turn around, they both squeal.*

'You look so good, Amy!' says Lee.

'So good!' says Dee.

I can't even stand to look in the mirror because I'm afraid I'll stick out like a dozen rows of Christmas lights. But when they push me into the bathroom and make me look, I realize that it kind of does look good. It fits perfectly.

The next time we went to the lake, I wore it. Aunt Hannah had bought Dee a new one-piece with little cut-outs, and Dee and Lee thought we were the three coolest kids at the lake. I felt weird with all the sparkles, but we were having so much fun together that it didn't matter. We did all the usual things – swimming, splashing Jay, eating fudge bars. I'd forgotten about all of that until just now.

'You OK, kiddo?' Dad asks.

'I was just thinking about how we used to come here,' I say. 'Remember that sparkly swimsuit Lee and Dee gave me?' Dad chuckles. 'Your mom gave Hannah a good talking-to over that.'

'I never knew.'

'Eh, she decided it wasn't worth fighting over. You kids seemed so happy.'

'We were.' We're all the way across the lake from the swimming area, but I can see kids playing, little ants on the sand or in the water splashing each other. I wonder if I ever would have got comfortable with that tankini, if Lee and

Dee together could have got me interested in clothes and make-up and all that stuff, in being cool. But I never had a chance to change, to figure out how I'd grow up. I'm a universe away from days at the lake and Christmas gifts.

Dad puts his arm around me, and I lean into him. We stay there until the sun starts going down.

Mom and I walk in the park, the same park where Dee and I used to roller-skate when we were little, where Jay and I used to play on the swings and the monkey bars. It seems smaller but also greener than I remember. It's full of life, and I get used to the feel of Mom's steps beside me.

She tells me about how she's a supervisor at the post office now, how Jay got his first report card with no Cs last semester and is going to play baseball in high school. She stopped going to church a few years ago, but she's thinking about going back. And she's learnt some new things to make for dinner that she hopes I'll like.

I tell her I'll like them.

We see TV reporters following us with cameras, but they don't come close. We pretend they're not there.

Every night we have dinner as a family, and even though he doesn't look happy, Jay stays at the table. I learn that he spends most of his time with a friend named Trent. And when Mom drags it out of him that he has a girlfriend named Nona, he smiles. I want to meet his friends, and I hope that Jay staying at the table is a beginning, a sign that someday I'll be able to.

Another week has gone by, and I'm doing all right. Lee

has called for me three times, but then she gives up on me and talks to Mom. She wants all of us to come over for dinner with her and Aunt Hannah. Mom isn't sure it would be right, but Lee insists. She talks and talks and lets Mom go and then calls back. She says the whole family needs to be together and Aunt Hannah needs us, and finally, Mom agrees.

An hour before we're supposed to leave, Beth calls. I hear Dad's side of the conversation, and he's repeating the words to a children's story. He's talking about a black bear whose best friend was a field mouse, and while he recites the words to the story, he smiles.

I told Lola and Barbie stories just like that. There was the one about Mr Otter and Mr Turkey, based on Mom's obsession with the high school mascot, but there was also the one about Mickey Mouse and Donald Duck, which was new to the kids because we didn't have a TV. I even told them the one about the sponge who lived under the sea in a town called Bikini Bottom. I loved telling them stories. I used to smile just like Dad.

I can hear them laughing.

More, Chel!

Chel, another one!

When Mom knocks on my door, I'm crying.

'Honey, we don't have to do this,' she says. She thinks I'm crying about the dinner.

'No, I want to,' I say. I blow my nose into a Kleenex.

'Dr Kayla says we shouldn't push you.'

82

I've seen her twice since I walked out, but I haven't said much. Mom thinks that means I'm not ready for anything. But Lee told Mom she's convinced Aunt Hannah not to ask me any questions, and I believe Lee.

I want to see her. I want to leave my room, because I've lived in one room for so long. I've had this week with Mom and Dad and Jay, but there's more out there. If I'm going to stay, if I'm going to be Amy, I have to leave this tiny world again.

'I'm going,' I say.

'OK, if you're sure,' Mom says.

'I am.'

14.

Aunt Hannah gives me a hug. Her long hair brushes against the side of my face, and she swipes it back as she pulls away from me. She's tall, maybe five ten. Her hair is going grey, but the way it blends in with the blonde, it's hard to tell. If it weren't for the dark circles under her eyes, she'd look much younger than she is. She smiles and says hello to my parents, but the smile is only in her mouth. She turns away from all of us and heads back into the kitchen.

'Hey!' Lee gives me a big hug. Then she hugs my mom and my dad. She gives Jay a smile and a fist bump.

'We shouldn't have come,' my mom whispers.

'It's all right,' says Lee with a wide smile. It's strained, but she's playing it for all it's worth.

A great racket comes from the kitchen. Metal crashes

against metal. Glass breaks. It sounds like Aunt Hannah is knocking over chairs, and then it sounds like she's knocked over the whole table. Dishes break and shatter, and there's a huge crash.

My dad hangs his head.

My mom wipes her eyes.

Lee's smile fades.

'All right, then,' says Jay. He locks eyes with Lee, shakes his head, and leads the way out of the house. We all follow.

'I'm sorry,' I say to Lee as we leave.

She sighs. 'It's not your fault. I'll call you later, OK?'

'OK,' I say. It's hard to see how it's not my fault. I could tell my aunt the whole story. But would that make her feel better? Wouldn't she still want to break things? It's hard for me to say which would be better, because I know.

As we drive home, I try to imagine what it would have been like if Dee had disappeared, but I had been left behind. Would I want to know what happened to her? Would I want to know that she suffered and that she changed and that her life was one minute of horror after another? Or would I want to believe that she had been murdered on that very day that she was taken, and that she wasn't suffering any more?

I don't really wish that Dee had died that day, but in a way she did.

I wonder if I did.

I close my eyes and block out my parents' whispers. They're talking about how we shouldn't have tried to see Aunt Hannah, how she's not ready.

Barbie's face pops into my head. She's holding her own doll, a Barbie in a nurse's outfit. 'Barbie,' she says.

'Yes, that's right,' I say.

'She's Barbie and I'm Barbie.'

'Yes.'

'I want a dress like this.'

'That's a nurse's dress. Nurses help people,' I say.

'I can help people,' Barbie says. She smiles, and her face is suddenly Dee's face. Not Stacie's, Dee's.

'Yes you can,' I say. I wipe the tears out of my eyes, because Kyle and Stacie will be back from outside any minute, and I can't let them see that something's wrong.

I made her that nurse's outfit. I used an old sheet and the sewing machine that Kyle picked up from some second-hand store so that he wouldn't have to go shopping in town as often. Barbie couldn't tell the difference. She loved it.

'Honey, are you all right?' Mom has opened the back door of the car and seen that I'm crying.

'I'm fine,' I say.

'I'm so sorry,' she says. 'I never should have let this happen. I should have gone with my instincts.'

'It's not . . .' I can't finish. If I tell her what it's not, she'll ask what it is. 'It's OK. I understand.'

86

15.

I have just gone to bed when I hear a knock on my window. I pull the curtain, and there's Lee, smiling. I open the window, and she climbs in. She's wearing a skirt and high heels and a face full of make-up, and her hair looks really poofy.

'Nice of you to dress up for me,' I say.

'It's not for you,' she says. 'It's for the party.'

'Um . . . party?'

'Yep. It's Saturday night. People have parties.' She turns on my desk lamp and heads for the closet, where most of my new clothes are hanging, untouched. She starts pulling things out.

'I don't know if I'm ready for a party,' I say.

'You are,' says Lee.

'You thought your mom was ready to have dinner with me,' I say.

'Mom's Mom,' says Lee. 'You're you.'

'Everyone's going to stare at me. They'll take pictures.'

'So?'

'So I'm going to end up all over the internet.'

'So?' She thrusts a skirt at me. It's black with a purple band around the waist.

'I bought a skirt?'

'Dee loved parties,' says Lee. 'Don't you think she'd want to go to a party?' She smiles as if this were a normal thing to say.

Dee, in fact, did love parties, only she rarely got invited. She was too bubbly, too talkative, too *much*. I suddenly remember Annie Gearheart's birthday party, only a couple of months before Kyle took us. I wasn't there because Annie was in Dee's grade, but Dee told me all about it. She was so happy to be invited, because Annie and her friends were cool and pretty, and Annie had a big house out in the country. But Dee had said something that wasn't supposed to be funny, and all the girls laughed, and that made Dee burst into tears.

I can't face them, she said. And then, *Do you think she'll invite me next year?*

'That was a sucky thing to say,' I say to Lee.

'Did it work?'

'Yes.' I pull off my sleeping shorts and pull on the skirt. This is crazy. I can't go to a party. But in ten minutes, I'm dressed and Lee is putting make-up on my 'actress' face.

'Hold still! There.' She turns me towards the mirror so I can see, but she turns me back around so quickly that I haven't seen anything.

And then we are out the window and in Lee's car, and I feel like I'm watching these two girls drive away into the night, like this is a movie, because I've only seen high school parties in movies, and let's face it, I haven't even seen that many movies. The last time I watched a movie, I was ten years old.

'Everyone's going to be nice to you,' Lee says. 'Believe it or not, I'm popular. People like me. I've told everyone that when they see you, they have to be nice. Nobody's going to make fun of you or anything. They were all sad when you got kidnapped. Everyone looked for you – all the kids at school helped. People cried a lot. Boy, you should have seen Vinnie Openheimer cry. He was all broken up for a long time. We're good friends now, so he called me when he heard you came back. He was like, we all have to hang out! I told him you probably weren't ready. I mean, it was almost like he thought you'd go out with him – can you believe that? A girl comes back from being kidnapped and he thinks, hey, she probably doesn't have a boyfriend!'

'Vinnie Openheimer?' I try to remember who she's talking about.

'You know, Mini Vinnie?'

'Oooooh.' I do remember Mini Vinnie. He was this really little guy who was always clowning around. He used to say really random things just to see how people would react. When he did it to the teachers, he'd have the whole class in stitches. In fourth grade, he sat two seats behind me.

'Hey, Mrs Woods!'

'Yes, Vincent?'

'There isn't any firewood in the parking lot.'

'There isn't what?'

'Firewood in the parking lot.'

'Vincent, why would we need firewood in the parking lot?'

'Well, there isn't any.'

'Vincent, I asked why.'

'Because there isn't.'

At this point the whole class burst into laughter, and Mrs Woods finally caught on. And then he threw a wadded-up piece of paper at me. It hit the back of my neck and slipped to the floor beneath my seat. Somehow I knew he'd thrown it because he liked me, and even though he was kind of a dweeb, I actually kept that piece of paper. It wasn't every day that somebody liked me.

'Well, he's not mini any more!' Lee continues. 'He's huge! I mean, not fat or anything, just . . . you'll see. Boy, will you be surprised! Don't worry if he tries to hit on you because he's harmless. He's actually a great guy. More meat, same dork. People still call him Mini except now it's ironic.'

'Uh-huh.' I remember Vinnie, and thinking about him makes me smile, but I can't really picture him. I know he was little, but his face is a blank.

'I can't wait for you to meet Marco,' she goes on. 'He's *muy guapo*, if you know what I mean.' She winks. '*Muy muy muy.*'

I have no idea what she means.

'And I've told you about Christina and Kara, right? Well, they're still fighting, so if things are weird, it's not about you. Remember how Christina told Amanda and Izzie about Kara's pumpkins, well—'

'Her pumpkins?'

'Kara grows pumpkins! Her family lives out Grey Wood Lane, you know, kind of by the big lake? And she brings them to the fair every year – we *all* go to the fair every year – but then Christina told some other people and everyone was laughing about Kara and her giant pumpkins. And she has the hugest boobs, you know – I guess you don't know. Trust me, when you see her, you'll know. Anyway, Kara thinks Christina was saying it *that way* but I don't think she was. I mean, yeah, she can sometimes be a little bitchy but she wouldn't make fun of Kara's pumpkins or her *pumpkins*, you know? Those are two things that are off-limits. Oh, hey, I almost missed the turn!' She takes a hard left, throwing me against the back of the seat. 'So this party is at Ben Heller's house,' she says, apparently done talking about pumpkins. 'He thinks he's awesome because his dad lets him have all the parties he wants. The dad is, like, never there. I think he really lives in Seattle or something with his twenty-year-old wife. So Ben is kind of a douchebag but he does have good parties. I mean, where *else* are we going to go in a town this size? The big lake? That's so over.'

I think about saying *yeah* just to say something, but there's no need. Lee is either too self-involved to notice that I'm not talking, or she's trying to make sure I don't feel like I *have* to talk. I think it's the latter. If she weren't doing this to be nice, why would she be doing this? It probably isn't going to help her popularity to bring her weirdo purple cousin to the party.

She pulls up across the street from a small ranch house with chipped yellow paint, which is obviously the party house. There's music coming from it that moves the street.

'Come on!' She gets out of the car.

I follow her.

Dee loved parties, I tell myself.

I love the river.

But it's not right for me to love that.

There was a river near the cabin, too, and the cold air rushing up from the water made me feel awake and alive. The thick bushes we had to climb through to get down there were barriers between us and Kyle. And the girls loved it. They were born there, born to walk on the riverbank, like I was.

The music blasts me as we get closer. In a way, the river is the same as music, because it's loud and it drowns your voice out. But when I sat by the river, I felt calm and protected. I watched my girls laugh and play, and for a few minutes, I could believe they had something positive in their lives. I never thought bad things when I was by the river. But this music seems like it was written just to bring the bad things out.

Inside the cabin, with the door locked. I'm getting up off the floor, slowly.

'What's your name?' he asks me.

I'm falling back from his kick in slow motion. Hitting the ground.

'Heeeey! Ben, this is my cousin Amy.' We're at the door now, and a skinny kid wearing a baseball cap and holding a cigarette is in the doorway.

'Hellooo, ladies!' says Ben. 'Welcome to *mi casa*.' He doesn't even blink at me. No double take. 'Beer in the fridge. Leave your donation in the jar.' He takes a puff off his cigarette and smiles at me.

I follow Lee through the dingy living room into the kitchen. Yep, it looks like a teenage boy lives here alone. There's stuff strewn everywhere. Clothes and video game controllers and Chinese food boxes. There are maybe ten people hanging around, and I breathe out a breath I didn't know I was holding. When she said 'party', I thought she meant something huge, but this is just a few kids hanging around drinking. This is something I can handle.

I just wish the music wasn't so loud, wasn't beating into my brain.

The bowl crashes into the sink and breaks.

She's screaming in the dark and I'm silent.

She's screaming at me and I'm running out the door with Lola.

'Hey, babe,' says a tall guy who must be Marco because he grabs Lee and gives her a big, wet, gross kiss. As he lets her go, I realize what *muy guapo* means, wink wink. The guy is gorgeous, with broad shoulders and deep brown eyes. Even the girl who was raised in a cabin can see it.

'Marco, this is my cousin Amy,' Lee says.

'Amy! Nice to meet you.' He sticks out his hand.

I shake it. I don't remember the last time I shook hands with someone. I also don't remember the last time I met a hot guy in real life. I don't think it's ever happened.

He turns around and grabs two beers off the kitchen counter. He hands one to each of us. 'Glad to have you back,' says Marco.

'Thanks,' I say. I try to remember if I knew him before, but I can't place him. I feel like I would remember.

'Isn't she a looker now?' Lee asks.

'Sure,' says Marco. 'But she's no Lee Springfield.' With that, he gives her another wet, sloppy kiss.

Three more kids have come into the kitchen, two boys and a girl. The girl has the most humongous set of *pumpkins* I've ever seen.

You must be Kara, I almost say.

'Kara!' Lee cries before I can stick my foot in my mouth. She runs forward and gives Kara a big hug. I brace myself for the introduction, for Kara's reaction to finally meeting the kidnapped cousin. But then I look up. Somehow I missed him for a few seconds. I don't know how I missed him.

A huge guy is standing in the doorway.

I drop my beer. It crashes to the ground, and the bottle breaks, and beer splashes on my legs.

Everyone stares at me.

I stare at him.

He pushes forward, towards me.

94

I step back. One step, two steps. He's between me and the door.

He passes me and pulls the trash can out from beneath the sink. He kneels down next to my feet and starts picking up pieces of glass. 'Didn't know you could get drunk off just holding it,' he says.

I stare down at him, frozen. His head is normal sized, even big. There is nothing small and skinny and weird about his head. This is not Kyle. Who is this?

'Thanks, Vinnie,' says Marco. He grabs a roll of paper towels off the counter and kneels down to wipe up the mess.

'No prob,' says the big guy. *Mini Vinnie.* He smiles up at me. 'I'd say it was the fumes, but I'm pretty sure it wasn't open.' His eyes are blue, not deer brown. His smile is a normal size. His hair is buzz-cut, not falling over his face. And his nose is crooked.

I take a deep breath. 'What?'

'Nothing. Hi, I'm Vinnie. Remember me?'

'Of course,' I say. I take another deep breath. People start moving again, like a movie reel catching and rolling forwards. Everything is OK. The truth is, Vinnie doesn't look anything like he did six years ago. If Lee hadn't reminded me, there would be no way I'd have recognized him.

He dumps the broken glass in the trash and moves it back under the sink.

'Thanks,' I say. 'Vinnie, and Marco.'

'Sure,' Marco says. 'I've done it myself.' He smiles,

tosses the paper towels in the trash, and turns back to Lee, who is deep in conversation with Kara and another girl, who, from the way she won't look at Kara, must be Christina.

Vinnie towers over me.

Not Kyle not Kyle not Kyle.

'So, how do you like exciting Grey Wood? Feel like going back to wherever you came from?'

What? I open my mouth to say something, but all that comes out is a choked breath.

He grabs another beer off the counter, pops it open with his keychain, and hands it to me. 'If you drop this one, too, you have to pay.'

I still can't think of what to say.

'Just kidding. Girls never pay.' He pulls a five-dollar bill out of his wallet and stuffs it in a jar on the counter, then grabs a beer for himself. As he pops it open, he grins down at me. 'That's OK; it's the usual response I get from girls. What are you talking about, Vinnie? Stop talking, Vinnie.'

'I . . .'

'But I never stop talking. Kind of like your coz over there.' A laugh spills out of me. I cover my eyes with my hand. Vinnie is trying to be nice to me. I know that. He's Mini Vinnie, the little guy with the *figurative* big mouth, the guy who was always cracking jokes and being totally random. It's just Mini Vinnie.

'So, seen any good movies lately?'

I take my hand down. *Mini Vinnie. Mini Vinnie.* 'No,' I say.

'Me neither. Read any good books?'

'Um . . .'

'Me neither. I hate reading.'

'I'm going to go to the library soon,' I say. 'I used to go to the library.'

'Just kidding – I love the library. I read lots of books. Well comic books. They're called graphic novels now, did you know that? I don't know what you know since you've been, like, in a cave for six years.'

'It wasn't a cave,' I say. 'It was a . . .' – *a cabin* – '. . . a house.'

'Oh, well, you should read some graphic novels. Get you started up again. Pictures. Easy.'

'I'll do that,' I say.

'I could let you borrow some. You know, if you don't want to go to the library. They have a bad selection there anyway.'

'OK,' I say. 'Thanks.'

Lee walks over with the other two girls. 'Come on, Vinnie, do you ever stop talking?'

'Said the pot.'

'Ha ha.'

'He's not bothering me,' I say. But even so, I'm ready to step away, to not be standing next to someone so big.

Lee grabs my arm and pulls me with them. She pulls me all the way into the living room, leaving Vinnie behind. 'Sorry about that,' she yells over the music. She goes over to the stereo and turns down the volume, then comes back to me. 'I hope he wasn't coming on too strong.'

'No, it's all right,' I say. The music pulses, but it's not so bad now. It's contained.

'This is Kara' – she points to the girl with the pumpkins, who has short, curly red hair – 'and this is Christina.' Christina is skinny with brown hair kind of like how mine would be if it were long. She's wearing jeans and a white tank top with the words *cool beats* written in red. 'Guys, this is Amy.'

'Hey,' Kara says. She smiles, but it's uncertain. She lifts her hand like she's going to hold it out to shake, and then she leans forward like maybe she's going to hug me, but then she rocks back on her heels.

'Hey,' Christina says.

We're all silent. Even Lee is silent.

I don't know what to do, so I take my first sip of beer ever. It's disgusting, but I swallow. I feel like wiping my mouth, but I don't.

'Remember the science fair?' Kara blurts.

My mind spins. Science fair. Science fair.

Kara talks fast, like she has to finish the sentence before a bell. 'It was you and me and Rowan Michaels, and Mr Fisher stuck us in a group together, and we had to extract DNA from a banana, only it didn't work, and then Rowan's dad helped us write it up so it looked like it worked, but it was all a lie. And we got an A, which was my first A in a science class ever.'

It comes rushing back to me. Kara was this girl who was sort of cool, and she didn't want to be stuck with me, and I didn't want to be stuck with her, and it was all a disaster.

But it's one thing we have in common. By bringing it up, it's like she's thrown me a rope, and I grab it.

'Yeah,' I say. 'It was a cool project.'

'It was terrible!' Kara says. She turns to the others. 'We couldn't get along at all. Remember how we got in a fight over which banana to use? You wanted one with spots, but I *had* to have the one that was perfect.'

Lee and Christina both laugh at this.

I laugh too. But the truth is, I don't remember that part.

'I moved here in eighth grade,' Christina says. 'So I guess we've never met before.'

'We're glad you're back,' Kara says, almost cutting Christina off. 'The whole town is glad. I remember looking for you.'

'*You* did?' I ask.

'Of course she did,' Lee says. 'We did that thing where everyone walks together and they cover a whole area. Everyone at school was there.'

That's what people do when they're looking for a body, I think. We're all thinking it.

'It means a lot,' I say. 'I never knew what was going on. I figured my family would look, but . . .' But there was never any chance of them finding us. Even that first week, when I kept telling Kyle that someone would find us, I never really believed it. It was like my parents and the whole town of Grey Wood and the whole ten years of my life were erased the moment we pulled up to the cabin. But none of it was ever gone at all. While I was there, Lee and Kara were becoming friends, and Christina moved to town, and Mini Vinnie grew into a huge hulk of a man, and my brother grew up, and my dad moved to Colorado and got fat and remarried with stepchildren. People just like the people here at this house had parties just like this one and went to school and graduated and went to college and got jobs and had lives and children, and I didn't even know it was all out here. I couldn't contemplate any world beyond our cabin and the river.

I miss them. I see Stacie's face. Her blue eyes stare at me. She is calm for one second. One second that turns into hours. She has stopped moving as if frozen in the frame of the DVR, her arms raised, her mouth open. She was calm even in her rage, just for that one second.

'Chel!'

'Chel!'

They're calling for me. Not in my memory, but now. Somewhere out there, they're calling for me. They don't understand why I had to leave. They ask for me every night.

'Daddy, where's Chel?'

'When is Chel coming back?'

'Daddy, where's Chel?'

'Daddy?'

I realize I'm still standing in the living room of this boy Ben's house, and my hand is over my face, and there are people around me. Slowly, I remove my hand.

Kara has moved next to Lee, and I can't see Christina. Marco is on the other side of Lee, and behind him, Mini Vinnie is staring at me.

My beer is on the ground. The bottle didn't break, but liquid spreads out on to the carpet. The music is still playing, now fast and urgent. I walk towards the door. One foot in front of another, until I'm through it. I walk between two boys who are sitting on the steps smoking. A weird sweet smell washes over me. I walk faster, until I'm on the sidewalk. I look both ways.

But there is nowhere I can go. They live in a world I can't get to.

'Amy? Or . . . Chelsea?' Lee comes up behind me.

'I'm all right,' I say. In the back of my mind, I realize that she called me Chelsea and that something about that is wrong. Or is it wrong that she first called me Amy?

'I'm sorry,' she says. 'I told them not to bring it up, but I guess there was no way . . .' She sits down next to me on the kerb. I never even realized that I was sitting.

'We knew people would look, but we didn't think anyone would find us,' I say.

'Oh,' Lee says.

'I'm sorry about the beer. Two beers.'

'Nobody cares about the beer.'

'Sometimes I go back. You know, in my mind. And it's like for a minute I'm really there and not here.' I think I'm all right now. I can see the street in front of me. Two girls are heading towards us, towards the house. One of them waves at Lee.

Lee waves back.

They look at me, then at each other, and then walk faster.

'I shouldn't have pushed you,' she says. 'I just thought you might want to get out, do something normal. Because I guess you couldn't go to parties, and maybe you wanted to.'

'I couldn't really want anything,' I say.

'Oh.' Lee is crying. She's trying to hide it, but she wipes a tear away with one hand.

'I don't know what I'm supposed to want – what Amy is supposed to want. I know I don't want to be locked in my room, though.' I put my arm around her. 'Thank you for making me come out.' A tear rolls down my face, too. I may not be ready for this, but I know I don't want to be locked up. She was right about that. I never want to be locked up again.

'Really?' She wipes her face again. 'I thought I'd just made things worse.'

'Really,' I say. 'What happens, going back there, it would happen whether I was here or alone in my room.'

'I guess you're working with that therapist lady,' Lee says.

'Yeah.' Actually, we haven't even got there. Dr Kayla is still trying to get me to tell her what happened to me and where Dee is. We can't get to her actually helping me until she finds that out, and I'm never going to tell her. I'm never going to tell anyone, even if it means that I can never forget, that I have to live with the memories my whole life. I don't want to forget anyway. I want to remember them, every minute of every day.

Dee would have loved to go to a party. Lee is right about

that, too.

'Let's go back in,' I say.

Lee eyes me sideways. 'Are you sure?'

'I won't try to have another beer,' I say. I guess Dee probably would have liked to try drinking, but that part of being a teenager will have to wait. Just being in a room with other people is enough weirdness for one night.

'If you want to leave, just say it,' she says. 'Or give me a look. I can see these people any time.'

'OK,' I say. We stand up and turn back to the house, and Mini Vinnie is sticking his head out the door. He waves at us and grins big. 'OK,' I say again. And I lead the way back through the two smokers into the house.

16.

I end up with Vinnie's phone number, scrawled on a piece of paper towel. He said he'd show me his comic books. Which is something that maybe I would have liked back when I was ten, but it's all right with me. I don't mind doing kid stuff, especially if it's going to be with a boy; kid stuff is a lot better.

I rub my hand over the paper towel as we drive home.

'I hope he didn't bother you,' Lee says.

'No, I like him,' I say. 'He treated me like I was normal. I mean, everyone was trying to avoid it, but he just brought it up straight out. Like, maybe you don't know what comic books are because you lived in a cave.' I smile at the memory.

'Oh my god,' Lee says. And then she starts talking. She

tells me about how the guy Ben who lives in the house used to date a girl named Felicia who wasn't there. '. . . so Felicia started going out with this *old* guy. His name is *Gordon* and he goes to college, but he's old to even be in college. Like, he must be *twenty-five* or something. And she brought him to the *prom* with her, and Ben was there with Holly but they're just friends, and he got *wasted* and that's why the whole wall on the side with the sliding door looks like it got attacked by a coyote or a pack of wild geese or something.'

'You mean he scratched up the wall?' I ask.

'I guess. And now Felicia is texting him again. But she's *still* going out with this old guy.'

I try to think of something to say, but I can't.

'And he's not even cute,' Lee finishes as she parks a block away from my house, far enough so that hopefully we won't wake my parents. 'I mean, at least Ben is cute, right?'

'Yeah,' I say, even though Ben is far from *muy guapo*, in my opinion. Maybe it's the fact that he looks like he doesn't shower. Maybe if he cleaned up, he'd be all right. I wonder if I'm supposed to think Ben is cute. Is that something all girls are supposed to know?

'Remember, I was never here,' Lee says. 'If Aunt Patty finds out I took you to a party . . .' She runs a finger across her neck dramatically.

I smile and put the paper towel in my pocket. 'You were never here,' I say.

She watches me while I walk the block back to my house, and I don't realize that I'm only taking shallow tiny breaths until I'm through the window, and I take a deep breath in, and the breath doesn't really catch. The room is dark, covered in shadows. The new twin bed sits in the same spot my twin bed used to sit in, before. And all of a sudden there we are, nine-year-old Amy and eleven-year-old Dee. I'm on the twin and she's on the trundle, the extra mattress that rolled beneath it. We're supposed to be asleep, but of course, we aren't. We're eating Red Vines liquorice sticks that we bought at the convenience store on our way home from school. We're giggling as we eat them, because it's illicit. We're getting away with something.

I blink and shake my head, and the scene disappears. I'm looking at the new bed again, and I'm alone in the room. I don't turn the light on, but I look at myself in the full-length mirror that's hanging on the closet door. In my skirt, with my new haircut and my make-up, I don't look like either Amy or Chelsea. I look like a completely new person. This is the person who met Lee's friends tonight, who got Vinnie's phone number and took her very first sip of beer. Maybe this is the person I'm supposed to be now, I think. Maybe I should just be this person, this new Amy. Maybe this Amy is the person I was supposed to be, who I would have become if the past six years had never happened. If I could forget, then it would be easy. But how can I be the girl who drinks beer and cares about parties and friends and boys when I know what it's like to be a mother? I know what it's like to love someone more than anyone could ever love their parents or their friends or a boy. But I can't know that, I think. I *have* to be Amy. It will be better for them if I pretend like they don't even exist.

I sit down on the bed and close my eyes. 'There was an old lion who was missing half of his hair,' I whisper. Lola liked this one the best. 'This was no ordinary lion that lived in Africa, but this was the kind of lion that lived by the river. He liked to eat crayfish and play with the snail shells . . .' I lie down. Maybe I can be this new Amy on the outside, but on the inside, when it's dark out and no one else is awake, I can still be myself, and I can still remember.

My dad is yelling at someone. I wake up in the clothes I was wearing last night.

'Get out of here!' my dad yells.

I change my clothes in a flash and wipe my face with an old T-shirt to get the rest of the make-up off.

'I'm calling the police,' my dad says. 'This is trespass!'

He must be yelling at reporters. They've been calling us, and now they've stopped being polite. I knew it was going to happen someday, but I still don't like it. I don't like to hear my dad yell.

The door slams. My dad is still yelling, but now he's yelling at my mom. I can't understand the words, though. I can't stand this. I have to make him stop.

'Dad,' I say, coming out of my room.

'. . . as if she's not a person, as if she's something to gawk at,' he rants. It's not just my mom in the living room. Jay is there, too. He's sitting in his usual spot on the couch with his arms crossed, as if the whole speech is directed at him.

My mom sighs as I come in. 'We're sorry we woke you,' she says.

Jay rolls his eyes.

'I'm sorry about the reporters,' I say to him.

My dad shakes his head and turns away.

'They'll forget about me pretty soon.'

'Not until they find Dee,' Jay says.

'Jay!' My mom's face goes crimson.

I don't think he's right. I think that they ended up forgetting about both of us after a while. My parents may not have forgotten, but the reporters did. Once some time goes by, they'll stop wondering what happened to Dee. I just have to let time go by.

'You could stop all of this,' Jay says. 'If you just tell them.'

'Jay, that is *enough*,' Mom says.

Jay looks down.

Dad turns back around to face me. I can see in his eyes that he agrees with Jay. If I would just tell them, things would be better. He thinks that Dee is dead, and if I tell him, then he'll be able to go back to Colorado. But that's not fair. Maybe he thinks that if I'm alive, so is Dee, and he really wants to save her. Maybe he wants to stay here with us, but he also wants to go home. I know how that feels because I feel exactly the same way.

I know Jay wants him to stay and never go back to Colorado. He still won't say much to Dad, but that's because he's hurting. If he didn't want Dad to stay, then none of this would hurt so much. But me telling the truth won't make Dad stay, and even if it could, I wouldn't. Because nobody matters as much as Barbie and Lola.

I go back to my room, and I stay there until Monday, when it's time for Dr Kayla.

She asks me about my childhood, about how Amy became best friends with Dee. I tell her that Dee acted young for her age, and I acted old. I tell her about how we used to go to the river, and how we used to have slumber parties, and how we used to sneak candy into my room at night.

'Candy was the best thing,' I say. 'Because our moms hardly ever let us have it. And it was our secret.'

'What kind of candy did you like?' Dr Kayla asks.

'Well, it's very bad for you,' I say. 'We shouldn't have eaten it.'

'But it was something fun you did together,' she says.

We couldn't do it any more, after. I shake my head.

Dr Kayla pulls out a package of Red Vines from a drawer in her desk and holds it out. 'Would you like some?' she asks.

My mom must have told her I like Red Vines. I know I didn't tell her.

'No, it's bad for me,' I say. I put my hand over my face.

Dr Kayla doesn't seem to notice when I do this. 'Why do you say that?' she asks.

'It's bad,' I whisper.

'Is that something this man told you?'

If I keep my hand over my face, maybe she will stop asking me questions. And now I'm thinking about ice cream. Chocolate ice cream and gummy bears and pretzels and muffins and Froot Loops. It's bad of me to think about these things. Bad people eat like this. They poison themselves.

'It's all right to have a treat once in a while,' Dr Kayla says.

'I know that,' I say. 'I ate some ice cream. At the mall.'

'How did that make you feel?' she asks.

I take my hand away from my face, but I keep my eyes closed. I remember the taste of the chocolate ice cream that Lee bought for me. 'It was good,' I say. I open my eyes. Dr Kayla is smiling.

I take a Red Vine, but I don't eat it. Red Vines were Dee's favourite, and I'm not ready for that yet.

The police are waiting outside with my parents; it's a man and a woman. The cops have a huddled talk with Dr Kayla, and my mom puts her arm around me, and I stand there and watch them, and then they come over to me.

'Amy, would it be OK if we ask you a few questions?' the woman cop asks. I think she's the same cop who came to see me that first night. She has short blonde hair and a large, flat nose. Her eyes are sad, and I know she's only doing her job. The last time she asked me questions, when I didn't answer, she went away.

'Yes,' I say. 'It's all right,' I tell my mom.

We go back into Dr Kayla's office. I sit in my usual chair in front of her desk, and Dr Kayla stands by the door, trying to look as if she's not there. For once, I'm glad she is.

She's not going to let them push too far.

'I know what you want me to tell you,' I say. 'But I can't.' It's the first time I've been honest with them, admitted that I know the answers.

'This man has told you that he has the power,' says the lady cop, 'but it isn't true. You have the power now. Once you tell us where your cousin is, we can go find her, and we can take this man away to jail.'

I have never told them that it was a man. All they know is what some random person saw, far down the riverbank.

'We are very experienced in bringing dangerous people into custody,' the man says. 'We won't let him hurt Dee.'

'I know you would try,' I say. I stare at them. I am going to sit here and stare until they give up and go away. But the woman won't just let me do that.

'Amy,' she says. She sits down next to me in the other chair in front of Dr Kayla's desk. 'We know that you love your cousin. We know that's why you're doing this.' She reaches out and takes my hand. She has brown eyes. There is a doll that she looks like, but I can't place the name. I don't understand how I could have forgotten. I can see the doll as if she's right in front of my eyes. And that makes me like this woman more. She could be like me.

'You don't know what I know,' I say.

'That's why we're asking you these questions,' the woman says. 'We want to understand. Amy, it's been more than two weeks since you came home. Every day that passes makes it harder for us to find her.'

*

111

In the forest, there was a tree. There were lots of trees, of course, but there was this one tree that was bigger than the other ones around it. I used to tell Lola and Barbie that the tree was magic, that there were fairies, and that was why there were mushrooms on it. The fairies lived in the mushrooms. Lola would always ask me, if there were really fairies, why couldn't we see them? I would say that fairies can make themselves invisible, and then I would put my hand over my face, and I would say, you can't see me, I must be a fairy. And then she would laugh and say that I was not a fairy, I was just putting a hand over my face. But one night, I saw her doing it. She put her hand over her face and then Barbie said, a fairy! And then Barbie put her hand over her face, and Lola pretended that she couldn't see her.

They knew it was just a game, but they also knew it was magic.

'That's enough for one day,' Dr Kayla says. I hear the cops shuffling around and the door opening and closing, and I know that Dr Kayla is still there. I can feel her breathing.

'You can take your hand away. It's just me,' she says.

I do it, but I look down at my lap. When the police look at me, they see either a crazy person or a monster. They see a person who would let her own cousin die instead of telling them what they need to know. It's right for them to see me that way because there is part of me that is a monster. And there is part of me that is crazy, because when you get beat up by a big man and you listen to your cousin being raped, and you disappear into the woods for six years, that is what happens. But there is another part of me that's not crazy, that's doing what's right for Stacie and for Barbie and Lola. They will not convince me that what I'm doing now is wrong.

Dr Kayla sits down next to me. 'Amy, your aunt has filed papers with the court to compel you to give a deposition. Do you know what that is?'

'No,' I say.

'It means that you would have to answer questions.'

'Or what?' I ask.

'Well, or be in contempt of court,' she says.

'I'm not going to answer,' I say. My mind spins. I shouldn't be surprised. Dee is Aunt Hannah's daughter. She would do anything to find her.

'My job will be to evaluate you and tell the court whether you will be harmed if you testify,' she says.

It isn't me who will be harmed. I say nothing.

'You will be able to discuss this with your parents, and you can get a lawyer for yourself.'

'Am I going to jail?' I ask.

'No,' she says. 'I can't imagine that anyone would send you to jail. Your aunt just wants answers. She doesn't know what else to do.' I'm still looking down at my lap, but I can see the lower part of her face, how her mouth turns a little bit up as if she's trying to smile, but she's sad. I don't think she wants me to go to jail. But I think she wants me to talk. She thinks that if she helps me, then I will want to talk, and everything will be OK.

'Thank you,' I say.

'You're welcome, Amy.' She puts a hand over mine and squeezes.

Tears well up in my eyes. Dr Kayla wants everything to be OK.

17.

My parents are livid. They can't believe Aunt Hannah would do this. But at the same time, they look at me with those sad eyes, like they wish I would just talk. No one will say it; even Jay isn't saying it as we sit at the dinner table. We eat in complete silence.

Jay gets up and cleans his plate, and then he goes to the freezer and gets out an ice cream bar. He takes it into the living room to eat, leaving the three of us at the table.

'We're going to get you a lawyer,' my dad says.

'Dr Kayla is not going to let this happen,' my mom says. 'You need time. After what you've been through, you deserve all the time you need.' But her eyes don't agree with what she's saying. Her eyes say that she feels what Aunt Hannah feels. It's only because she loves me that she can hold it back behind her brown eyes, eyes like mine.

No one says anything else, and we're all done eating, but no one moves to get up from the table until the phone rings.

Dad jumps in his chair, and he knocks over his water glass. It goes everywhere, soaking into the tablecloth. He curses and picks up his glass as Mom goes to answer it.

'Hello?' she says. She stares at me with those sad eyes. 'It's for you.' She holds the phone out.

I think that it must be Lee. I wonder if she had anything to do with what her mom has done. She said she doesn't want to know, but maybe that isn't true. Maybe she wants to make me talk, but she'll pretend that she doesn't. All of her being nice to me, it could be a trick. But if that's true, I can't let on that I know.

I take the phone. 'Hello?'

'Amy! It's Vinnie,' says the voice.

'Oh, um . . .' It takes me a second to remember. It's like the party two nights ago happened in another life, that parallel world where Amy never went away.

'So I knew you probably wouldn't call me. I mean, why would you? But Lee gave me your number, and she told me I could call but not to bother you, so I'm not trying to bother you, all right?'

'All right,' I say.

'Well, I was wondering if you want to hang out, like we talked about?'

'Um . . . when?'

'Well, tonight. You don't have plans, do you? We don't

have to hang out at my house. I mean, that was a stupid idea. Who wants to do that? We could go to the library, though. They have graphic novels. Or maybe you like geography. I hear they have a lot of maps. I mean, atlases.'

'Atlases?'

'All kinds of atlases,' he says. 'Africa, Venezuela, Europe.'

'That sounds . . .' I know I don't want to stay here right now. I know I can't take another minute of my mom's sad eyes, of the silence. Even though it's all my fault.

'Dumb, I know, but that's me. I'm good for dumb.'

'It sounds great,' I say.

'Cool. I could pick you up.'

'OK,' I say.

'Great!' He hangs up fast. I guess he was worried that I'd change my mind.

My mom is staring at me.

'It's OK,' I say. 'It's just Vinnie. Mini Vinnie Open-heimer. Lee introduced me to him again. He wants to take me to the library.'

'I don't know,' my mom says.

'I need something to read,' I say. Now that my mom is trying to stop me, I know I need to get out of the house. Nothing could be more important. If I don't get out, I'll start to scream. It wells up in me, and I stuff it back. It's like when you're sick and you're trying not to throw up. I almost can't hold it back, but I do. But the scream is still there.

'Honey, we're going to have to prove that you aren't able

117

to talk about what happened,' she says. 'What if somebody sees you?'

'I'm going,' I say. I think this is what normal teenagers do. They fight with their mothers over going out. I go into the living room, and Jay is watching TV and finishing his ice cream. As I walk in, he hurriedly flips the TV off.

'Good luck,' he says.

'What do you mean?' I ask.

'You'll never hear the end of it. You weren't using drugs, were you?' he mimics. 'Were there any parents there? What about girls? You didn't answer your phone. What was I supposed to think?'

What if you were kidnapped? That's why Mom is always worried about him. It's just one more way I ruined his life.

'I'm sorry,' I say.

'Amy, come on, I didn't mean it's your fault.' He takes a last bite of ice cream and swallows it with a grimace that says *cod liver oil*, not *sweet*.

'It is, though,' I say. 'Everything.'

'Amy—'

But I don't wait to hear what he has to say. I know what he really thinks, and it's true. If I had never got in the car, if I had run, if I would just tell them, they would be happier. But I didn't, and I can't. It's too late. I grab my Safeway bag, go out the front door, and sit on the kerb to wait for Vinnie. I can see my mom peeking through the living room window. I put my head between my legs, and I scream without opening my mouth. I scream and scream and scream until I see feet in front of me. They are big, floppy man feet.

118

'Hey,' Vinnie says.

I jump up. 'Hey.' I run towards his car, which is parked right across the street. It's an old Toyota Corolla, and he rushes in front of me and opens the door. I jump in, and I guess he takes his cue from me, because he runs around to his side and stuffs himself in the front seat. The car is too small for him and he's bent over as he puts the car into gear, and we shoot off down the street. A few seconds later, we jerk to a stop at a stop sign. I think his bad driving has rattled the scream out of me.

'Are you OK?' he asks, gunning it again. We shoot across the intersection and careen along.

'Y-yes,' I say.

'It seemed like someone was chasing you.'

'My mom doesn't want me to go out,' I say.

'Oh, well, I can see that. She's a mom. She probably thinks about you like you're still ten.' We speed around a corner and then take off again. 'My mom doesn't want me to drive, but since I got my licence, she kind of has to let me.' He says this as if they're the same thing, my mom believing I'm a little girl and his mom having a realistic fear that he will kill himself while driving. 'You made it through that party all right,' he says. 'Anyway, lots of crazy people go out. You can't keep them all in.'

'Right,' I say. 'True.'

'Not that you're crazy,' he says, pulling into the library parking lot. We hit the kerb in front of the parking spot, and I'm thrown back against my seat. 'Unless you are. That's OK, too.'

'I think I'm a little crazy,' I say.

'Oh, OK, cool.' He jumps out of the car, runs around to my side, and opens my door.

I step out, and I can feel him above me. But there's less of him than there was of Kyle. I didn't notice that before, how Vinnie is thinner. Because Vinnie isn't skinny. But Kyle had some fat hanging off him. No matter how healthy he ate and how much he exercised, he couldn't get rid of it. Vinnie is solid. He probably doesn't have any fat anywhere on his body.

He takes a step back, and we walk across the parking lot with a foot between us. The parking lot seems long and looming. It takes a lot of steps to get across it.

'I guess you need a library card,' he says as he holds the door open for me.

'I had one,' I say.

'Great. You just need to renew it. So what do you think? Graphic novels? There's the teen section.' He points. 'I always head straight for fantasy. You know, dragons?' He holds up his hands like they're claws and grins big.

'That's your dragon?' I ask.

'Sure.' He hisses. 'That's what dragons sound like.' He hisses again.

I burst out laughing.

The lady behind the desk glares at us, but she's laughing a little bit, too.

'I had this story about dragons,' I say as we head for the fantasy section.

'Which one was it?' he asks.

'Well, I made it up. There was this dragon that had green wings. But she wanted red wings like her sister.'

'Did she breathe fire?'

'Yes, but that didn't matter,' I say. 'All dragons breathe fire, but only some of them have red wings.'

'What about gold? Seems like I'd worry about how much gold I had, if I were a dragon.'

'I don't think they knew what gold was,' I say.

'Who didn't know?' he asks. He pulls a book off the shelf and examines the cover. He acts like this question is nothing at all.

I can't believe I said that. I pick up a book, too. This one is not about dragons. It's about a lady wearing improbable armour that shows off her boobs. She also has a sword that's probably too big for her to use. I try to remember if I taught the girls about gold or not. I must have taught them about money. That must have been something we talked about. Kyle used to count it. He had a wad that he kept in his pocket all the time, like he was worried that we would steal it. Even after years had gone by, after he stopped locking us inside the cabin, he still kept that money in his pocket.

'I'm sorry,' Vinnie says. 'I know you don't want to talk about it.'

I keep looking at the book. I want to go away into my mind now. Why am I always going away when I don't want to, and now that I want to, I'm still here?

'Hey, want to do something more fun? I mean, books are nice but they kind of make you think about things, don't they?'

I nod. I'm not sure what he means, but suddenly the tall shelves are placed too closely together. They lean over me. The books seem to hover on the shelves as if they might fall at any moment. Or jump. I want to get out of this building.

'We'll just check out a few so your mom thinks we were here the whole time.' He heads for another section of the library and starts pulling books off the shelves. 'Graphic novels, teen stuff,' he says. 'And this one's new? What do you think?' It has a picture of a girl on the cover, but her head is cut off. She's facing away from the camera, too, looking off into the distance, her dress flowing around her feet. Vinnie doesn't wait for me to answer, just brings them all up to the counter. I stand behind him, hoping the lady checking out the books can't see me. I want to put my hand in front of my face, but I don't. If I do that, people will just look at me more.

It seems like it takes another hour, but finally Vinnie takes the books and leads the way back out the door. His jeans are dark and new, I notice. Not like Kyle's, which were faded and ratty. And Vinnie wears a T-shirt that hangs loose and doesn't stick to his belly. His hair is shorter and there's no grey in it. There's nothing about Vinnie that's like Kyle at all.

Vinnie throws the books in the back seat of the car and turns to me. 'So I guess you don't know how to drive,' he says.

'No.' That's just one more thing Kyle took from me. I'm supposed to have my licence now. I'm supposed to be terrorizing my friends the way Vinnie terrorizes his.

'Want to learn?'

'From you?' I blurt. I put my hand over my mouth.

He laughs. 'You know what they say – if you can't do, teach.' He smiles, and his mouth is normal sized, and his eyes light up. He's not mad at me at all. He waves at the parking lot in front of us, which is attached to the parking lot for the elementary school next door. It's almost all empty. 'Plenty of space and nothing to hit. This is where my mom used to take me.'

'I don't know.'

'Come on, you'll love it. Driving is what freedom's all about.' He opens the driver's side door and waves an arm.

'Freedom sounds good,' I say. I slide into the driver's seat.

'There's a thing under the seat.' He reaches between my legs and pulls a lever. With both hands he moves my seat forwards with me in it. Before I can do or say anything, he's pulled away again and is running around to the passenger side. He hands me the key. 'Let's get this party started!' he says, grinning.

I put the key in the ignition. Ten minutes later, I'm doing a circle around the parking lot, and the grin on my face is bigger than the grin on his. I imagine slamming my foot on the gas pedal and pulling out into the street. And then? I could go away. I could go somewhere where no one knew me, where no one would ask any questions. Instead, I make another circle and another. I stop and start and turn and park and start up again.

Vinnie talks. He tells me about all the kids we went to school with together before and what happened to them, who got tall like him and who is still short and who got ugly and who got hot. 'You're lucky you missed middle school,' he says. 'Middle school was terrible. In sixth grade I got beat up all the time. See this scar?' He points to something on his chin. 'But then *I* got big. I don't see why that means you have to beat people up, though.'

I drive faster, around and around and around.

'Once I got tall, people said I should start playing basketball, so I did, but then after a few practices, people started saying I should maybe not play basketball. Somebody said I should join the chess club, so I did that, but chess is hard. You know?'

I stop the car and start it again.

'Anyway, high school is better. People still call me Mini Vinnie, but nobody tries to beat me up. I joined the choir. Want to hear me sing?' He doesn't wait for an answer, but launches into some song I've never heard before, something about the stars and the moon colliding. But his voice is actually good. I don't realize that I've completely stopped the car until it's over.

'That was really good,' I say.

'Thanks. I think I've found my calling. Something that doesn't require coordination.' We're both silent for a few seconds. It's getting dark outside. The library has closed and the final couple of cars have left the parking lot. 'Do you want to go home?' he asks.

'I don't know,' I say. I know my mom is worried about

me. She will be going insane with worry. My dad will be angry, but he'll be doing something with it. He's probably talked to seven lawyers already, trying to make sure I don't have to talk. It isn't right for me to be out here while they're upset for me. But I still don't want to go back.

Vinnie reaches over me and turns a rod next to the steering wheel. The car's lights come on, blasting the parking lot with their beams. 'We don't have to go back,' he says. He puts a hand on my shoulder. He lets it sit there for a second, and then he gives my shoulder a little pat. He looks down at me with big blue eyes, all serious.

I squirm.

'I'm sorry,' he says. 'I thought when someone was upset you were supposed to . . . I don't know.'

'It's OK,' I say. 'It's not your fault.'

'You don't like people touching you,' he says. 'I get it.'

'I'm sorry,' I say again. 'Lee told me . . . she said you were asking her . . .'

'It's all right,' he says. 'I'm an idiot.'

'I don't know why people like boys,' I say. 'What boys and girls do.' I can't look at him, so I look out across the parking lot. All that space, and I could start the car again. I could go anywhere I want now, but in my mind, part of me is back in the cabin. Part of me is in the bathroom with Lola, and I am singing to her, and we're pretending there's nobody else there. We're pretending she came from nowhere, and there's no such thing as what boys and girls do at all.

Vinnie lifts a hand like he's going to try to pat my

shoulder again, but then he doesn't. 'Most boys aren't like that,' he says.

I know what he thinks. He thinks somebody raped me. But nobody did. Nobody did it to me, so I don't have a right to feel this way. The worst things didn't happen to me; they happened to her, and I forgot. I forgot that she was what he did to her, and I blamed her for who she became. I don't have a right to even be sitting here in this car, learning how to drive with this boy who wants to be my friend. It should be her sitting here, not me. She deserved to be here.

'You know, lots of people have issues,' Vinnie says. 'Maybe you can join a support group.'

'I don't know if it's the same,' I say. That's an understatement. Nobody can understand what's inside me. And they shouldn't. Because something inside me is wrong.

'Take me, for example,' Vinnie says. 'I go to a support group. It's for kids who don't know what's going on.'

I look at him out of the corner of my eye. His face is serious in a different way now, and his hands are in his lap.

'Like, don't know whether they like boys or girls,' he says.

'You don't know if you like girls?' I almost laugh. It seems like nonsense, after what Lee told me and the way he looked at me a minute ago.

'I think I like girls, but I also think I like boys,' he says. 'It's confusing.' Before I can say anything, he rushes on. 'It's in Portland, the support group. My mom takes me every other Saturday. She thinks I need to talk to people who understand because she doesn't.'

126

'Does it help?' I ask.

He shrugs. 'Yeah. At least I know I'm not the only one. Like, there's nothing wrong with me. Or at least, not *that* wrong.'

I stare at the parking lot.

'OK, I know it's not the same,' he says. 'I'm sorry.'

'No,' I say. 'Thank you.' There probably is a support group out there for girls who got raped. And if that was my problem, maybe it could actually make me feel better. But where's the group for girls who were silent while their best friend got raped? Who loved something that came out of it more than life? Who want something back . . . I close my eyes. I want to go there in my mind, but I can still feel the car and the parking lot and Vinnie sitting next to me and even my parents waiting at home. Vinnie does this to me somehow. He keeps me sitting at least part way in the present, and I don't know if I like it.

'Nobody at school knows,' he says. 'Except Lee. You know, in this town . . .'

'Being different is a crime,' I say. I think about how Dee was different, how she was bubbly and too talkative and always wanted to be a part of everything, and for some reason, that made her weird. But she never stopped trying to be a part of things, even so. She was the resilient one then. She was the one I would have thought would survive. Tears leak from my face. She cried when they excluded her. She was weak in that way. I should have realized that she was weak, and I should have been strong. I should have found a way to make him turn to me, but instead, I hoped he wouldn't. I prayed he wouldn't. I prayed he would never do it to me.

'Hey, you don't have to cry,' Vinnie says. 'I still like girls, too. You still have a chance with all this.'

That was the most inappropriate joke ever. I keep crying, but part of me is laughing. I shake my head.

'Do you want to break things? I've got some recycling in the trunk. We can throw my dad's beer bottles against the library wall.'

'I want to be different,' I say.

Vinnie doesn't answer. I don't look at him. I know that when he stops talking, it's serious. If he isn't talking, then I'll talk. And I want to. I want to talk about Stacie, and about my babies, and about every single thing that happened. About who I was when I was Chelsea and what I did and what I didn't do. Who I should have been, what I should have done.

'I want to be a good person,' I begin. I can feel it coming, but I can't stop it. 'I want to be the one who protects. The one who's stronger. The one who stops the bad person from . . .'

Vinnie waits.

'I want to want . . .'

'What?' he asks.

'To be the one who died,' I say. 'But I don't want that. I didn't want it. I didn't want it.' I collapse into sobs, and Vinnie puts his hand on my shoulder again, and I don't shake it off. I lean on the steering wheel and close my eyes and just sob.

18.

A good person, a good friend, a good cousin, would have wanted to trade places. A good person would have wished she could be the one lying on the ground, her face still, her hair bloody. But would a good person have wanted to leave those children with a mother who was broken, a mother who was no mother at all? There was no way to be a good cousin and a good mother. There is a part of me that knows that, that knows it wasn't wrong of me to love those children, that it will never be wrong for me to love them. But there is another part of me that knows that loving those children was a betrayal of the worst kind.

You wanted them, I hear her screaming. *You wanted them.* But I didn't. I didn't want them any more than she did. I just had the capacity to love them. Dee's heart, which was so big before and so forgiving and so open, got closed up. I think it started before he raped her. It even happened before she was Stacie. The moment Kyle touched Dee, when he grabbed her by the arm that day at the river, that was when she stopped talking. She lost her voice, and after that, everything followed.

We had been in the cabin for about six months when I figured it out. Stacie didn't figure it out herself. When she didn't get her period, she was glad. She had never wanted it, and she thought it had magically gone away. If Kyle noticed, he didn't say anything. This was before he ever let us leave the cabin to go down to the river, so we were all there in the little room with the doors locked from the inside and the key around Kyle's neck. He had his dolls lined up on the table, Barbie and Lola and Chelsea and Stacie all together with some others.

'Barbie, you are looking beautiful today,' Kyle said. 'Why, thank you, Kyle,' Kyle said in a small, breathy voice. 'It is so nice and warm inside now that you have finished bringing the wood in for the stove. I want the very best for you, dear one.' Kyle made the Barbie doll walk across the table, like she was heading for the woodstove.

Stacie hadn't had her period in two months, and she wasn't feeling good, either. She didn't say anything, but I noticed she was eating slower and sleeping longer. We sat on the bed doing nothing, just watching Kyle with his dolls.

'Stacie,' I said.

She didn't really look at me.

'Once you get it, it isn't supposed to stop,' I whispered.

'Yes it is,' she said.

'No, it isn't.'

'It wasn't supposed to start.'

'I love you, Barbie,' Kyle whispered to the one wearing the nurse's outfit. He ran a hand down her little plastic body. 'You are my favourite Barbie of all.' He whispered back. 'And I love you.'

'Stacie doesn't get hers,' Stacie said. She stared at the doll Stacie, which Kyle was holding in his other hand now.

I leant my head in as close to her ear as I could. 'Dee,' I whispered, barely making any sound.

Kyle's little head snapped up. He smashed the nurse Barbie to the table.

'You're pregnant,' I said, louder than I meant to. I stared at Kyle as he got up from his chair, still holding the Stacie doll. His eyes changed from childlike to angry as he walked towards us; they glowed hard as his steps tensed.

I held up my hand to protect myself, but his shadow leant over me. He didn't strike.

'Is it true, Stacie?' he asked. 'Stacie, is it true?' Now he was talking to the doll.

Stacie burst into tears. She couldn't talk. All she could do was cry.

'I'm sorry,' I said. 'It's not true. I take it back.' I hugged her, but she didn't hug me. She just cried.

Stacie's stomach got bigger, but the rest of her didn't grow. She didn't get taller or stronger. The baby didn't give her anything. All it did was take away. First she couldn't eat without wanting to toss everything back up, and when that passed, she had trouble walking because of the extra weight and the way it all sat in her belly and made her off balance. It kept her from sleeping, and she would lie on her side in the big bed with her eyes open. Kyle started sleeping on the side towards the wall because Stacie would have to get up and pee during the night. She would roll off the bed and stumble as she tried to walk, and she would make her way slowly past my camp bed and into the bathroom, and she would stay there for a long time.

After a while, the baby started moving around in there. The first time it happened, Kyle was away. He had driven into town to get us supplies, and so we were locked inside the cabin. I had already done all the chores I was supposed to do, so I was sitting next to Stacie on the big bed, reading *Hawaii* by James Michener for the third time. We didn't have much entertainment – no video games or iPad or computer. For books, we had the King James Bible, three novels by Louis L'Amour about cowboys, and *Hawaii*. I think they were all in the cabin before Kyle got there, because I never saw him pick one up. Over the years I read them all about a thousand times. When Stacie was first pregnant, I could already have recited by heart how the Hawaiian Islands formed out of volcanoes in the ocean and how the people came across the ocean in little boats. It was nice to imagine myself as one of them, out there in the water with all that space, not confined in a single room. Stacie was curled in a ball with her feet almost touching me. Suddenly, she sat up. She was wearing a pink velour sweatsuit, already four sizes bigger than she'd been before.

'What happened?' I asked.

She clutched her stomach. 'It moved.'

'Oh.' I wasn't sure what to say.

Her face twisted.

'Again?' I asked.

'It's kicking me.'

'That's what they do,' I said. 'Jay kicked my mom, and she laughed.' I remembered her sitting in the big chair in the living room. It was just a flash, like a photograph in my head. My mom sitting there holding her stomach, laughing. *He's a rowdy one, Amy,* she said. *Amy. Amy.* The name flipped through my brain. I held on to the picture. I was looking up at my mom from below. Her belly was so big, and there was a ring on the hand over her belly. And the old afghan that our grandma made, lying over her lap. It was as clear as if I were looking right at her now.

'I don't want it.' Stacie scooted off the edge of the bed. 'I don't want it.'

'It's OK,' I said. 'It's normal.'

Tears exploded from Stacie's face. 'I don't want it. I don't want it.' She stumbled against my camp bed and pushed it aside. It rolled over, and its frame clanged against the hardwood floor.

I stood up. 'It will come out,' I said. 'It will come out and everything will be fine.'

'I want it out now.' She kicked the overturned bed out of the way and stomped towards the little kitchen. 'What will hurt it?' She opened a cupboard and slammed it shut again, then opened the next one. 'Cereal. Soup. Pasta.' She slammed the cupboard and bent down beneath the sink. 'This.' She pulled a gallon of bleach out and slammed it on the counter. 'This.' She pulled out a container of dishwashing soap. 'This.' She pulled out a spray bottle of cleaning fluid. She turned back towards me. 'One of these things will do it.'

'They'll kill *you*,' I said. I reached for the spray bottle, but she slapped my hand. 'Stacie, come on.'

She pushed me in the chest. I fell back into a counter. She ripped the cap off the bleach.

'No!' I grabbed it from her, and bleach flew out of the top. It got all over her pink sweatsuit and my purple nightgown.

She grabbed for it, but I threw it away. It landed on the floor next to my overturned camp bed, the liquid flying with the bottle. Where it landed, the bleach spilt out and the smell overwhelmed the room. Stacie picked up the dishwashing soap.

I reached for it, but she was quicker. She kicked my leg and ran past me, opening the cap as she went. I hobbled after her, and with her big belly, she was slower. I caught her just as she rounded the corner towards the bathroom. As I grabbed for the bottle, she put it to her mouth and took a long gulp. I smashed it away from her, and it fell on the floor, too.

Bubbles frothed around her mouth, and she grinned at me. 'It's going to die,' she said.

'You need to throw up.' I pushed her towards the bathroom.

'No.' She pushed back against me, and this time, her belly helped her. I pushed, and she shoved me, and I couldn't move her an inch.

'You have to get it out!' I was crying now, too. 'Stacie, you drank soap!' I didn't know what drinking soap did. All I knew was she had to get it out of her. I didn't care about the baby then. I never knew it was going to be Lola. I just didn't want Stacie to die.

'No.' She shoved me harder. 'No no no no.' Then she shuddered and leant forward and threw up all over the floor. 'No!' She fell to her knees, screaming. 'No! No! No! No!' She threw up again. 'No.' She put her head in her hands and sobbed. Her belly heaved. The smell of the bleach we'd spilt filled the whole cabin. All the windows were closed and locked, too, so there was no air coming in at all. I knew that was bad.

'Come on,' I said. 'Let's go in the bathroom.'

But Stacie wouldn't move. I brought her water, and then I cleaned up the vomit and the bleach and the dish soap, and all she could do was sit there and sob.

I am sobbing into the steering wheel for so long that Vinnie calls my parents' house. He tells them that we're having a good time and I'm doing fine and we decided to go out for some ice cream. He says that I got a lot of books at the library and I need my own library card. He says, 'No, she's just worried you're still mad at her. OK, I'll tell her. Don't worry, Mr MacArthur, we'll be home before too long.' Then he pats me on the back again. He pats me the way you hit somebody who is choking, only softer. And by that time, I've cried so much that I don't think there are any more tears in me. I sit up, and my eyes are a fog.

'You want some water?' Vinnie asks. 'When I cry, I get thirsty.'

'You cry?' I ask. My voice comes out hoarse. I guess I am thirsty.

'Sure. Guys cry. I try not to do it in front of people, though. Gotta keep up appearances. I'm Big Vinnie now. That's what my mom says.'

I try to laugh and start coughing instead.

'Let's go to Dairy Queen,' he says. 'We can get you some water and also, if we get ice cream, I didn't just tell your dad a big fat lie.'

We trade places in the car, and then we're on our way, speeding and careening around corners. We go to the drive-through and order two large Blizzards. I get mine with M&Ms just like I used to do when I was a kid. But as Vinnie digs in, I let mine sit there. I already had ice cream once, with Lee. It was OK then, even though Dee wasn't there to share it. And it didn't make me a bad person, and it isn't going to hurt me. Slowly, I stick my spoon in the cup and raise it to my mouth. Just like the chocolate ice cream was still good, the Blizzard is still good, too.

'You wanted them.'

I don't answer her. I can't say it isn't true, not with them only a few feet away.

'*You wanted them.*'

'I may not know what happened,' Vinnie says, 'but I know you guys didn't kidnap yourselves. That means whatever happened wasn't your fault.'

Kyle slams the door in my face. I am out in the night, and they are inside.

'I'm glad it wasn't you who died.'

I swallow my bite of ice cream and turn to look at Vinnie. Even though he's pushed the driver's seat back as far as it will go, he still looks awkwardly scrunched. He fiddles with his spoon, digging a hole in his ice cream. 'Thanks,' I say.

'Your parents will be, too,' he says.

'But not Aunt Hannah,' I say. 'Not Lee.'

'They'll understand,' he says. 'They deserve to know the truth.'

I take another bite of ice cream, but the taste is gone. 'It's not just about her,' I say.

'What do you mean?' He slurps the ice cream off his spoon.

Don't say it, Chelsea, I think. *Don't say it.* But I have to tell someone. They're in my heart and my head and now they're in my throat, bursting out. They're too strong and too big to keep inside me. 'Dee had two kids,' I say. 'They're still there, with him. If I tell anyone anything, he'll kill them. That's what he said he'd do, and I believe it. If you knew him, you would, too.' My voice shakes as I say it, and then something snaps inside me. I take another bite of ice cream without tasting it. I am looking in on this scene

137

from outside the car. I am watching calmly. A boy in the car almost chokes on a bite of ice cream. He spits it back into his cup. The girl takes another bite.

When Lola was first born, before she was old enough to be a person, Kyle mostly treated her like she was his precious doll. He didn't get angry with her often, not when she cried all night and kept us all awake or stunk up our whole tiny cabin, or needed feeding and bathing and watching. Kyle would hold her and coo to her and change her diaper. It was like he was Lola's father and, even though I was only eleven, I was her mother. When he wasn't hitting me or throwing my food away, there were times when I could almost forget. Times when for a few minutes or an hour or even a day, I could believe we were a family. It was one of those times he told me about his.

He was sitting at the table, holding her in his arms. She squirmed and reached for his face, and he smiled that huge smile, and his eyes laughed.

'Aren't you a doll?' he cooed. 'Aren't you?'

'She's better than a doll,' I said. I was sweeping the wood floor of the cabin, and I clutched my broom. Why did I say that? But Kyle didn't get angry.

'Yes,' he said. 'Yes, you are.' He wrapped his arms around her and turned in his chair. Stacie was sitting on the bed. She watched all of us but said nothing. 'When I was a kid, they were my favourite things.' He looked at me, then at Lola. I'd never seen him smile like that, as if he was actually happy.

'You had dolls then?' I asked. I'd never thought about him as a kid. It didn't seem possible. Based on his face, I guessed he was in his twenties now. But how could someone so large have ever been small?

'My sister had dolls,' he said. 'Boys aren't supposed to have dolls. Are they?' He poked Lola in the stomach. She giggled. 'But then she died and Mommy didn't want to throw them out. Daddy wanted to but Mommy didn't, so she hid them in my room. Didn't she?'

The broom twitched in my hands, but I couldn't make myself sweep. If his sister died, that was sad. But he didn't act sad.

'Daddy caught me with one once. She was a Barbie. Cowgirl Barbie, with the little vest. She had high-heeled boots for her little high-heeled feet.' He rubbed Lola's bare foot. She giggled again. 'He hit me with his brown belt. That's how I got the scar on my back. You've seen it, Stacie.'

I'd seen it, too. He got dressed in front of both of us. But he looked at Stacie now. His eyes searched for her. His mouth closed up small so it didn't look like a clown mouth any more. It looked almost normal.

Stacie nodded and looked away.

I ran the broom across the floor. I had completely lost track of the pile of dirt.

'Barbie was my friend, and he took her away. But I had other friends, didn't I?' His eyes moved to the row of dolls lined up on top of the bookshelf and spilling over on to the bed. There were three more Barbies in that row.

'What about your mom?' Stacie asked. 'Did she hit you, too?' She didn't quite look at him when she said it, but there was an edge to her voice, mean.

'Mommy wanted Felicity back, didn't she?' He grinned at Lola. His clown face was back. 'She wished it had been me and not her who got so sick. All your daddy had was his dolls, baby, isn't that right? But now he has you, and you're *better* than a doll, aren't you?'

I kept sweeping. I was making a new pile of dirt, but every time I tried to sweep more dirt into it, I would sweep too hard, and the whole thing would break up. Kyle had bad parents. Maybe that explained why he was this way. But that didn't make it right. We weren't dolls; we were people.

'Sounds like your parents didn't love you,' Stacie said. If I had said that, he would have hit me. But nothing she said ever made him angry like that.

'Some people are supposed to love you and play with you and treat you nice,' Kyle told Lola. 'But if they don't, they get what they deserve. Yes they do.'

I kept sweeping.

Stacie didn't say anything. I didn't look up to see what was on her face. I could hear her breathing, though. She had a little bit of a cold, and she wheezed, in and out, wheeze, in and out.

'They never knew, did they? One night they were having dinner like every day and by bedtime Daddy got to be alone with his dolls. And everything in the whole house belonged to him. Just like how things are now, isn't that right?'

Lola began to cry. Kyle stood up, cradling her in his arms, and brought her over to Stacie. He set Lola down on the bed, and Stacie put one arm around her. The arm was shaking.

I swept faster, trying not to think about what Kyle had just said. Kyle had just told us that he murdered his parents, and he hadn't even blinked an eye.

That night, I lay on my camp bed next to the double bed, and I tried to imagine what Kyle's parents had been like. Had they looked like him, big people with little heads? Was his dad a bad man, too, or had Kyle made it all up? How did Kyle's sister die? I wondered if I should have been sad about some of it, if Kyle's past was supposed to be tragic. But Kyle didn't seem upset. He acted like he got everything he ever wanted. I could hear Stacie breathing, and I knew she was awake. I wished we could talk about it because maybe if we could at least talk about it I would be less scared. But he was between us, and we couldn't risk waking him up. No, it wasn't *we* who couldn't risk it; it was me.

Kyle would only kill Stacie if I ran away, if I told anyone. She was his doll, and as long as she was his and no one tried to take her, she'd stay alive. But Kyle never wanted me. He had no reason to keep me at all.

Lola was in her crib, which was at the foot of the bed. I wished I could hold her, but I couldn't risk waking her up either.

Kyle was going to kill me. Someday, he'd decide to do it. *I have to make sure he needs me,* I thought. *He needs me to take care of Lola.* I couldn't clutch Stacie or Lola or anyone, so I clutched my blanket. I wrapped my arms around it like it could protect me. And I shook so hard the bed vibrated beneath me.

Now that somebody knows, I'm not sure what I should do. Vinnie said he wouldn't tell anyone, but I don't know if I can trust him. I think he's a good guy, and he will probably want to do what's right, but he might not understand what that is. He might think the right thing is to run over to Aunt Hannah and tell her. I reach into my Safeway bag and hold on to the Stacie doll. We're still in Vinnie's car, and now we're sitting outside my house. I have a stack of books in my bag, too. They've squashed Stacie a little bit.

Why did I tell him? I am bad at keeping things inside. I used to think I was good at it, before. I was the one who didn't talk as much. But I couldn't hold back what I knew about Stacie being pregnant. She could have gone on for months pretending that it wasn't true, but I had to ruin it for her by saying it out loud, and now I might have ruined everything. Why couldn't I keep my mouth shut?

I wish that if you didn't say something, then it wouldn't be true. But it's all true whether I say it or not.

'I had fun today, hanging out,' Vinnie says. Apparently he's decided to ignore the part where I dissolved into tears and burdened him with my secrets.

'Me too,' I say. 'Thanks for teaching me how to drive.' I'm crushing the Stacie doll with one hand, and I pull my bag in close to my body. I'm staring out the car window at the mailbox with MacArthur on it. Something I didn't notice before is that the lettering is fading. Pieces of the red paint are chipped off, too. If I weren't looking, that red paint would still be chipped.

'I'd never say anything,' he says. 'If it was, like, my mom or somebody I had to protect, I wouldn't tell anyone either.'

'I don't want them to grow up with him,' I say. 'But the second he sees anyone coming, they'll be dead.' I don't look at him. I keep looking at the mailbox.

'If you tell, I'll kill them.'

The door slams.

I stumble down the three steps.

I know Kyle's kind of love. Once, I thought I was the one he'd kill, because he didn't want me. But now I know it's the other way. He let me go because he never wanted to own me. I was the buy one, get one free. But the things that are his: Stacie, Lola, Barbie. They're his or they're no one's.

Lola, a baby, less than a year old, crawling.

Stacie, sitting in the kitchen chair, watching her cross from where she was sitting towards the door.

Me, at the stove, cooking chicken. Pieces I'd just cut up, the cutting board and knife in the sink, smeared with goo from chicken innards. The chicken beginning to sizzle, bits to pop.

Kyle, opening the door.

It opened in, and it whooshed in front of Lola. She began to cry, falling back on her butt. She yowled.

Kyle picked her up off the floor. 'Oh, did I scare you, baby?' he cooed. He bounced her, but she kept yowling. Her cries grew louder. 'Baby, baby, baby,' Kyle said, but it did no good. The door was still standing open, cold night air blowing in. I walked around the edge of the counter, past Stacie, ready to take her, but he carried her outside, walked down the three steps from the porch to the driveway.

We all heard it at the same time, the roar of a car engine, the grating of tyres over gravel.

Kyle turned back towards me, gripped Lola tighter, and made a motion with his arm.

I slammed the door shut.

'What is it?' Stacie asked, standing. 'It's someone – someone's found us.' Her eyes lit.

We grabbed hands. It was the first time in months we'd done that. We rushed to the window and looked out. A car was pulling up the hill.

Kyle stared straight at us through the window. He put a hand around Lola's tiny neck and very slowly, shook his head.

'Maybe the cops know how to deal with people like that,' Vinnie says. 'Maybe they can talk him out of it. They do it on TV all the time. There's this guy who gets on the phone with the bad guy inside the building, and the bad guy sweats, and all the hostages cry, and then at the last minute everyone gets out OK.'

I don't remember ever seeing anything like that on TV.

I guess I've missed a lot of shows in the last six years. 'But you know him,' Vinnie says. 'It's up to you.'

I can't go inside. Not with this rattling around in my mind. Not when I went and said it out loud, and now someone is talking to me about it, out loud. But there's nowhere else for me to go. I wish Vinnie would start driving again and we could speed out of here, and I would never have to face my mom or my dad or Jay or Aunt Hannah or Lee. I would never have to see in their eyes how much they want to know the truth or face maybe being dragged in front of a judge. I would have to keep lying my whole life, but I wouldn't have to lie to the people I care about. It's hard to keep lying to them.

Especially when I made that choice, when I saw the look in Kyle's eyes that night, when we saw that car nosing up towards us. When I grabbed Stacie and pulled her down, so no one would see us in the window.

'You wanted her,' she said to me.

'No,' I said. But I held her hands. I held them and stared into her eyes, and she stared back. She knew the choice I made that day.

I push the Stacie doll down to the bottom of my Safeway bag. 'I can't tell them,' I say. 'You can't tell them either.'

'I won't,' Vinnie says. And I believe it. I have to.

19.

Six years is a long time. It's a long time to be constantly terrified and angry and sad. Sometimes if you want to survive, you have to make the best out of whatever kind of life you have. I could have refused to take care of the babies. I could have refused to let Kyle call me Chelsea, and I could have kept calling Stacie Dee. I could have let him throw my food away and starved to death.

I could have jumped in between Stacie and him every time he did it to her and let him knock me to the ground. I could have made him kill me.

In the moments when he smiled, when he showed a little bit of affection, I could have turned away. I could have spit in his weird little clown face.

But I wanted to live. I wanted to have moments when

the world wasn't dark and angry and sad. I wanted to have something to love.

The bathroom door opened. That was how Kyle would do it. He didn't care what you were doing in there. If he wanted to come in, he would just come. I could feel him standing above me. He blocked out half the light from the little bulb hanging from the ceiling. I was twelve now. Lola was a year and half old, and Stacie was pregnant again with Barbie. She wasn't too far along yet, though. We were both trying to pretend it wasn't true.

I couldn't help myself. I retched again. I had been sick for an hour, ever since I ate the last of the bologna sausage as a midnight snack. I didn't look at him as he came in. I didn't want to hear the lecture. Somehow it was my fault that I was sick. It could never be his fault, for buying old bologna from the half-price bin. We could never have sugar or white bread, but old processed meat, which happened to be really cheap, was no problem. He never saw any inconsistency in that, because whatever he did always made sense to him.

'Are you all right?' he asked. He sat down on the floor behind me. His legs were so long that one of his feet knocked against my rear as he adjusted himself.

'Bologna,' I whispered. 'Was bad.' Here it comes, I thought. I leant forward against the toilet, waiting to see if there was any more in me. Maybe if I kept throwing up he would at least not come any closer.

'Oh.' He shifted himself, and his foot knocked against

147

me again.

I thought I was done throwing up, so I closed the toilet lid and stood up. When I turned around, I saw that there were tears in Kyle's eyes.

'I was thinking about my sister,' he said.

I turned on the tap and filled a glass with water, hoping it wouldn't come back up again.

'Felicity was a beautiful little girl,' he said. 'Everybody said so. They gave her all the dolls. The pretty ones. Those were the ones she liked.'

I didn't know what to say. I wasn't sure if he even wanted me to say anything. So I sat down on the toilet lid and sipped the water.

'They looked at me like I did it, but I didn't. I didn't mean to. Nobody ever died from the flu before.' His shoe squeaked against the bathroom tile as he shifted himself again. 'Like I wanted to get the flu and then give it to her so she would die, that's how they looked at me.'

I took another sip of water. He was really crying now, tears rolling down his face. With Kyle, you could never be sure what tears meant. Sometimes he might be sad, but sometimes he was angry. When Kyle cried, you never knew what he might do.

'I never wanted it to happen. Just because I wanted her dolls, that doesn't mean I wanted her to die, does it?' He looked up at me. 'I loved . . . she was . . . it was just the *flu*. Nobody dies from it. Nobody.' He began sobbing, huffing and snorting and making noise.

I set down my glass of water and tore a few sheets of

toilet paper from the roll. I handed them to him.

He took the toilet paper and blew his nose.

'It's not your fault,' I said. I'd learnt by now to say whatever I thought he wanted to hear. I knew the truth didn't set you free, it got you hurt.

'But they thought it was.' He wiped his face with both hands.

So you killed them.

'They were supposed to love me.' He sobbed into his hands. His fingernails were thick and yellow. He dug them into his forehead. 'If they had just loved me like they were supposed to . . .'

'It's not your fault,' I said again.

'It's *not*,' he said. 'It was *them*.' He removed his hands from his face. His red eyes stared at me. 'You know I would never hurt you,' he said.

'I . . .' I swallowed, trying to keep myself from retching again. The water I had just drunk churned in my empty stomach.

'Anyone who loves me back, I would never hurt them. You and Stacie, and Lola, and all the dolls, I would never hurt any of you.'

'OK,' I said. Except raping Stacie, hitting me, starving us all. *None of us will ever love you*. The truth stuck in my throat, trying to push its way out like the bad bologna. I swallowed it with more water.

'We're all going to be together,' he said. 'For ever. A real family.'

For ever. Until he dies, I thought. *Someday, he'll die.*

Stacie stood in the doorway, holding Lola. 'She wants you,' Stacie said, and she set the baby on the floor.

'Dada!' Lola said, crawling towards him. 'Dada!'

Kyle scooped her up off the ground. 'Well, hello, baby.' He smiled at her, full big clown smile.

Stacie disappeared from the doorway.

'You are never going to get sick,' he said, cradling Lola. 'You are never going to get the flu or eat any bad bologna. You are never going to be sad. You are going to know that people love you. Me and your mommy and your Auntie Chel. We all love you, and we'll keep you safe.'

'Dada!' Lola said. Her big blue eyes lit up, and she reached for his face.

In the main room, a light came on.

Kyle's smile disappeared. We both knew a second before she started that this time it would be really bad. He shoved Lola at me, and I took her, and she began to cry.

Stacie was screaming. She wasn't screaming words, just screaming. Loud and long and wild. Something hard hit the floor. Something else crashed.

I stepped out of the bathroom just far enough to see. Kyle was holding Stacie. There was blood on her arm, blood dripping on the floor, and a serrated knife on the ground that must have had her blood on it. All the rest of our silverware was on the ground, too.

'Let me go!' she screamed. 'Let me go!' She squirmed in his arms.

'Shh,' Kyle said. 'Baby, shh.'

I took Lola back into the bathroom and closed the door.

Why does she scream now? I thought. *Why now and not when he's doing it? And why does he stop her from hurting herself, but he won't stop hurting her? How can he possibly think this is love?*

'He cried for his sister, but he killed his parents,' I whispered.

'Dada,' Lola said.

'Yes, Dada,' I said. 'Why is he this way? Why does he do this?'

Stacie was still screaming.

I closed my eyes, and it was like I closed my ears, too. There was no more yelling. What Kyle had done to his family, what he had done to Stacie, what he had done to me, that was all gone. I held Lola close to me, and I rocked back and forth. 'Once there was an otter,' I began. 'An otter who wanted to be friends with a turkey.'

Lola was warm, and I could feel her little heart beating. She touched my face with one of her tiny little hands. 'Chel!'

'Lola, you said my name.' I opened my eyes and looked at her round face, with her blue, innocent eyes.

'Chel!'

In the background, there was noise. But I couldn't hear it. I only heard Lola's sweet little voice. I smiled. 'Do you want to hear the rest of the story?' I said. 'The otter wanted to be the turkey's friend, so he lifted his nose out of the river . . .'

A day goes by, and then two. Vinnie doesn't tell my secret. I told someone the truth, and yet it's like I didn't. It's like everything is the same. Just like I thought, my dad has already found a lawyer to fight for me. The lawyer tells the judge that I'll be harmed if I have to talk. He brings in a report from Dr Kayla, who says I'm not ready. But the judge says I have to go into court with the lawyer so he can talk to me himself. I'm supposed to go with Dr Kayla and the lawyer and my parents.

I could tell them that Dee is dead, but that won't stop them from looking for Kyle. Aunt Hannah and Lee will want to send him to jail for what he did. They won't stop and their lawyer won't stop until I tell them where he is. I know that this lawyer my dad got can't stop that for ever.

But Dr Kayla said they won't send me to jail. If I don't talk, there's really nothing they can do. So on the third day after I told Vinnie, the day I'm supposed to go in to see the judge, I stay in my bedroom.

My dad knocks on the door. 'Honey? It's going to be fine. The judge isn't going to ask you any details. He's just going to ask you how you're feeling. We went over all this with the lawyer.'

'I'm not going,' I say. I'm wearing shorts that I bought on my shopping trip with Lee and a purple top. I'm also wearing the ugly pink beads, and I'm holding my Stacie doll. I'm doing this for her, too. I'm doing this for the person she was before, the one who always wanted to have kids someday. That Dee would have done anything to protect them. I can't bring her back or change what happened, but I can do this for her.

You wanted them, I hear her scream.

You would have wanted them, too, I think. You would have loved them more than anything in the world. I picture Dee right here in this room on the trundle bed eating Red Vines, smiling. I picture her on roller skates as we whizzed through the paths in the big park.

'I wonder who I'm going to marry,' she says. She skids off the path and stops herself against the play structure with the tyre swings. I totter after her. I was always more cautious on roller skates. She never seemed to worry about falling, just whooshed off on the sidewalk or the grass or into the street. Now we're standing on sawdust.

'Probably somebody rich,' I say.

'A millionaire!' She pulls off her skates and jumps up on the tyre swing. 'And he'll have blue eyes and long hair like a knight.'

'I don't think there are knights any more,' I say, climbing on the next tyre swing.

'I said like a knight,' she says, swinging. 'And we're going to have six children, and they'll have blue eyes and dark hair just like him. Well, maybe a couple will be blonde like me.'

'If they're rich, I guess they can dye their hair however they want,' I say.

She laughs. 'Six beautiful, rich children. And we'll live in a mansion. You and your husband can live right next door.'

'We'll have two mansions and twelve kids,' I say.

That was Dee. That was Lola and Barbie's real mother.

And she was still there, part of her, for a long time. I remember that day the car came, those long minutes under the window. Minutes when she could have jumped up, pounded on the window, run out the door. *You wanted her,*

153

she accused me. But she was silent. To protect Lola, she sacrificed herself, too.

We heard the door slam behind Kyle, but even then, I didn't want to stand up. In case the man was still out there, in case there was any chance he'd see us. The first thing I saw was Kyle's legs, the bottoms of his ratty brown cargo pants.

Lola let out a cry, and I began to breathe again.

But the man must be gone. The first person to ever come up here in close to two years, and we'd let him go. Stacie dropped my hands and stood up.

'I saw you looking out,' Kyle said, his voice whiny and high.

'I'll take her,' Stacie said. I looked up and saw Stacie hold out her arms. Lola was still crying, flailing her little hands. I stood up, too, but Kyle didn't look at me.

'You wanted to talk to him.'

'No, I didn't,' Stacie said. Her voice was flat. 'Just give me Lola so I can feed her.'

Kyle burst into tears. He pulled Lola closer, and she screeched.

'She's just crying because she's hungry,' I said. I could smell the chicken that I'd left on the stove burning. Kyle smelt it, too, and he headed for the stove, moving Lola to one arm. He turned the stove off, plucked the frying pan off the burner, and tossed the blackening chicken into the garbage.

'Stop crying,' he said to Lola, tears still streaming down his face. 'Stop!'

Lola screamed harder.

'I can feed her,' Stacie said.

Kyle turned back towards us. His face was streaked with tears, but his eyes were hard. He cradled Lola with both arms again. 'No one's eating tonight. Not you, not Chelsea, not Lola. You've been bad.'

'She's just a baby,' Stacie said.

'She looked at him, too,' Kyle said. 'She made him ask questions.'

'She's too young—'

'No.' He leant down into Lola's face. 'You've been bad.'

Suddenly I remembered the day I told Stacie she was pregnant, how Kyle had been playing with that Barbie and saying he loved her, how he'd slammed the Barbie on the table. I stepped forward, reaching for Lola. 'I'll take her,' I said. 'I won't let Stacie feed her.' One more step and then another, and finally, I was close enough.

Kyle shoved Lola into my arms. He leant against the kitchen counter. 'You're all bad,' he said.

We sat there for hours, with Kyle staring at us, afraid to move. I held Lola while she cried her lungs out. Stacie leant against the window that we'd both wanted so badly to look out of, wanted so badly to use to signal that man. Later that night, when Kyle was finally asleep, she took Lola into the bathroom and fed her. And that wasn't the last secret night-time feeding. Even when the girls were too old to nurse, Kyle would sometimes take their food away. And we'd stash food together, hiding it in odd places like in the backs of high cupboards or underneath clothes. We'd take a little at a time so Kyle wouldn't notice it was missing and then use it to feed the girls. Stacie always helped with that. Almost until the end.

I haven't given her enough credit, for everything she did. For everything she didn't do. For all the years she held out, before . . .

I squeeze my eyes closed, search for another memory, a day or an hour or even a moment when she was Stacie, but she was still herself. When she would agree with what I'm doing. I know there are more, but I'm stuck back under the window. My hands grip hers, and she grips my hands back.

You wanted her.

My dad opens the door and peeks his head in. He frowns when he sees my purple shirt. I'd been wearing other colours, and this doesn't look good. It looks like I'm really crazy like we want Dr Kayla to say. I set the Stacie doll down and try to look not crazy.

'You don't have a choice, honey,' he says. 'I promise it will be OK. Your mom and I will be right there.'

'I have a choice,' I say.

He sighs and tilts his head that way he used to do when he was annoyed. Like when I took Jay's ball and wouldn't give it back to him.

'Someday I'll tell you and you'll understand,' I say. I wonder when that will be. When Kyle dies, how will I know? Will the girls be able to find me?

'Amy.' He sighs again and sits down next to me on the bed. 'There is a court hearing. We have to go.'

156

My mom stands in the doorway now. She wrings her hands in front of her chest. Her eyes flit back and forth between us. I see Jay behind her, standing in the doorway of his bedroom, staring. Mom is wearing a floral print dress like the kind she used to wear to church. It doesn't look natural on her any more.

'I'm not going,' I say. 'If they want to put me in jail, they can do that.'

'Nobody is going to put you in jail,' my dad says.

'OK,' I say. 'Good.'

My dad doesn't even try again. He goes back out of the room, and my mom stares in at me while he calls the lawyer and tells him that I won't go. In her eyes, she is saying, *Tell me.* Behind her, Jay's eyes are saying, *Tell them.* I make my eyes empty. I say nothing with my eyes at all.

Many hours later, after everyone else is asleep, I'm curled up on my bed, still wearing my clothes, holding the Stacie doll close. I'm trying not to think about anything, but I see them like they're right there. I see Barbie the day she was born, all messy and squealing. I see Lola jumping, trying to catch a fly. I see Stacie sitting on the bed, staring with those blank eyes. I see Kyle smiling. I feel his hand connect with my face, the hardness of the floor that comes up to meet me. I hear their voices saying my name. *Chel! Chel!* I hear the door slam in front of me. I hear the gravel crinkling beneath my feet. The night air swirls around me as I pass the line, the end of our world, the point beyond which horrible things are supposed to happen. I feel my steps taking me down, past the edge, away from them.

And suddenly: *Stacie is pregnant with Barbie, probably seven or eight months along. She's sitting up on the bed with her back leaning against the wall. One hand sits absently on her belly, and her face is calm. Two-year-old Lola is on the bed, too, playing with a rag doll, one I made myself out of an old T-shirt and cotton balls. The doll's face is drawn on in marker, but Lola doesn't care. She's named it Poopa, and she loves it.*

'Mommy, Poopa wants to say hi,' Lola says, scooting over to her.

'Well, does she?' Stacie says. 'Did you hear that, Barbie? You've made a new friend.' Kyle had already named the baby, even though, of course, we didn't know it would be a girl. He was so sure he'd get exactly what he wanted.

'Mommy, they're friends already,' Lola says. She presses the doll's face against Stacie's stomach.

'I wish I had a friend named Poopa,' says Stacie, patting the doll's head. She looks up at me, where I'm standing with my broom, afraid to move and spoil this.

'It's a good name,' I say.

'Brilliant.'

'What's "brilliant"?' Lola asks.

'Like smart. Like if you know a lot of things,' Stacie replies.

'Brilliant!' Lola says, taking the doll back. 'Brilliant!' It becomes her new favourite word, and for the few weeks until Barbie is born, whenever Lola says it, Stacie looks at me and smiles.

I open my eyes to find Lee sitting next to me on the bed. The window is open. I sit up and stare at it.

'You didn't move the whole time I was climbing in,' she says. 'But you weren't asleep. Your eyes were open.'

I wipe the drool off my chin. I must have fallen asleep at least for a while.

'The judge set another date,' Lee says. Her hair is in a ponytail, and she's wearing sweatpants and a T-shirt. She's not dressed for a party this time.

'I'm sorry,' I say.

'No, you're not,' she says. She says it flatly, like it's just a statement of fact.

I look away from her. She's right. I know I'm doing the right thing.

'Picture this, Amy,' she says. 'You have a daughter who you love more than anything in the world. She's your oldest daughter, and before you had her, you never really loved anyone. You didn't love your daughter's dad, not really. He was just a guy you grew up with, someone who could give you what you really wanted in life, to be a mother.'

I close my eyes. I want to put my hands over my ears.

'So this daughter, she's everything to you. Even when you have another daughter, who you love, you know you'll never love anyone like you love this girl. When you finally divorce the husband you never loved, you focus everything you are on the girls.'

'I'm sorry,' I whisper.

Lee is silent for a minute. 'And then you lose her,' she finally says. 'Even though six years go by, you never allow yourself to give up. You keep her room the same as it always was. You set a third place at the table. When you go to the movies with the daughter you have left, sometimes you even buy an extra ticket.'

'She did that?' I ask.

'Actually, I set the table,' Lee says. 'She made me do it.'

We are silent.

'Do you think she would have liked to know that, Amy? That Mom believed she was coming home?'

'I don't know,' I say. And I don't. What difference would it make, when she could never get there? Maybe it would have made things even worse. But maybe it would have given her hope. Knowing what I know, I wish I could go back and tell her.

'I'm not saying this to make you feel bad,' Lee says. 'I just want you to understand. Mom freaked out in the courtroom. She screamed and cried and had to be carried out by the bailiff. Now she's asleep thanks to a ton of pills. Before you came back, her hope almost wasn't real. She hoped Dee was alive, but she didn't expect her to come walking through the door. Now she does. It's like right after she was kidnapped all over again. You gave her hope, Amy, and it's making her crazy. It's killing her.'

I wipe tears out of my closed eyes, but I say nothing.

'Amy, please look at me.'

Slowly, I turn my head. Her eyes are so sad, even though they're barely wet.

She picks up the Stacie doll from where I must have let it drop when I fell asleep. 'This doll is always wearing pink, and you wanted the pink beads,' she says. 'I know what this

160

means. It means this doll represents Dee.'

I kind of nod and shake my head at the same time.

'It means you loved her.'

I reach for the doll, but she holds it away from me.

'She wouldn't want her mom to suffer, would she? To not know? I thought it would be better for all of us. I thought the woman who cooks every night for two children would never be able to handle the truth. But this is worse, Amy. It's *worse*.' She's squeezing the doll so hard that her hand shakes. She realizes she's doing it and eases up. She looks down at the doll and smoothes its pink dress. 'I didn't come here to say that. I never wanted to push you. I know whatever is going on with us, what happened to you must have been worse.'

Not what happened to me, I think. But that truth isn't what Lee wants to know. She thinks there's only life and death, staying away or coming home. She doesn't know about the difference between Stacie and Dee, between being whole and being shattered.

'I came here because I just wanted to talk about her. That's all. I won't try to pressure you, I promise.' She looks down at the doll as she speaks. She probably means what she's saying. Everything she's done so far has been to help me. But she also wants to know the truth. And she's going to learn it. It has a life of its own, now that it's out there. Vinnie knows, and soon everyone else will, too. I can't stop it, but I can't let it happen either.

I don't know what to do, so I sit perfectly still.

'And I want to do something to remember her,' Lee

says. 'I want to help you, but I need to remember her. I can't pretend she never existed. That's what you want, but I can't do it.'

'I don't want that,' I say. But that's the result, I realize. So few people really knew her in the short time she had. If no one can ask me about her, then I'm wiping the rest of her away. She wouldn't want that. She always wanted to be included. She'd want us to remember.

'What do you think Dee would like to do, if she were here now?' Lee leans the doll against the wall, so she's facing us.

'She'd want to eat Red Vines,' I say. But immediately I know that's wrong. It was twelve-year-old Dee who wanted to eat candy. Eighteen-year-old Dee would want to be making out with some boy in the back of a movie theatre, or hanging out with her eighteen-year-old friends. I don't actually know what eighteen-year-olds do. But Lee doesn't care whether I'm right or not.

'OK,' she says. 'That's what we'll do. We'll get some Red Vines.'

I never agreed to go with her. I know I can't go, because she's changed her mind about not knowing. But I don't feel like I have any control over my body as I pull myself over the windowsill and land on the grass of our side yard. Lee has used the card with me that she has figured out will always work. Dee would want to live, and she would want us to remember.

20.

Lee drives for a minute in silence. It feels weird around her. Her silence makes me want to say something, and I want it to be something normal. I want to keep more of the truth from spilling out.

'I had a good time with Vinnie,' I say. 'He taught me how to drive.'

'He told me,' she says.

I freeze. But he can't have told her *that*.

'Maybe we should call him.' She hands me her phone.

'It's late.' According to her phone, it's 1:00 a.m.

'Dee wouldn't want to just hang out with me,' she says. 'She didn't like me all that much.'

'That's not true.'

'Sure it is. I remember she had this pair of shoes. They

163

were too small for her. She grew out of them. She couldn't have used them at all any more, so I asked if I could have them. Because they fit me perfectly. But she wouldn't give them to me. Not until Mom made her. She threw a fit about it, too. She threw them at me. Broke one of the straps.'

'It sounds different when you tell it,' I say.

'I'll bet.'

'It was just a pair of shoes,' I say. 'Sisters fight.'

'Usually they fight and then they make up,' she says. 'Then they play a game of cards on the living room carpet and sneak candy into their bedrooms and talk all night. They band together to get their mom to make mac and cheese instead of tuna casserole.'

'She wanted to,' I say. 'She felt bad about the fight, too.' I realize that I don't know whether she did or not. We were never allowed to talk about the families we left behind. I felt bad about how I'd been mean to Jay, not letting him hang out with us. Did she feel the same way? She must have.

'Big sisters share make-up with their little sisters,' she says. 'They teach them how to do their hair.'

'I think you would have been the one teaching,' I say.

'Then the little sister teaches,' she says. 'Somebody teaches somebody.' She turns abruptly, and we're heading down River Road. I take a deep breath, but we drive right by the place it happened. 'Call Vinnie,' she says.

'I—'

'Just call him,' she says.

164

So I do. It takes me a minute because I don't understand how her phone works. But finally, I call his number.

'Lee?'

'It's Ch— Amy,' I say. 'It's Amy MacArthur.' I say my whole name more for my benefit than his.

'Oh, hi. Want a late-night driving lesson? Nobody out on the road. Smart.'

'No, it's just . . .' I look at Lee, but her face is blank. 'Lee and I are hanging out.'

'Meet us at the Publik Mart,' Lee says.

I repeat it for Vinnie.

'Okey-doke,' he says. He doesn't ask any questions. I wonder if he's used to Lee calling him in the middle of the night and insisting he show up someplace.

'You must be really good friends,' I say.

'We dated freshman year,' Lee says. 'Nothing much happened, but yeah, he's been a good friend. One of the best.'

'You dated Vinnie?'

'You probably think I'm out of his league,' she says.

'Well, I guess, I mean . . .'

'He doesn't look like Marco,' Lee says. 'But sometimes the hot guys, they expect you to be hot on the inside, too. They expect you to be pretty and perfect and well adjusted and normal. Vinnie would never expect that.'

'But you—'

'I'm the girl whose sister was kidnapped,' she says. She turns the corner into the Publik Mart. It hits me that this is also the bus stop. This is the place I stepped off the bus into

165

Grey Wood. This is the place I became Amy again. *Amy MacArthur,* I think. *Amy.* Lee's face is lit by the overhanging lights above the gas pumps. Even with her hair pulled back and no make-up, she's beautiful. If you look carefully, you can see the differences between Lee and Dee. Dee's face was rounder and more childlike. Even at eighteen, even after everything that happened, she still looked younger than her age. Lee has more angles. She looks like she's thinking something deep. Dee always looked like she was *feeling*.

Vinnie pulls in as we get out of the car. He gives Lee a hug and grins at me, arms open.

I lean in to him, and he gives me a quick squeeze.

'So what are we doing?' he asks. 'I already took her to the library and Dairy Queen. If we want to take her someplace new, we'll have to go to Portland.'

'We're getting Red Vines,' Lee says. She leads the way into the store. We're the only people in there, except for the cashier; a thin, balding man who's practically asleep on his feet. He barely looks up as we walk in.

Vinnie hasn't acted like he knows anything. I can trust him, I tell myself. Lee trusts him, so I can, too.

Lee buys three large packs of Red Vines. Vinnie buys a Coke. I don't have any money, so I don't buy anything. We head back out to the parking lot and stand next to Lee's car. She tears the plastic off the box and puts a vine into her mouth.

Vinnie looks at me. Obviously he thinks Lee is acting weird, too. But I don't know if I should tell him why, or if I even can. Instead, I take out a Red Vine and start eating. I used to love these as much as Dee did, and I haven't had one in six years. Even though I shouldn't be enjoying this night at all, I like it. I savour the texture of the candy, the taste of the sugar. *Amy MacArthur*, I think. *I am Amy*.

Lee eats another vine. Vinnie eats one. I eat another.

'When Dee disappeared,' Lee says, 'Vinnie was the first kid to talk to me. Everybody else was afraid. It was like having a sister disappear was catching.'

'Since I'm an only child, I was immune,' Vinnie says.

'It was probably three weeks before anyone else tried,' Lee says, ignoring the joke. 'I mean, people would say they were sorry or ask how I was, but it was just bullshit. Nobody wanted to know the answer.'

'Not everyone was like that,' Vinnie says.

'I don't know,' Lee says. 'Maybe not everyone. But most people. My friends stopped calling me. Right when you would think they'd be there, if they were your real friends. All the friends I have now are different. Christina and Kara, I met them once we started high school.' She swallows the last of a vine and looks at me. 'I know it's not the same. I know. I was the lucky one. But it was hard for us, too.'

'I know,' I say.

'That's why Jay's hurting,' Lee says. 'He knows it's not fair of him to complain, to be angry about what happened to *him*. But he's only fourteen. And he was eight when his whole life fell apart.'

'I know,' I say. 'He hates me.'

'He doesn't hate you,' Lee says. 'He missed you, too.

167

Everyone was sorry for the parents, and they forgot about him. He's mad because you were alive the whole time, and he thought you were dead. He was so sad, Amy.'

'I didn't forget him. I thought about him all the time.' I thought about those blackberries every day. I wasn't supposed to think about him, but I did. When it was dark and everyone was asleep, that's when I'd let myself remember.

'You tell him that,' she says. 'You're lucky you still have him.' She grabs another Red Vine and shoves it in her mouth. She chews and chews, and there is too much vine in her mouth, and if this were any other moment, it would be silly. If Dee were here, we would be laughing. Instead, our eyes fill with tears. Even Vinnie wipes a tear away as he puts an arm around Lee's shoulder.

Lee finally swallows the last of it, and then she reaches for the half-empty box. She holds it up. 'To Dee,' she says. 'I know you're dead. I've known it since the first day Amy came back, and you didn't. I know horrible things happened to you that I can never even imagine, and he killed you. But I'm not going to forget. Mom's not going to forget, ever.' She takes a breath and opens her mouth like she's going to say something else, but then she throws the Red Vines on the ground. They spill out on to the pavement, and she folds her arms over her chest.

'Lee . . .' *What, Amy?* I think. Are you going to tell her it's not true? When Vinnie already knows? When really everyone already knows except Aunt Hannah, and everything that happens to Aunt Hannah happens to Lee? Am I really going to keep doing this to them?

Vinnie pulls Lee closer, but he doesn't say anything.

'I said I didn't want to know,' Lee says quietly, her chest heaving. 'But I do. Not just for Mom, for me. I want to say goodbye to my sister. I want to have somebody to blame for what happened to us. I want to see this man in jail, to point my finger and say, *He did this*. I want whoever killed Dee to pay.'

The door slams in my face.

There is blood in Stacie's hair.

I'm shoving things into the Safeway bag. I'm shoving the Stacie doll in.

Now Vinnie's arm is around me. He has moved in between us and is pulling both of us close. I don't know how much time I've lost, but it's like Lee hasn't moved.

'She's dead,' I say. 'But that's all I can tell you.' My hand goes to my pink beads. But the beads aren't for Dee; they're for Stacie. Stacie's not who we're mourning. I reach up and unhook the beads. I let them roll around in my hands. Somewhere, there are two little girls who are worth everything. They are worth Lee's pain, and Aunt Hannah's, and mine. They are even worth everything that happened to Dee. I have to believe that, or I will die. I will fall down on the ground right here at the bus stop and I will never get up. Unless Lola and Barbie are alive, and they are a reason to keep standing.

'Where is she?' Lee asks.

I shake my head.

'I want to know where her body is,' she says. 'Mom will

never believe it without a body.'

'I don't know,' I say.

Her face is calm and silent. Her eye is open, one blue eye staring up.

'You do know,' she says. 'You know where *he* is.' Lee has turned towards me. Vinnie's arm is still around her, and now it's like he's holding her back, like he's afraid she'll attack me. But she just *looks*.

Barbie is crying, but Lola has stopped. Lola is grabbing the back of my leg.

I put my hand over my face.

'Lee, come on,' Vinnie says. 'You don't know what she went through.' His voice is far away from me. I am far away from me. *Kyle is crying. He is bending over her, feeling for a pulse. Baby, baby, he says. Barbie clings to me. There is blood on her face, too, a little stream coming from her hairline.*

'Amy, come back. Chelsea.' Lee shakes me. It works. I snap back. Vinnie is behind her, staring down at us, hands raised like he doesn't know what he should do. Lee's face is on a level with mine. 'If she's dead, can't we just have her body? Can't my mom have that?' Tears stream down her face now. Her hands grip my shoulders.

'I don't know where he buried her,' I say. 'That's the truth.'

'Lee, stop,' Vinnie says. He pulls her away from me. He pulls her all the way around the front of the car. 'You're just pushing her away. You'll get your answers when Amy can handle it. OK?' He holds Lee by both shoulders. 'OK?'

'OK,' Lee says. She turns back to me. 'I'm sorry. I know

I promised. I wasn't lying; it's just hard. It's hard to be there for you and my mom both. And she was my sister. Not just her daughter, not just your friend, but *my* sister. I get to care, too.'

'I know,' I say. I realize that I have admitted to another person that Dee is dead, and now it truly can't be stopped. But it could never be stopped, really. When I decided to come home, I put everything in motion.

'I'm sorry,' Lee says. She walks back to me and puts her arms around me. She pulls me in, and I press my hands against her back. Here she is, comforting me, when I'm the one who has ruined her mom's life, and hers.

After a long time, Lee finally lets me go. She reaches on top of the car and takes the second pack of Red Vines, and then she sits down on the ground. The parking lot is gross with gas stains and dirt and who knows what else, but she doesn't seem to care. She rips open the package.

Vinnie sits down next to her and takes a Red Vine.

I sit down, too.

'My mom planned Dee's whole life,' she says, mostly to Vinnie. 'What classes she was going to take in high school. And when she would be allowed to date, and what her curfew would be. And now that she'd be eighteen, we're getting college brochures in the mail.'

'Knowing will help her,' Vinnie says. He pulls Lee close, and she puts her head on his shoulder.

I don't know what to say, so I chew a piece of candy. Even through everything, it's still sweet.

'Now I have to tell her,' Lee says. 'I know Amy can't do

it, so I have to. But unless she sees the body, she'll never believe. She'll keep on looking through those college brochures, trying to find the right one for her. Last month it was Reed. This month it's Stanford. Dee got a lot smarter since she died, I guess.'

'She could have gone to Stanford,' Vinnie says. 'She was smart.'

'She didn't even like to read,' Lee says. 'She couldn't stand sitting alone and being quiet.'

'She would have been in every club,' says Vinnie. 'Wasn't she in a play over the summer? Maybe she would have been a star.'

'She would have tried,' Lee says. 'Even if they didn't give her the part she wanted, she would have kept going back. She never gave up. Never let all the shitty things about life get her down.' Lee folds a Red Vine and chomps through it. There were days, even weeks, even months, when I'd forget that Dee used to be like that. The kind of person who kept trying, who cried easily but then smiled. The person who would love a doll named Poopa and a little girl learning to say *brilliant*. She was buried inside Stacie, but she didn't disappear for ever. Maybe not until Barbie was born, maybe not even ever. If it had been her who came home, she might have recovered. Even after everything, she still could have had a chance.

'She deserved to go to college,' I say. It's just one of a million things she deserved, one of a million things that Kyle took.

Vinnie holds up two Red Vines. 'To Dee Springfield,

172

superstar,' he says.

'To Dee.' Lee lifts her candy.

'To Dee,' I say. Across the parking lot, a car turns in. It drives slowly towards us and pulls into the nearest parking spot. A man gets out and heads for the Publik Mart while the woman sits in the passenger seat, checking her phone. Ordinary people are living their lives. All around town, people are sleeping through a regular, mild summer night. Tomorrow morning, they'll wake up and go about their days. In the morning, Aunt Hannah will wake up, too. Lee will tell her that I admitted that Dee is dead, and there will be more questions. I know I can't keep my secrets for ever.

I watch the woman get out of the car as the man returns. He hands her a pop, and she twists the top off. I haven't had a pop in six years, and now I may never have one. Now I know that the life with candy and pop and family and friends isn't something I can ever have.

My knuckles are bleeding, and the door is closed. Kyle won't let me back in. Not tonight, maybe never. It's not until I reach the edge of the tree line, until I pass the place that was the end of our world, that I realize I'm free. Kyle has let me walk away. And I was from a town called Grey Wood.

I didn't know where else to go. But I should never have come back here.

Once Kyle found out Stacie was pregnant with Lola, he began bringing home dresses. They were pink and frilly and looked like they cost money. Stacie wore the dresses, but she wore her sweatpants under them. Stacie hadn't been eating very much, but now Kyle made her sit at the table until she ate every single thing on her plate.

'Come on, Stacie,' he said to her. He picked up her fork and stabbed a piece of chicken with it. 'Don't you want our little angel to be strong?' He said it with a soft voice and a weird cadence, like he was already talking to a baby.

She ate mechanically, whatever he put in front of her, and she barely ever said a word.

Kyle began taking us both out for walks, because fresh air was supposed to be good for the baby. He held Stacie's hand like she was his precious little girl who might get hit by a car while crossing the street, even though there were no streets because we were in the middle of nowhere. He held my hand tight because he was afraid I'd run away. He held my hand so tightly that he was cutting off the circulation.

But I had been inside that cabin for months, and I was so happy to be outside that I was about ready to laugh and also about ready to cry from joy. I didn't care that Kyle was holding my hand, because we were getting close to the river, and it wasn't that different from the river back in Grey Wood. I pulled them forwards, trying to race for the river-bank. Kyle followed me, gripping my hand, and Stacie shuffled, almost letting herself be dragged.

We started going out every day, and I felt like a weight that was on my chest had lifted, and I could finally breathe. Kyle bought a couple of used picture books, and he started reading them to Stacie's stomach. He ordered me to get firewood and cook dinner and clean the whole cabin, but as long as I did it, there was less chance he'd hit me.

He talked to the baby like he already knew it was a girl.

'Heeeey, little sweetie pie,' he said to Stacie's stomach.

Sometimes I saw tears leaking out of Stacie's eyes when Kyle talked like that, but he didn't seem to notice. I was just so glad I wasn't locked up inside any more.

When Stacie was maybe eight months along, Kyle had gone out into town, and so, as usual, we were locked inside the cabin. This was a few months after Stacie had the breakdown where she drank soap. She said she wasn't going to try it again, but I didn't trust her. Whenever Kyle left, I was terrified she would do something I couldn't stop. Now she was lying on the little bed, facing away from me, crying.

I climbed on to the bed, sat next to her feet, and pulled my legs into my chest. 'It's not going to be that bad,' I said.

She kept sobbing.

'Mom had two babies, and she's fine.' I had only the vaguest idea of what having a baby was like. I had only seen it on TV, where there was a lady in a hospital bed, and she screamed for a while, but then everyone was standing around looking at her while she held the baby, and she looked happy. I also once saw a show where a lady had a baby in the back seat of a Jeep, but that didn't look so bad either.

'I hope I die,' she said.

'You won't die,' I said.

'People die,' she said. 'Sometimes the baby won't come

out, so they have to cut it out, but he'll never take me to a hospital, so I'll just die.'

'No,' I said. I threw myself on top of her. 'No, no, no. I'm not going to let that happen.'

'I wish it would,' she said.

I hugged her tighter.

'Get off, you're squashing me,' she said. There was a hint of lightness in her voice when she said it.

'See, if you don't want to be squashed, then you don't want to die,' I said, and I sat up again.

'OK,' she said. She kicked me with one foot. And I knew that even though she was really sad, she didn't want to die yet.

But now that she had made me think about it, I couldn't stop. I thought of a thousand more ways that she could die, like if she started bleeding, or if she got sick, or if the cabin caught on fire. Even when I was outside by the river, it started creeping into my brain. What if she died? Then I would be left all alone with Kyle.

21.

I hear my mom on the phone with Aunt Hannah. My mom keeps saying that I haven't said anything, but Aunt Hannah is screaming. I can't hear the words, but I can hear the noise from where I sit in the living room. Jay sits next to me with his arms crossed. He is still, but tears leak from the edges of his eyes. I want to tell him again that I'm sorry, or reach over and hug him, but the chasm is still between us. Nothing I do or say will help.

My dad is in the kitchen with my mom. He has his hand on her shoulder as she talks.

My mom turns around and looks at me, and I know that there's no point in denying it, now that Lee knows. Lee has told her that I admitted it, but Aunt Hannah won't believe it until she hears it from me.

'Tell her that Dee is dead,' I say.

Jay puts both hands over his eyes and takes a deep, halting breath.

My mom can't tell her. She hands the phone to my dad.

'Hannah,' my dad says. 'I'm so sorry.'

Aunt Hannah is still screaming.

'She wanted everyone to have some hope,' he says. 'But she realized that it wasn't fair to you. It was hard for her to tell us, but she did.'

Aunt Hannah is asking how. She is asking when.

'It's hard for her to talk about,' my dad says. 'She's been through something none of us can imagine.' He pauses. 'We'll find out before too long, Hannah. We'll find this guy. I promise.'

This is what I was afraid of. Now they'll expect me to tell them where he is so they can arrest him. But he's not going to let himself be arrested. Now that they know about Dee, the rest of it will come out. And I can never let that happen.

About a year after Kyle took us, I washed tiny, newborn Lola in the sink. She was kind of ugly, kind of shrivelled. But she had her mother's blue eyes, and she was waving her arms and legs, and she was warm and alive. She didn't know that this was a sad place. She didn't know that her mother was kidnapped and raped and sad or that her father was a monster. She didn't know about the town of Grey Wood and the river there and all the people who had stopped looking for us.

'Hey,' I whispered. 'Hey.' I held her in both hands, wet and dripping. I was afraid that if I did anything else, I would drop her.

Kyle laid out a towel on the counter.

'Here you go,' he said. He took the baby from me and set her down, and then he dried her off with the towel. He patted her gently and leant his face in close to hers. 'Aren't you just the most beautiful little princess,' he said. 'Your name is Lola, yes it is.' He picked her up, wrapped in the towel, and he took her over to Stacie, who was curled up in a ball. 'Here is your beautiful daughter,' he said to her. He set the baby down in the circle between her head and her knees.

Stacie reached out a hand and touched Lola's, but she didn't say anything.

Kyle got down on his knees and touched the baby's other hand. 'Lo-la. Lo-la.'

Stacie rolled over so that she was facing away. The baby waved her arms and let out a loud wail.

I went over to the bed. 'Stacie?' I asked.

But she didn't answer.

'Mommy is tired from having you, yes she is,' said Kyle. He poked the baby in the stomach.

I cooked food, and Kyle made Stacie eat it. He cooed at her like she was a baby, too.

At first, we put Lola's crib next to my camp bed. Pretty soon I started to talk to her. I didn't talk in baby talk; I talked in whispers. Even though she didn't understand yet, I started telling her stories. I told her about a river where there was no one around, and there were fish and birds and snails and crayfish. I explained how to bait a hook with a worm and where the best place on the river is to fish. I remembered the plots of some of the books I used to read, and I told her what I could remember. I didn't tell her about anything real. I decided that she didn't need to know about that other world, the world before. If she didn't know about it, then she wouldn't miss it. She would never be sad the way Stacie was.

Kyle only waited about a month.

He told Stacie he loved her.

I took Lola into the bathroom and sang to her. I sang all the church songs I could remember, and I sang the songs from the boy bands and everything else I could remember from the radio. I sang, and she giggled, and pretty soon she was making noises like she was singing, too, and we were alone in the world, and nothing that's true was really true.

'Would you like to talk about your breakthrough?' Dr Kayla asks during our session on Monday.

'I didn't mean to tell anyone,' I say. I'm holding the Stacie doll and also the book that has the girl with no head on the cover. I haven't started reading it yet, but I've got through half the graphic novels.

The police have stopped poking around as much now that they know they aren't going to find Dee. But I know they've traced my bus ticket. They've figured out where I got on the bus, and so they're out there looking for him.

But they've been out there looking for three weeks, ever since I've been back. They've probably looked everywhere by now and not found him. They don't know who they're looking for. All they know is that he's tall and white. There are thousands of men in Oregon who look like that.

'How did you feel when she died?' Dr Kayla asks.

'She was my best friend,' I say. *I am sitting by the river. Two-year-old Lola is with me, and Barbie is about to be born. Lola understands that something big is about to happen. She knows that Mommy has a big belly and that there's going to be another kid, but I don't know if she really understands what that will mean. I hold on to her because if I don't, she will just run down to the water. She will go anywhere there is a path and pick up anything not nailed down.*

'Chel!' she says. She picks up a rock and taps it on the ground.

'Rock,' I say.

'Rock!' she says. She tries to wriggle out of my hands, but I won't let her. I am not going to let her go.

'If you tell me how you feel, then I can help you work on how to deal with your feelings,' says Dr Kayla.

'I think maybe she wanted to,' I say.

'You think maybe Dee wanted to die?' Dr Kayla asks.

'She was sad because he raped her,' I say. I can feel my breath going in and out. And I hear something like a river. I can't really see Dr Kayla's face.

'How did that make you feel?' Dr Kayla asks.

'I was glad it wasn't me,' I say.

'That is a normal way to feel,' says Dr Kayla. 'It's OK to want to be safe. Every person on this earth wants to

181

avoid being hurt.'

'But she was my best friend,' I say.

'You deserved to be safe,' Dr Kayla says. 'You didn't hurt her; he did.'

'But I could have shared it,' I say. 'I could have taken it half the time, and then maybe she wouldn't have been so sad.'

'Take a minute to think about it this way,' Dr Kayla says. 'If Dee was really sick, and she was in the hospital, you would be sad for her, wouldn't you?'

'Yes,' I say.

'But then if you got sick, that wouldn't cure her, would it?'

'I don't know,' I say.

'Yes, you do,' says Dr Kayla. 'You know that when you get the flu and you give it to someone else, you don't magically get better. Now you're both sick. What the man did to Dee is just like that. If he also did it to you, it would not have made her better.'

'If he was doing it to me, he wouldn't be doing it to her,' I say. 'He can't do it to both of us at the same time.'

'Do you think that would have made Dee happy?' Dr Kayla asks.

'Maybe,' I say. 'Maybe for a few minutes.'

Dr Kayla purses her lips and gives a little half smile with sad eyes. She's trying to tell me that it's not my fault. She's trying to tell me to blame Kyle. And I do blame him. He is a monster. I hate him with every single piece of my heart. I could have killed him in his sleep. We had a knife in the kitchen, and I could have done it with that. I would lie awake and think about it, but then I would think about Lola and Barbie, and I would imagine what would happen if Kyle woke up and killed me instead. And then they would only have Kyle and Stacie for parents, and neither one of them could handle that. If I tried to kill Kyle, it might be like killing them.

And now they're alone with him.

But they aren't dead. Not yet.

But I don't really know that. I won't know if they're still alive and if they're safe until I see them again. The cops will think they can protect them, but they didn't see the way Kyle's big hand curled around Lola's tiny neck. They haven't felt the hardness of Kyle's hand, the swiftness of Kyle's kick. The only way to protect them is to make sure that no one finds them. I have to go back and convince Kyle to take us all away to somewhere far from that bus stop, somewhere no one will ever find us.

I let a few more days go by. If I stay in my room, I think, I can have these days. I can hold out for a little while without talking to anyone, without any chance of giving any more information away. I read all the rest of the graphic novels, and then I read the book with the picture of the girl with no head. The book is about a regular girl who lives in a small town that is not that different from ours, and she falls in love with two boys, and her father has a drinking problem. In the end she picks the right boy and goes away to college with him, and she also gets her dad into rehab. I don't quite understand the part about the boys. I don't see why they were so attractive, and at the part where they have sex for the first time, I skim. I don't understand why she wants to do that.

Nobody pressures me for more information. I hear my dad on the phone with the police. They talk quietly, but I can tell that they haven't found him. I want to know how close they are, but I don't want to ask. Anything I say might give them away.

I also hear my dad talking to his wife, Beth, and Liam and Beatrice. My dad says that he misses them, but he doesn't know yet when he'll be back. There's a smile in his voice when he talks to them, and it reminds me of how he used to be. He's really trying to have a do-over, and I want him to have it. He deserves a family that won't fall apart.

It's probably good that I'll never meet Liam and Beatrice. It hasn't been good for Jay to be my brother.

As I think this, Jay knocks on my bedroom door. I can tell it's him because it's kind of loud and kind of restless. His fist goes *tap-tap tap-tap*.

'Come in,' I say.

He steps into the room and looks around.

'Hey,' I say.

'Hey.' He sits down on the floor, because there's nowhere else to sit except the twin bed, and that's where I am. I'm sitting with the book next to me, closed. While I was thinking about my dad and his family, I was also thinking about the girl in the book. She had sex, but she didn't get pregnant. She didn't get sad, and she went away with the boy on purpose.

'Hey,' I say again.

'Lee called,' he says. He fidgets with his hands and doesn't look up at me. He's so tall now that he kind of slouches while he sits. His bony shoulders poke through his T-shirt. The brown hair on the top of his head sticks up. It's the same colour as my hair.

'Oh,' I say.

'She wanted me to tell you that she's sorry she pressured you. I guess she didn't want to face you, if you were mad.'

'I'm not mad,' I say. 'She's right. Dee was her sister. She deserved to know the truth.'

Jay shrugs.

'She went through a lot, too,' I say. 'You both did. I know that.'

'It's not about us,' he says. He's still not really looking at me, but at least he's talking. These are the most words he's said to me in days.

'It's OK,' I say. 'I know Dad left because of this, and Mom was sad. Lee made me understand – it's not all about me. You have a right complain and be angry and talk about how much things sucked.'

'What really sucked was that you were dead,' he says. 'I missed you.'

'I missed you, too,' I say. Lee is right. I need to tell him, before it's too late. Before I leave again and he thinks I never cared at all.

'Lee made me understand some things, too,' he says.

185

'I've been a total asshole.'

'It's all right.'

'No, it isn't. She said . . . I mean, I can guess what happened to you. We all can.' He fiddles with the carpet, still not able to look at me. I know what he thinks, and I can't tell him he's wrong. It would lead to too many more things. So I pick something true to say, something I hope he can understand.

'I couldn't leave,' I say. 'I never wanted to be there. Not for a single second. I thought about you all the time. You, Mom, Dad. I wasn't supposed to, but I did. There wasn't a day or a night or a minute . . .' I can't finish because I'm about to burst into tears. I don't want to break down now. I want to have a minute with my brother. 'I want things to be the way they were. More than anything.' *Just for today,* I think. *I want this one day.*

He looks up and wipes his eyes. 'We could play a game,' he says.

I nod. I don't trust myself to speak.

He gets up and goes out and brings back Sequence. I haven't moved from my spot. I haven't even moved my hands.

He opens the box and pulls out a piece of paper. 'Here's our score sheet. Remember this?' He smiles. 'Looks like I was three games ahead.' I can tell that it's my handwriting on the paper. For every game in the house, we had a score sheet and kept track of who had won what. Whenever someone got far ahead, the score sheets would disappear. I guess Mom didn't want one of us to feel bad and threw them out. But I'm glad she didn't throw this one away. I'm not sorry to see a record of this kind of loss.

'We'll see about that,' I say, and I slide off the bed on to the floor.

At the cabin, there were no board games. There was one deck of cards. It had a pattern of red diamonds on the outside, and there was a hole punched through the middle of the whole deck. The cards had hardly ever been used when Dee and I got there. By the time I left, they were falling apart.

Before Kyle let us outside, before we knew Stacie was pregnant, there was nothing to do besides playing cards and reading the same books, unless we wanted to listen to Kyle play with his dolls. The other things I did were clean and cook, but there was only so much of that to do. So we played. We played everything we could remember: rummy, gin rummy, speed, spit, spite and malice, casino, war. We even played cribbage, marking our scores on paper towels. Sometimes when we were playing something fast-paced, like spit, Stacie would smile, and she would move like she used to move.

After Lola was born, though, Stacie didn't play as often. When Lola was old enough, I started teaching her easy games like crazy eights and go fish, and we tried to get Stacie to join us. Sometimes she would, but other times she would just stare off into space.

Jay wins our game of Sequence. After all these years, I've pretty much forgotten all the strategy. But I don't mind. I feel like I'm a kid again, and I'm hanging around the house with my little brother on a boring summer day. Back then, I didn't appreciate this. I wished that something more exciting would happen. I didn't wish that I was getting invited to parties and all that stuff like Dee. I wished I would get abducted by space aliens and go on an adventure. For some reason, I always imagined that this would happen at the river. I would be down there one day – sometimes I would be alone and other times I would be with Dee or Jay – and a giant flying saucer would float down, and then a door would open and an alien would stick his head out and invite me to go with them. So I guess it really wasn't an abduction that I was daydreaming about; it was an invitation. The aliens were going to take me away from my normal life.

'I used to dream about getting taken away on a spaceship,' I say.

'Yeah, I know,' Jay says. 'You were weird.'

Jay's phone rings. He looks at it.

'It's Lee,' he says. 'Hello? Yeah, I told her. I don't think she's mad.' He looks at me.

I take the phone. 'Hi,' I say.

'I'm so sorry,' she says. 'I never should have pushed you that way. My mom was so upset that day. I felt like I had to do *something*. But I could have gone about it better. I could have asked you in the daytime, given you a chance to get away.'

'It's OK,' I say.

'No, it's not. I . . .' She trails off. I don't like it. I can't stand it when she doesn't talk.

'How's Aunt Hannah?' I ask.

'She's dealing,' Lee says. 'She knew it all along, just like I did. But she wants more. She wants to know everything that happened. She thinks that if she knows everything, somehow that will make it better.'

'It won't,' I say.

'I know that,' Lee says. 'But I can't help it. I want to know, too. Now that I know she's dead – I mean, now that I can't deny it any more – it feels like a hole has opened up in this house. It's like a whirlpool made of everything we can imagine about what happened, and everything is getting sucked inside, and the only way to stop it is to . . . I don't know . . . plug the hole . . . with the truth.'

Lola is screaming.

She's wiggling in Kyle's arms.

'Amy?'

'I don't want to think about it,' I say. It's like the room around me has disappeared, and Jay has disappeared, and everything is filled with light. *I'm looking at the wood wall of the cabin. I can hear Lola screaming. And Barbie is crying some-where, too. She's behind me, but I can't turn around. And Stacie is lying on the floor, dead. She's on her back, and her head is kind of twisted wrong. Her blonde hair is hanging over part of her face, so I can only see one of her eyes.*

There is a second where nobody moves. We all stand there staring at her. We don't know she's dead yet. We all hope she might still be alive.

'I'll ask her,' I hear Jay saying. At some point he must

have taken the phone from me. 'OK. I don't know. I said I'll ask her. Goodbye, Lee.'

Jay snaps into focus, still sitting on the floor. I am back in my bedroom. The Sequence game is half put away.

'You won the game,' I say.

'Yeah.' He puts the paper in the box without marking down his win, though. That's not right. He's supposed to care that he just won the game. 'What just happened, Amy? Where did you go? Does your doctor know this happens? Does Mom know?'

I gather up the rest of the cards. I didn't want to go back there. This whole time I've been back, I've gone to so many other times, but I haven't gone there. Not for real. Not all the way. I don't want to go back there again.

I am at the bus station. I buy a ticket, and it costs me all the money that lady who picked me up gave me except six bucks.

This is where everything starts. There is nothing before that.

'Amy, you should let them help you. We want you back. Me, Mom, Dad, Lee. That guy Vinnie. Everyone else in town, too. Everyone looked for you. Everyone cares.'

'They care about Amy,' I say. I put the lid back on the box. But I didn't pack everything right. The lid will not go on straight. It looks like it might fly off at any moment.

Jay squints at me.

'He gave us different names,' I say. 'My name was Chelsea, and Dee was Stacie.'

'Who gave you different names?' he asks. There's an

edge to his voice. He doesn't understand why I'm doing this.

I shake my head.

He picks up the game box. As he lifts it, the box top shifts. It rises up on one end, close to coming part way off. 'Aunt Hannah deserves to know,' he says, his voice quiet. 'So does Lee. And Mom and Dad. And me.' He looks up, right into my eyes. 'We deserve to know because we love you.'

'Jay, I love you, too.'

Mom opens the bedroom door. She sticks her head in and looks around, as if she expects the room to be destroyed.

Jay wipes his eyes, gets to his feet, and pushes past Mom out of the room. At least I said it. I won't go away again without him knowing.

Mom comes in. 'You were playing a game?' she asks.

I nod.

'Well. That's good.' She sounds like she's not sure. I'm not sure any more either. Jay is never going to stop wanting answers. Aunt Hannah and Lee will always want answers. Mom and Dad will always want answers, even if they never actually ask. Everyone who ever knew us wants to know what happened, and they'll want to know until I finally tell them. I've waited a few days, but I can't wait any longer.

Mom steps forward and pulls me into a hug. Her long hair scratches my face. It reminds me of when I was little, when her hair was always falling on me. It smells the same now, like apples. 'All that matters is that you're back,' she says. 'You don't have to say anything else until you're ready.'

I hug her back. 'What if I'm never ready?'

'It doesn't matter,' she says. She lets me go and pulls away. 'I just want you to be healthy. If you can tell Dr Kayla, maybe that will help you.'

'Maybe,' I say.

Mom smiles. Her eyes are a little sad, but the smile is real. She thinks the *maybe* means something, but I don't mean it. I hate having to lie to her. It's not fair.

The room shifts.

He is pushing me.

    Lola is screaming.

    Barbie is crying.

    They are both crying.

    He is screaming.

    'Get out! Get out! Get out!'

    I push back, but he's too strong.

    'Take everything!' He lets go of me and grabs my clothes. He throws things at me. A shirt. Jeans. A Safeway bag.

    I reach for Barbie, but he's in between us.

    'Never come back here!' He pushes me, and I fall back. I hit the floor, and I know I can't stay here. I know if I try to stay, he'll kill me. I crawl to the bag and throw things in. A shirt. Jeans. The Stacie doll. She fell to the ground – I shove her in. I grab Stacie's pink jacket.

    He lifts me up and heaves me back, out the door, and I fall again on my backside.

He slams the door, and I hear crying. Kyle, Barbie, Lola. Screams.

I am pounding on the door.

I am screaming.

'Let me in! Kyle, they need me. I'm their mother. They need me!'

He opens the door, but he's still between me and them. He's so big, I can't even see them.

'They need me. Kyle, please.'

'They're mine! You can't take them!' Tears stream down his face. His cheeks are red. He's pouring sweat.

'I didn't mean to.' All I can think of is the girls, in there with him.

'If you tell, I'll kill them.' He slams the door again.

I step back over the porch, stumble down the three steps. I am outside and they are inside, and Kyle means it. I have to leave.

'. . . in two hours,' my mom says.

'Oh,' I say. I have no idea what she just said.

'You didn't forget, did you?' she asks.

Two hours. She's talking about my next appointment with Dr Kayla.

'No, I didn't forget,' I say.

'OK.' She smiles, and she looks like she wants to hug me again, but she doesn't. She turns to leave.

'Wait,' I say. I run forward and hug her. I press my cheek into her cheek. 'I love you,' I say. I wish it wasn't the last time.

'I love you, too.' She squeezes me.

'I know.' I squeeze her back. 'I understand that more

than ever.' I close my eyes and feel my mother's arms around me. I feel her heartbeat. Her hair flies across my cheek. She thought I was dead. She changed my room. But she never stopped loving me, not for a single second. She thought about me every hour of every day. She'll never stop thinking about me. I wish I could take all that away. I wish I could wave a magic wand and make her forget, so she could be a woman with one child, and have that be the way it's always been. Because I know there is only one thing I can do now, and it's going to hurt her.

22.

I don't have any money. My parents have paid for every single thing I've needed since I got home. But even if I had money for a bus ticket, I couldn't take the same bus back. That bus stopped a bunch of times. Every single stop is a chance for someone to see me. My face has been all over the TV, and it will be again once they realize I'm gone. I wonder how much it would cost to hire a taxi and whether I could steal it, but I know as soon as I think it that it's crazy. The taxi driver would turn me in. But I need help from someone. And only one person knows enough to understand why I have to go.

It's after midnight, and it's completely dark except for a streetlight way down the block. I sit on my bed and look out my bedroom window. I wonder if I can trust Vinnie.

He seemed to understand why I wasn't telling anyone, and he didn't slip even the tiniest bit when we were with Lee. But he thinks I should tell. He's just like everyone else in that way. They all think that everything will be better once the truth comes out. I know now that it's once, not if. I can't keep it to myself for ever. One day the truth about the girls will slip out. I will say something, or Vinnie will, or somebody will just know. And when somebody realizes, I don't think I'll be strong enough, just like I wasn't strong enough to deny to Lee that Dee was dead.

I should never have come home. Every second that I'm here puts them in danger, because I'm weak. There's a part of me that wants to talk. There's a part of me that wants to spill out every single second. Words and tears would come out, and then I wouldn't have to carry them. Then they would belong to someone else.

I want to tell Mom. I want to tell Lee. I even want to tell Aunt Hannah. As long as I'm here, I will never be strong enough to be silent.

As long as I'm not with them, I will want to tell someone about them.

This is not my home any more. I am not Amy. I wish I were Amy, but Amy is dead as much as Dee. *Amy MacArthur.* The name rolls around inside my brain. For six years, I hardly let myself think it. And now I have to put it away again. I have to be Chelsea, no last name, a living doll, and I have to be her until Kyle dies.

I like it here. I like being in my old bedroom. I like seeing the MacArthur mailbox. I like walking down this familiar hall. I like seeing my mom and my dad and Jay. I like not having to be the one to cook and clean. I like going to the library. I like being alone, in the quiet, with a door between me and the rest of the world.

Tears roll down my face. I can no longer see out the window. And I have blocked out this thing for so long, this awful truth, this truth that has kept me from leaving for days now, even though I've known I should – that has kept me here for an impossible month. I like being away from them. I never have to give another bath, make another meal, clean up another mess. I like not having to take care of anyone but myself. Now I'm sobbing. I don't want to go back. I don't want to see Kyle. I don't want to remember.

But I can't stand to forget them. What if I stay here and I begin to forget? What if I stop having these spells where I'm suddenly there, and I only have normal memories? Then I will never be able to see them. I will never be able to hold Barbie or play with Lola or tell them stories. I will never be able to see them laugh. I will never see Stacie again.

What if my memories fade away?

I know that no matter how much I want to stay here, I can never let them stay with him alone. I can never risk the chance that I might tell someone about them. I can never stay here and be Amy.

I've made my decision, but I don't do anything about it. I stare at the window, and I cry until I can't any more. And then I sleep for a whole day. I don't sleep very well. I lie awake and picture myself packing up my Safeway bag and leaving, and climbing into Vinnie's car. And then we drive away into the night. Or then the police come, and they swarm us, and they ask me and ask me and ask me. And then the loop starts over. I am packing my Safeway bag. The Stacie doll goes in first, then my clothes, the purple clothes. I have to leave most of the things Lee bought me behind. I am packing; I am packing; I am packing.

My mom knocks on the door. 'Amy? Are you all right? It's almost time for dinner.'

'I don't feel good,' I say.

'You'll feel better if you eat,' she says.

'Can you save something for me?' I'll need to eat before I leave. But I can't face her. I can't tell her goodbye, and I can't act like everything is normal.

'OK, honey,' she says. But she's still there. 'Should we take you to a doctor?'

'It's just a little bug,' I say.

Finally, she goes away. I hear the bare murmur of voices from down the hall. I just made some progress with Jay, and now it's over. Dad will go back to Colorado. I told Mom and Jay that I loved them, but not Dad. If I go out there now and say it, he'll know something is going on. But they know I'm alive, I tell myself. It won't be as bad for them this time.

I force myself to sit up. Now, while they're distracted, is a good time. I pick up the phone and listen to the dial tone. The paper towel with Vinnie's phone number is sitting on top of the stack of books on the windowsill. I dial.

'Hello,' he says.

'Hi,' I say.

'Amy! Hey, how are you?'

'I'm OK,' I say.

'Great! Are you ready to go back to the library? We could do something else, too. Lots to do around here if you like nature. We could go for a hike. Now that I have a car, there's lots of places. Unless you don't like hiking. Maybe you want to go to the beach. We can drive to the beach, or—'

'Vinnie,' I cut him off. 'I need a favour.'

'OK, sure, Amy. Whatever you need.'

I take a deep breath. It comes out more like a gasp.

'You can drive if you want,' he says. 'You're already better than I am.'

'No,' I say. 'What I want is for you to drive.'

'Oh, OK, sure,' he says. 'Where do you want to go?'

'I want to go back,' I say.

'Back?'

'Back.'

'Oh.' There is silence.

'Vinnie—'

'Are you sure that's a good idea?' he asks.

'If I stay here, I'm going to tell,' I say. 'I told you what happens if I do that.'

It is dark, and I am packing. It takes longer than it did when I was imagining it. I pick up each piece of clothing. Most things I haven't even worn. There's a dress that comes up far above my knees. It still has its tags on it. There's a pair of sandals that are not that practical for walking. It doesn't make any sense to take them. I pack two pairs of jeans and four T-shirts, and I wear my new athletic shoes. I wear the jacket I arrived in – Stacie's pink jacket. I also take the book with the headless girl on the cover. I know it's wrong of me to take it because it doesn't belong to me, but there's something about it. When I'm back, I'll have plenty of time to read it again, to understand what she liked about that boy she went off with.

Never come back here! I hear him scream. But I haven't told anyone. When I come back, it will be just me. He won't hurt them if I come back alone. He'll have realized that he can't take care of them, realized they need me. And we can all go somewhere else, somewhere no one could ever follow me. I try to think of what I'll say when I walk up that long hill, when I open up the cabin door. *It's just me. I'm alone.* I imagine myself yelling it. *It's just Chelsea! I'm all alone!*

If he doesn't let me back, I'll . . . I shut off the thought. My mind fills with solid black. There is no if or then or but, just one step and then another.

I take my bag into the empty kitchen and open up the refrigerator. My mom has left me a dinner. It's already on a plate covered in plastic wrap. I take it out, and my stomach is churning into knots. I'm the furthest thing from hungry. But I eat it. I eat a slice of meat loaf made with oatmeal instead of breadcrumbs. I eat four red potatoes and six pieces of broccoli. I eat it all cold, but it doesn't matter. It still tastes good. It tastes so good that I almost don't let myself taste it. It's just food, I tell myself. I'm only eating because I have to eat. I want to wash the dish, but I'm afraid that will make too much noise, so I just leave it in the sink.

I take one last look around the kitchen. It hasn't changed much since I was a kid, but now I'm seeing it from a different angle. This is where Mom made food for us. And I know why she did it now. I know she might not have always liked it, and maybe some days she wished someone else would do it. But she had to make sure we ate. It wasn't just because she loved us; it was because we followed from her like a hand follows from an arm. If we didn't eat, she couldn't have eaten. And if we died, she would never be whole.

There is a pad of scratch paper by the phone. I didn't plan to leave any kind of note, but now I can't help myself. I can't let Mom and Dad worry more than they have to. This time, they have to know that I'm leaving of my own free will and I'm OK.

'Mom and Dad,' I write. And then I add, 'and Jay.' He deserves to be included. 'I have to leave. I hope someday I'll see you again, and I'll be able to explain everything. Please don't follow me, and don't call the police. I have a good reason for doing this. Please trust me. I wish I could stay.' I don't know what else to say. What I've written isn't enough. It sounds like it was written by a robot. But I don't have anything better. 'I love you,' I write. And then I sign it, 'Amy'. I write the *A* the way I used to when I was a kid, with a big round *A* and the tail of the *Y* curling around the whole word. Then I make two little round dots in the *A*, so it looks like the *A* is a sort of half-smiling face. It doesn't fit with the note I just wrote, the one with no personality at all. It doesn't fit with anything about me now. But I leave it. I head back through the living room and out the front door, closing it as quietly as I can. I walk down the driveway and turn right. I walk past the MacArthur mailbox with its chipping paint, and I keep walking two more blocks until I get to the place where I'm supposed to meet Vinnie. But he's not here yet. I think about sitting down on the kerb, but I'm too restless. I pace up and down the sidewalk beneath a sign that says *2 HOUR PARKING*. And then I hear the unmistakable lurch of Vinnie's driving, and the car skids to a stop in front of me.

But it's not just Vinnie. Lee is in the back seat.

I freeze.

Lee jumps out. 'Amy, don't be mad,' she says.

Vinnie rolls down the window. 'I'm sorry,' he says. 'Lee called me right after you did.'

'So you told her?' I whisper-yell.

'I didn't tell anyone,' Lee says.

'Why are you here?'

'If you want to go back, that's your choice,' Lee says. 'We shouldn't lock you up any more than he did.'

'But.'

'But nothing,' Lee says. 'We just want to help.'

I don't believe her for a second, but I climb into the front seat. I can't go back to my house. I will just have to think of something. I will have to be strong enough to take whatever they throw at me.

Vinnie starts driving. I haven't told him where to go, but he has figured out that he needs to head for the highway.

'What are you going to do when you get there?' Lee asks.

I say nothing.

'Are you going to get revenge? Like, try to kill him?'

I say nothing.

'You don't *like* him, do you?'

'No, I don't *like* him!' I yell.

Vinnie jumps, and the car swerves.

'But you want to go live with him again?' Lee asks. Vinnie didn't tell her everything. I let my breath out. Lee doesn't know about them. Maybe she will let me go. She can't care about me that much. 'Amy, there's this thing called Stockholm syndrome,' Lee says. 'It's when you start to identify with your kidnapper. Like, because you spend so much time together—'

'I don't *identify* with him,' I snap.

He lifts Barbie in the air. He spins her around.

He slams the nurse Barbie on the table.

He puts a hand around Lola's neck.

'OK, well . . .' Lee searches for words.

'But you lived with him for so long,' Vinnie says. 'Maybe you don't realize that there's another way. That you can stay with your parents. You can stay if you want to.'

'You *know* I can't,' I say. He knows. Why is he doing this? Why does he have to make it harder? But he's driving. We're heading north.

'What if he kills you, too?' Lee asks. She leans forward,

sticks her head between the two front seats. 'You saw what happened to my mom. Do you want your mom to be crazy, too?'

It's not fair of her to say this. I sit perfectly still. I stare ahead out the windscreen. We are getting closer.

'Amy, this isn't about you.' Lee's voice is hard now. 'If you cared about your mom and your dad, you would stay.'

I care about them, I think. But I don't say it. I'm not capable of speaking. It's like I'm not even in the car. I left a note for them. They will know I'm alive. But they won't know if I die.

'Never come back here!'

The door slams.

There is blood in Stacie's hair.

Barbie is crying.

'Dee would want to be free,' Lee says. 'She would want you to be free, too. You were her best friend, Amy. She loved you. You were more her sister than I was. She would want you to stay.'

She wouldn't want anything for me. She would barely even know me. But the old Dee. The old Dee. She would have loved them. She would have wanted me to go back for them. *Lee doesn't know. She doesn't know.*

Stacie grabs Barbie by the hair.

'We could call the police,' Lee says. 'We could have him arrested, and he would never hurt you again.'

I can't take a full breath. Air is rushing by us. Vinnie's car is old, and the wheels rattle against the highway. He speeds around a curve. The window next to me is open a crack. I

204

put my hands over my ears and close my eyes. I squeeze them shut. But I can hear my breathing.

'Amy, let me do this,' Lee says.

'Let her be,' Vinnie says. 'Lee, don't.'

'We can't just let her go back,' Lee says. 'She needs help.'

'Lee!' Vinnie yells.

The car careens around another turn.

'Vinnie, can't you see how wrong this is?' Lee asks. 'I'm doing it.' She's holding her phone. I can't see it, but I know it. She's about to call the cops. She's about to kill them.

I click open my seat belt and lean the seat back as far as it will go.

'Ow! Amy!' Lee screams.

I slide between the seats and fall on top of her. I can't even see her. I grab blindly for the phone. My hand hits her face, her arm, her chest. My legs are kicking behind me. I'm trying to press against anything, anything to keep me on top of Lee, to stop her from calling.

She turns her face away and holds her hands up.

The phone tumbles away from her. I collapse on top of her and try to push myself up, try to see where it landed. But I can't see anything. Everything is a blur. I think I'm crying. Or maybe we're underwater. Maybe Vinnie has crashed the car into a lake and we're going to drown. Maybe that's why I still can't breathe. But we're weaving back and forth. We're still on the road. I'm on top of Lee. Her hands are touching me. She's pushing against my chest. She's trying to lift me off of her, but she's not strong enough.

'Amy. Amy,' Lee says. 'Get off me!'

She was going to call the cops. She was going to kill them. I push away from her, and I punch her in the side of the face. She was going to kill them. She was going to kill my kids. The car jerks, and I roll away, still half on top of Lee. I fish under the seat for the phone, but I can't find it. And I realize the car has stopped, and outside the window there is a silent, unmoving tree, and there is no wind, and the door opens next to my head, and I look up and see Vinnie. His blue eyes stare down at me out of his normal, round face. Three large zits sit in a row across his chin.

Vinnie grabs me by the shoulders and pulls me from the car. I let him pull me. The blur in my eyes has cleared. There are tears on my cheeks, but none in my eyes any more. I set my feet on the ground and lean against him.

'Are you OK?' he asks.

'Don't let her call,' I say. My voice is small, almost nothing. But it took breath to say it. I am breathing. My eyes search for the phone.

Lee is still in the back seat. She's sitting up now, and she has it. I try to leap forward, but Vinnie holds me.

'Lee, let's talk about this,' Vinnie says.

The face of the phone is smashed up. Lee tries to do something with it, but it doesn't work. The phone is broken. She can't call. I lean into Vinnie.

I watch Lee. She throws the phone into the back seat window. 'I'm trying to help you,' she says. She turns to look at me. The left side of her face is turning purple. I must have done that. But I'm still not sorry. I don't care if

206

she is their aunt. If she does anything to bring the cops, I'll kill her.

'Let's just chill out for a minute,' Vinnie says.

'You were never going to help me,' I say. I point at Lee. 'You just wanted to stop me. You think I'm crazy. But I'm not crazy.'

'Yes, you are,' Lee says.

'She doesn't really think that,' Vinnie says. 'She just wants to make sure nobody hurts you again. His arm squeezes me. 'I don't want him to hurt you.' His voice is quiet and earnest. He says it slowly, not like when he makes a joke. He means it. And that means he'll never let me go.

Lee slowly steps out of the car. 'I'm sorry,' she says. 'Vinnie is right. I didn't mean it.' Her face really looks terrible where I punched her. But she's still beautiful. She's still a sharper version of Dee. 'Let's stay here for a while and calm down. Think about what to do.'

I can't look at her. I hurt her, and it wasn't fair of me. She doesn't know that helping me means hurting them. She would love them if she knew. I'm a bad person. But I'm not only bad. I love my children. No matter what else I do, there's that. I look past Lee, and I see that Vinnie's keys are hanging from the ignition. The car is parked crookedly on the shoulder of the country highway, a two-lane road lined with trees. We are standing in a shallow lane of gravel.

The driver's side door is even open.

I take a step away from Vinnie, act like I just need some space. I walk slowly around the car and put one hand on my face. I don't cover my eyes, though.

'We have all night,' Vinnie says. 'We can stay here for a while.'

'There has to be another way,' Lee says. 'You deserve your life. You deserve to do everything – everything Dee would have wanted to do. We can help you have that.'

She's trying to manipulate me again because Dee is dead. I remember a time when I was at Dee's house. There was a little boy who lived next door to them. His name was Josiah. Dee would play tag with him in the backyard, and she would laugh. I can see Dee laughing. I can see Josiah running away on his stubby little legs. If Dee had had Lola and Barbie in her old life, that's how it would have been. I'm standing next to the driver's side door now.

I slide in, slam the door shut, and turn the key.

'Amy!' Lee calls.

I floor it. I swerve out on the highway. The back door is still open. They both must be yelling now, but I can't hear them. I keep my foot on the gas pedal. I am speeding away from them. All I can hear is the noise of the wind.

When she was still at least partly Dee, we were driving up this very highway. And the wind rushed past us, and the wheels rattled against the road. And the trees seemed to be running by.

Dee and I held hands. She reached back from the front seat, and I leant forward. Her hand was cold but sweaty. She sat perfectly still. I squirmed, trying not to move.

Kyle was humming. Mmm hmm hmm. Mmm hmm hmm.

I wondered what would happen if I got the door open. Could I jump out, or would I die? Could I get Dee to do it with me? You are not supposed to get in the car. Once you get in the car, you're dead.

For a while, I thought that was a lie. I thought that even though we had to be with Kyle, we were alive.

I am humming as I drive Vinnie's car. Mmm hmm hmm. Mmm hmm hmm. The song had no words. He loved to hum it when he was playing with his dolls. A long amount of time passes, and this highway winds around and around and every exit looks the same. I was looking for the road signs six years ago, hoping to see something that would help us. I thought I would remember for ever, but now . . .

I have no idea where to go from here. As this realization hits me, I let up on the gas. I could have already passed the turn.

I try not to imagine what Vinnie and Lee are doing. They will need someone to pick them up. What will they say? They both want to protect me, and they think that means dragging me home. Lee wants to call the police. She might have used Vinnie's phone to call them already. Why didn't I take it from him? Why didn't I think of that? I panicked. I saw the keys in the ignition and the open door, and I just went for it. Now I have hardly any time. I have to find them, and find them fast. I have to get them away from here, somewhere no one will ever find us. I have to make Kyle understand.

I shouldn't have stolen Vinnie's car. Vinnie was the only

one who knew, and he kept my secret. He taught me to drive. I hope that after we leave, he finds the car. Maybe I can apologize someday. Kyle is a lot older than me, and someday he will die. And then we can come home again, and I'll apologize to Vinnie. Maybe I'll buy him a new car.

But Kyle isn't that old. I think he's probably about thirty. It will be a long time before he dies.

Unless.

They can't know I killed their daddy. They don't understand how things are. I can't kill their daddy.

I drive on. I see an exit towards the town where I got on the bus, and I take it. I'm driving below the speed limit now, looking for another turn. When the lady drove me to the bus stop that night, I didn't pay close enough attention. Why didn't I pay attention?

My hands slip on the steering wheel. Sweat is pouring out of my palms. It's like how when we turned a corner, my hand slipped out of Dee's hand. I have to keep my hand on the wheel. I turn a corner now, a soft corner, and there's a sign with a picture of a stoplight. And there, far down the road, is the stoplight itself, and something clicks together in my brain. My heart beats faster. When we reached this point before, Kyle began to slow down. He changed the way he was humming.

'We're almost home, ladies,' he said. 'Aren't you excited to see your new home?'

That's when my hand slipped.

Dee grabbed for it again, and again it slipped. Our hands slid past each other.

There's a break in the trees before the intersection. There's an old gas station that is closed and falling apart, and there's a sign that says gas is $1.56 a gallon on a pump that isn't connected to anything. This is where I take the left turn.

I ran down this hill.

I was carrying my Safeway bag with the Stacie doll, and my jacket was only half zipped, and I didn't know where I was going. And I stopped next to that disconnected pump, and it was dark, and a woman stopped for me. A white woman wearing business clothes with an empty car seat in the back.

'Are you OK?' she asked me.

'I need to get to a bus station,' I said.

'Can I call your mom for you?' she asked. She looked me up and down as she said it, and she hesitated, as if she wasn't sure I was as young as I looked, or maybe like she thought I was going to rob her.

Now I turn the car left across the main road. I drive slowly up the long hill. There are two more turns, one on to a steep paved road and another that's gravel. And then off the gravel road is a road that's just dirt. I wipe my hands on my jeans, one after the other, and I grip the wheel. Each time I have been on this road, there was no going back.

23.

I pull off the road before the second turn. I can't drive all the way up, or Kyle will know I'm coming. If he knows I'm coming, he will hide, or he will do something. I need to be able to tell him that it's just me, and convince him to take me back.

I wouldn't take me back.

I would want to kill me.

Sometimes I want to kill me.

I pull in as far as I can, but that isn't very far. There are too many trees. The car isn't hidden at all. It's just a little way off the road. Anybody who was looking would find it. That means I can't leave it here for long, not with Vinnie and Lee down there, not with Vinnie still having his phone. I have to get them and then . . . I don't know where we'll go, but we'll go somewhere. Another cabin, another river. Anywhere they won't find us.

I run up the hill. My feet pound on pavement. I'm carrying my bag over one shoulder, and it's slamming against me. I hold on to the straps and keep running. Up up up. I am leading them up this hill. If I don't get myself up and then all of us down again, we'll be found. Maybe they're better off without me. If I take the car back down the hill now and drive away, if I drive away east and end up in Idaho, maybe the cops won't find me, and if they don't find me, I can never tell anyone that they exist or where they are.

But Vinnie might tell Lee now. He might already have told her. Lee won't stop until she finds them. She'll tell Aunt Hannah, and Aunt Hannah will not stop.

I don't want to be a mother.

But I am.

I am.

I make it to the next turn, and up I go, on gravel now. This road has dirt, too, and weeds growing up in the road. No car but Kyle's goes up this far any more. There are no neighbours. There was a fire, Kyle told us. A fire in the nearest house, and the family ran out in the night, and later they came back for their chickens and cows, and now it's just us, he said. Us and the river and the dolls and the night.

I can't go back now. It would make sense to go back, to the car, to Idaho, to Wyoming, to Canada. I don't even know what those places look like; I just know they're not here. But it's not possible. I slow down as I reach the dirt road, the one with hardly any gravel at all. It's dark. By rights I shouldn't be able to see anything, but my eyes have got used to it since I left the car. There are stars and the moon out. Maybe they will all be asleep, and I can walk in, and . . .

Maybe I can take them.

The thought strikes me. I fall back a step and then two. If I could get inside without waking Kyle, if I could get them to be quiet, if I could walk them out into the night. If I could get them back to the car, all without Kyle ever waking up. That is the solution to all my problems. I'll tell them that they can see their daddy later. I'll say that we're just going on a little trip for fun. They'll be all right. They'll miss him, but it won't be like I killed him.

It won't be like . . .

I shiver. I'm frozen in the middle of the dirt road, halfway up the last hill. There will be a little curve in the road, and then the cabin will come into view. I have to be quiet if I'm going to do this. Now that I've thought of it, I can't think of anything else. I can't imagine going back and staying with Kyle, not trying to take them away with me. I don't know how I even thought I could do that, when this plan is obvious, when this has to be the only way.

I begin to walk again. I can see only the road in front of me now, as I place one foot in front of the other. I know there are trees on either side of me. I pass the spot beyond which I never went, the cluster of four trees together that marked the boundaries of our lives. I pass it and I don't falter in my steps. It's not a real boundary; I know that now.

I ran down this road and past it once, and now I know that I can again.

But I'm home now. I'm walking through my backyard. I lived here six years, and I know every tree and every bush and every pit in this road. I know all the squirrels and the snails and the grass. I know the stars, each one by names Lola and I made up. I knew enough about constellations to know there were some, but the only one I could remember was the Big Dipper. So we made up the rest, sitting there in the place where the trees parted to leave room for the cabin, but as far from the cabin as you could go without entering the forest. That was two years ago, when Lola was three and Barbie was one, but when Barbie was old enough, we showed her. And she wanted to play with the pinecones. She didn't care about the stars at all.

The cabin sits dark and small in its clearing. Kyle's Subaru is parked crookedly to the side. It has seen better days. It's old and dirty now, with two windows taped over with duct tape. I used to think driving was so hard, so impossibly out of reach, but I just did it. I drove all the way here on the highway. Now I have two things I can do. I can walk past the line, and I can drive.

I slow my steps, making sure not to make a sound. One step after another, and I'm in front of the three stairs that lead up to the tiny wooden porch in front of the door. One stair, two, three. I reach for the doorknob. I'm ready to scream, to tell Kyle it's just me, no cops. But not yet. Not until I at least try. The doorknob doesn't turn. It rattles the tiniest bit, and I pull my hand back. I wait. Two seconds, three. There is no sound from inside. I peer in the little square window. There is no curtain and never was one. I can see to where the beds were . . . I strain my eyes. They must be there. My heart beats and my head pulses and my eyes blur. They must be there. And then I see her. Lola is sitting up on the camp bed where I used to sleep. She is staring right at me.

We stare at each other.

I put my finger to my lips.

She stares.

I wave her towards me. My hand shakes. She's wearing a frilly pink nightgown. It's frayed at the edges and, I know, faded from bright pink to dull. Her blonde hair is messy around the edges of her face. She slides off the bed and takes a glance behind her. I can't see what she's looking at; it's either Kyle or Barbie, or maybe both.

I beckon her. I don't know if she can see my eyes. They are saying, *Now. Please. Quiet. Please, Lola, please.*

She takes a step forward, then another, then another. She disappears from view under the window, and there is the faint click of the lock, and then the doorknob turns, slowly, and the door moves inward. Lola pulls it with care, making no noise.

I kneel on the porch, my face pressed into the crack.

She opens it wider. 'Chel,' she whispers. Her blue eyes stare into mine. She's frightened; it's as if she thinks I'm a ghost.

I hold my hand steady in mid-air. I might reach out to grab her any second. I might pull her in close, and I might burst into tears, and she might burst into tears, or she might scream.

'I've come back for you,' I whisper. 'And Barbie. I would never leave you. You know that.'

'Daddy said you can't,' Lola whispers. She learnt how to whisper from me, thank God. Together we learnt how to have our time, how to not set Stacie or him off.

'Daddy is sometimes wrong,' I say.

She stares at me. Maybe I went too far with that. She'll never believe it. I struggle to find something else to say, some way to convince her. She needs to be quiet. She needs to come out, and let me come in and get Barbie.

I hold out a hand.

Lola slides through the door.

I pull her into my arms. The tears fall. I can't hold them back, but I'm quiet. Her arms circle around my neck. She's crying, too, but miraculously, she's just as quiet.

'He said you meant to, but you didn't,' she says.

'I didn't mean to,' I say. 'I didn't mean to.'

'Daddy says she's up there.' Lola looks up at the stars.

I wipe the tears off her face. 'Yes, she is,' I say. 'She's up there, and we need to go that way.' I point at the road.

Lola begins to shake.

I pull her in. 'It's OK, baby. I've been down there, and it's good. There are a lot of people who love you. You'll be happy.' That's not what I planned to say. Everything I planned is forgotten.

She is still shaking. I can't wait any longer. Kyle could wake up at any second.

'You need to stay here,' I say. 'I'm going to get Barbie, and then we'll go. OK?'

'OK,' Lola whispers.

I almost gasp with relief. 'OK. I'll be back in one minute, baby. One minute.' I carefully set her aside, and she stands on the porch in her nightgown. She's only wearing socks on her feet, and her face is wet with tears, and she's shaking, but she stays quiet. She is so strong. She is the strongest little girl ever. So I can do this. I can be the strongest mom.

I rise to my feet, and I push the door open a little more. The hinge creaks. I step in on my tiptoes. It's darker inside, and it takes my eyes a second to adjust. Kyle is lying on the bed. Barbie is behind him, on the side of the bed next to the wall. I can't get to her without reaching over him, and I can't carry her away without her agreeing, without convincing her to be quiet. But she's only three. She can't understand the way Lola can.

There must be a way past him. This can't end here, with Lola outside and Barbie inside. I can't leave without Barbie. I step forward, one step, two, three. I am standing over Kyle. He is lying on his right side, one giant ear facing up, mouth slack. He's snoring gently. Breathing. Fast asleep, but how fast? My vision blurs, and I rock on my toes. This is the same as when I tried to get Dee, when I tried to run. I cut the rope and got the key, but when I woke Stacie up, I woke Kyle, too.

Barbie is smaller, I tell myself. *I couldn't carry Dee, but I can carry her.*

My vision clears, and I see Barbie. She stirs in her sleep. I reach over Kyle with one hand and tap her cheek.

She opens her eyes and stares at me.

I smile and pray she can see me, pray she recognizes me, pray she doesn't wake Kyle up. I reach out both hands. I am leaning dangerously far. I hope I can lift her from this angle.

'Chel?' she says sleepily.

I get my hands on either side of her, and I lift. I lift her up off the bed and my arms are straining and she goes over Kyle's head, and I pull her close to me, and I step back. I take another step back, and another.

Kyle is still sleeping.

Another step. I turn slowly. I step out through the door. 'Chel?'

I pull the door shut behind me, as quietly as I can. 'Yes, it's me, baby. It's me and we're leaving. Lola?' She is still on the porch, still waiting, still shaking. 'Lola, you'll have to walk. Can you do that?'

Lola doesn't walk. She takes off down the steps at a run. She races out across the dirt of the driveway and heads down the road. Her lack of shoes doesn't slow her down at all.

I burst into tears, and this time they're not quiet. I run after her, carrying Barbie, and Barbie begins to cry, and we make a great noise as we all run, down the hill and down and, finally, we run past the imaginary line, the one that used to form the border of our whole world. Lola doesn't stop but begins to walk, and I catch up to her, and we don't look behind us. I take her hand, and we keep walking. I look up at the stars and I think, *If you're up there, Dee, if you're watching over them, thank you.*

I was down by the river, carrying Barbie in a sling across my belly that I made myself out of a sheet. Kyle had bought that sewing machine at the flea market, and I made all the girls' clothes now, and I repaired all of Stacie's and my clothes.

Barbie was only five days old, and I was thirteen. She was so tiny that carrying her was almost nothing at all. She'd come earlier than we expected, but then, we didn't really know the date she was conceived. It could have been any one of a million nights. Each one of them, Stacie was so quiet that it seemed like she wasn't even there. I would take Lola into the bathroom, and through the door all I heard was the sound of Kyle breathing, heavy and strong. I tried to pretend I didn't know what he was doing to her, that it was really just Lola and me. Kyle would pretend, too, after.

Why are you in the bathroom? he'd say. As if what he did to her was nothing.

Now Barbie seemed too small and fragile, and I held her close and listened, making sure I could feel her and hear her, every second. It would be time to feed her soon, and I couldn't do it. I would have to take her back inside to Stacie and wake her. But I didn't know how she'd react. Barbie's birth was worse than Lola's – more painful, longer, awful.

Kyle came through the bushes. His large feet crunched on the rocks; his shadow cast itself over me.

'Where's Lola?' I asked.

'Stacie's awake,' he said. 'She's with her.' He sat down next to me, on the small rocks where the grass peeked through. The river flowed in front of us, foaming and loud. But Kyle's voice carried easily.

I looked up at him. His hair was longish. He cut it himself, when he thought of it, and it never looked anything like normal. But today it looked worse. It was tinged with grey already, and it was plastered against his head, the back longer than the front, pieces sticking out over his ears. He hunched his shoulders, leaning over his great body.

'Is she . . .' I didn't know how to ask it. I couldn't say a bad word about Stacie. Kyle wouldn't hear of it. One time I got frustrated with her and called her a bad name, and Kyle slapped me across the face. He slapped me so hard that my head hurt for days.

'She's quiet,' he said.

She had been quiet, after the birth, for a couple days. And then she had not been quiet. She had screamed and cried and thrown the dishes around the room until they were only pieces on the floor, and I went scrambling after them while Kyle held Barbie in the sling and picked up Lola in his arms, and as I picked up the pieces and swept them and vacuumed the floor to catch the tiniest of the shards, she screamed at me.

You want them. You want them. You want them, she screamed, and her face was red and blotchy from crying, and she could barely sit up, because she'd hurt herself destroying everything so soon after giving birth. Finally her voice gave out, and she could no longer scream at me. She collapsed into tears and rolled away from me on the bed.

At the river, I held Barbie close. Stacie wasn't right. I never wanted to be a mother. I never wanted how it happened. But this baby was precious. And Lola was precious. They were innocent, and they loved us, all of us, no matter what we did or who we were, and how could you not love someone like that?

She hadn't hurt Lola yet, then. But since the birth, I didn't like to sit there and leave Lola alone with her. Something had happened to her during those twenty-four hours of pain, something that opened the fracture inside her and broke her apart. I began to stand up, but Kyle pulled on my arm. I fell back into the rocks, clutching Barbie close.

'Where's Stacie?' he asked. There were tears in his eyes. He wasn't asking where she was, but what had happened to her. Why was she no longer the girl he had followed around the streets of Grey Wood? Why was she no longer his little doll?

'That day,' I began. I knew I shouldn't say it. I knew that the fact that I was holding Barbie might not keep me safe. But I opened my mouth, and it came out. 'When we were at the river, before you took us, she had just got her period.'

He stared at me. His eyes were filled with tears, but hard. He did nothing. Barbie and I still sat there on our rock.

'She was upset,' I said. 'She didn't want to grow up.' I had just turned thirteen, and I didn't have my period yet. I could feel it coming, though. I had boobs now. They weren't large, nothing near like what I thought I wanted, before. Now, I hoped they would stop growing. I hoped the blood would never come, and I could be a child. Kyle loved dolls, but he liked women, too. Women made him feel *that* way. At least, you had to be a little bit of a woman. Not a whole woman like our moms. But you had to have boobs, and blood. Those things made Kyle feel it.

'She's my Stacie,' he said. He hung his head low over his body.

You raped her, I thought. That was something I couldn't say. He already knew it, of course. But he acted as if that were nothing, as if what he did to her at night and these babies had no relation, as if Stacie could possibly be the same, after that.

I wasn't the same, and it wasn't me.

'She doesn't like them, but they're beautiful.' He turned his face back to me. 'Aren't they?'

I nodded.

'I don't hurt her,' he said.

I put my hand on Barbie's head and pulled her even closer. I curled around her, and I could see nothing, not Kyle, not the water, not the rocks; nothing.

'I don't mean to.' His voice came through the blur, over-rode everything. He was plaintive, almost whining, a sad tinge to his voice. 'I love her,' he said. 'Why does she have to be this way when she knows that I love her?'

I couldn't answer, could barely breathe.

'You love her, too, don't you?'

'Yes,' I said. He knew I did. He knew that was why I would never try to run again, even before Lola was born. I would never leave Stacie. I knew he meant it when he said he loved her, and I also knew what his love meant.

'I'm going to stop,' he said.

Stop? I let out a little gasp. Did he really mean it? And what if he did? What if he stopped with her and turned to me?

Barbie began to cry. She was hungry. I had to take her back to Stacie, the only one who could feed her.

'There won't be any more,' he said, 'if she doesn't love them. And if she doesn't want it.'

'I think . . .' I choked on my words. 'I think that will help her,' I said.

And he really did stop, and very soon after that, I got my period. But he didn't start doing it to me. He told me to clean this and change that diaper and cook and sew, but that was all he asked me to do for him. We both tiptoed around Stacie, and kept the girls away from her as much as we could. We watched and waited and said only kind things, no matter what we received back. But by that time, the cousin who had been my best friend was gone, and the doll who Kyle said he loved was gone, too.

24.

We're walking slower now because Lola's feet are hurting after running over gravel, and so she takes each step carefully. Barbie isn't wearing shoes either, and she's heavy, maybe even heavier than she was only a month ago. I'm sweating and stumbling down the hill, suddenly exhausted. But I can see the bend where I left the car now, and I get new strength. We only have to make it that far.

I didn't mean to.

I will tell them how much I loved their mommy.

I will tell them that their mommy loved them.

She was going to cut the dress to pieces. She had the sewing scissors in her right hand. But Kyle was saying, *We'll have more children. We'll be a family. Everything will be perfect.*

And Barbie got away from me. She ran towards Stacie because she loved that pink princess dress. 'Mommy, don't cut it,' she said.

Dee grabbed her by the hair, and she said, *This is your fault.* She pulled out a whole clump of Barbie's hair.

I was screaming, *Stop. Stacie, stop. Stop. Stop.*

You wanted them, she screamed.

Barbie was bawling.

Lola tried to go to her.

I pulled her back, and Stacie wrenched her out of my arms. She threw Lola, and Lola fell.

You wanted them.

No, baby doll, Kyle said. He picked up Lola. Barbie ran to them, and so did I.

You wanted them. She raised the scissors.

Mommy, no, Lola said.

Stacie rushed towards us with the scissors raised.

I jumped in front of them. I grabbed the lamp.

I never thought about how hard to hit her. I never thought about where. I just swung.

We all heard the crunch as the base of the lamp broke. And she fell like it was slow motion. She landed on her back with her hair covering one side of her face. One blue eye stared up at us.

Kyle got down on his knees. *Baby, baby. Baby doll. Wake up, baby doll.* He sobbed.

Lola and Barbie were hiding behind me but saying, *Mommy? Mommy?* and peering around me while my hands instinctively went out to hold them back, because in the movies they jump up again, the monsters.

But Stacie didn't jump up. She was no longer a monster. She was a body with Stacie's face, which I could not see yet was Dee's face. All I saw was the screaming, the hands on Barbie, Lola flying, and more screams, and the face distorted, and the lamp sitting on the little end table, and the crying, and Kyle, *Baby doll, wake up. Baby, wake up.*

But I'll never tell them that I saw Stacie as a monster. She wasn't, not until he made her that way. I'll tell them I didn't mean to, that I only wanted to calm Mommy down. I only wanted her to stop. That's the truth. I wanted to take them away from there while Kyle took Dee on their 'honeymoon', and I would have come back for Dee with the police. That's what I would have done, if she had made it through that day. I wanted all of us to be together.

'Chel. Chel.'

Whose voice is it?

I can't see anything, but I'm sure my eyes are open.

'Chel.' It's another voice, a smaller one. Barbie.

I shake my head. It rubs against something. Slowly, I sit up. I'm looking through the windscreen of the car, and there is a gas pump. $1.56. I am at the gas station. *We* are at the gas station. The airbag is open. My chest aches.

'Barbie? Lola?' I turn around in my seat, awkwardly; the airbag is too big to let me do much.

'Chel!' Lola squeezes into the front seat and wraps her arms around me. Barbie hangs on to Lola.

'What happened?' I ask. It's coming back to me, though.

I was there. I was back there in the cabin on that day, with the lamp, and the screaming, and Kyle's face, and I was outside with them inside, and it was Dee's face after all lying there. That's where I was, on the drive back down the hill.

I rub my eyes. Yes, we are at the gas station. We have not got far enough. How much time has passed? Only a few minutes, surely. But I can't drive with this airbag out. And I don't have a phone. I should have insisted that Mom buy me a phone.

'Chel, you wouldn't answer,' Lola says.

'I'm sorry, baby,' I say. 'I got lost in my head. I'm sorry.'

'Where's Daddy?' Barbie asks.

'Daddy's sleeping,' I say. 'We didn't want to wake Daddy.' But he's probably awake now. He's probably noticed that they're gone.

'Where are we?' Barbie is crying.

'We're not very far from home,' I say. 'We're not far at all.' This is meant to reassure her, but Lola knows it doesn't reassure me. She leans into my face.

'You didn't want to crash,' she says.

'No, baby, I didn't.' We can't walk down the street, not with Lola still in socks and Barbie barefoot. Lola has walked as far as she can already. Her little feet must be killing her, but she doesn't complain.

'We put Mommy by the river,' she says. She plops down in the passenger seat.

I could have killed them. I never thought about that. I knew I had these blackouts, these times when I went

228

elsewhere. I never thought it would happen now. I should have thought about it. What if . . . I gasp for breath. I have to remain calm. They are all right, I tell myself. I just have to think of a way out.

'Daddy was sad.' Lola rubs her left foot.

Barbie climbs on top of her.

'I was sad, too,' I say. But the truth is, I wasn't sad enough. Every time I started to think about what I did, I pushed it away. I buried and buried and buried and acted like it didn't happen, like she had died and there was no context, like she was just gone. But you can't make something nothing just by closing yourself off. Because someday your mind will break, and you will be driving down a steep hill with two precious babies in the back seat, and you will almost kill them. That's what happens when you bury things.

I close my eyes. If I can just go away again, this will not have happened. I just want to go away again.

'Chel! Chel!' Lola pulls on my sleeve.

I open my eyes. There is another car in the lot. Its lights are on. My lights are on, too, I realize, spilling all over the pump.

People are getting out of the other car.

My driver's side door opens. Hands grab me and pull me out of the car. I am on the ground now, facing up to the stars. Lola and Barbie are both crying, but Lola is talking, too.

'Who are you?' she's asking.

'I'm Lee,' Lee says. 'I'm your auntie.'

'Chel's my auntie,' Lola says. 'You're a stranger.'

'We're both your aunties,' Lee says.

'I can't talk to strangers.'

'Chel.' Barbie is tugging on my sleeve.

'Hi, baby,' I say. 'I'm OK, baby.'

'Well, hello there,' Vinnie says. 'Amy's going to be all right. She just needs a little rest.'

'Her name is Barbie,' I say. 'Like the doll. And that's Lola. Girls, this is Vinnie and your Auntie Lee. It's OK to talk to them. They're not strangers.'

'Nice to meet you, Barbie and Lola,' Vinnie says. His face appears over mine. 'Did you hit your head?' he asks.

'I don't think so. The airbag came out.'

'OK,' he says. But he looks worried. His eyebrows squeeze together.

'I'm sorry I stole your car,' I say. 'And crashed it.' We need to get out of here. I need to tell him. 'Vinnie—' But I just want to close my eyes again.

'What do you see?' he asks. 'Do you see stars?'

I do see stars. Lots and lots of them. But those are real stars, not the kind of stars he means. 'No,' I say. 'I'm OK.' I sit up. Lee is sitting on the ground with Lola, who is standing very still, watching me.

Barbie grabs me as I sit up.

I put my arm around her. I'm supposed to be holding her, but it feels like she's holding me.

'I set up my car so I can find it by GPS,' he says. 'Lost it twice in the mall parking lot already.'

'Oh my god.' I'm so stupid that I didn't think of that,

230

that I thought I could get anywhere without them finding me.

'Lee and I rented a car from some guy at a mechanic's shop,' he says.

'I'll pay you back,' I say.

'I think the car might be stolen,' Vinnie goes on. 'That guy was sketch.'

'We're three felons now,' Lee says. '*Grand Theft Auto*, Oregon edition.'

'We have to go now,' I say.

'Is he close?' Lee asks. 'Vinnie, he must be close.'

'Yes,' I say. 'He's very close.'

Lee takes out a phone – it must be Vinnie's. The phone that caught me with its GPS, that I stupidly forgot to break. 'There's no reason not to call now, is there?' she asks.

'Other than us being felons,' Vinnie says.

I look around. I feel my arm around Barbie. I guess there isn't any reason. I guess the cops could come and take Kyle away now. But the thought doesn't make me feel good. It doesn't make me feel anything, really. I know I don't want Lola and Barbie to be anywhere near him, but at the same time, he's the only daddy they know.

'No, there's no reason,' I say. I hold out my free arm for Lola.

She walks over to me and lets me put my arm around her, too.

Lee dials the phone, just three numbers. There is a pause that seems to take a million years.

'I have information about the kidnapper of Amy

231

MacArthur,' she says. 'Yes, I know where he is.' She tells them what road we're on, and she looks up at the street sign and names the cross street. She tells them about the old gas station. Then she looks at me.

'Up the hill,' I say. 'Take a left and then a right. And then there's a dirt road, and there's a cabin.'

'Who is the auntie talking to?' Lola asks. She stares at Lee. I realize she has never even seen another adult woman before. Dee and Kyle and me were the only adults in her whole world. She'll think everybody is a stranger.

'She's talking to someone who's going to help us,' I say. But I don't know if that's true. What Kyle has done has already happened. If the police catch him and put him in jail, it won't do us any good. The girls won't understand why their daddy is in jail. Dee won't be alive again. If the police catch Kyle, then I'll have to see him. If he slips away and escapes, then maybe I'll never see him again.

But he won't do that. He won't really care about getting caught now. He's lost Stacie, the girl he was obsessed with since he first saw her walking to school, more than six years ago. He's lost me, who he owned, too. He hit me over and over again, and he didn't want me the way he wanted her, but I was his. Until I took Stacie away from him, he wanted to keep me. And now he's lost the girls, who were the last things he had.

'Does anyone else live up there?' Vinnie asks.

'No,' I say. 'There's just a burnt-out farmhouse.'

'Well, somebody's coming down the road,' he says.

I look up. There are headlights coming towards us. I

can't see the driver in their brightness, but there's only one person it could be.

'Daddy!' Barbie pipes into the silence.

'Why doesn't she get up?' Kyle asked me. We were outside on the porch this time, us and the girls, while Stacie lay inside on the bed, face to wall. It was getting cold, and we were all bundled up, me in an old thrift-store coat two sizes too big and the girls wrapped in blankets. I was fourteen, and Barbie had just turned one year old then. Actually, she was thirteen months. I had this idea in my head that until a baby turned a certain age, you were supposed to count the months. I didn't know when months stopped and years began, but I knew she was thirteen months then. I held her on my lap while Lola sat with a magnetic tray of letters, another thrift-store purchase, or maybe theft. Kyle didn't take us into town with him, so I could never be sure. I had no way of knowing how much he'd inherited from his dead parents or what he had left.

Lola moved the letters around sort of haphazardly. It was time to get some more books, I thought. She might already be behind, without having any preschool or anything. I had to make sure she learnt something, even if she was going to live up here with just us for her whole life.

'I don't touch her,' Kyle said. 'She was supposed to change back.' He was crying, tears rolling down his big face.

I tried not to let it show, that he gave me goosebumps, that my whole body stiffened. That I was thinking, *You raped her you raped her you raped her.*

'We need to give her more time,' I said.

He turned to me. He was wearing an old thrift-store coat, too, but his was too small on him. The hood didn't fit over his head and hung half way back, and the sleeves were too short. He reached out a large hand, thick with long but stubby fingers, and he touched my face. He ran one finger across my chin.

I sat so still, I was almost frozen into stone.

'You haven't changed, have you?' he said. He was looking me right in the eyes. I noticed that his deer-brown eyes weren't ugly. They weren't all that different from my eyes. I must have noticed that before, but he had never looked at me, not this way.

I had changed a lot. But I didn't want him to notice that.

'Chelsea, you're beautiful, too,' he said. 'You're really the mother of these children. Our children.'

I took this chance to look at Lola, to watch her moving the letters around into shapes rather than words.

'We'd all be lost without you,' he said. He pulled his hand back, and I was still, hoping, praying he would look away. And he did.

'I'm doing my best,' I said.

'I want to marry Stacie,' he said. 'When she's eighteen, we'll go into town and do it. We'll get the certificate. Rings and everything.'

He was going to take her into town? *What about us?* I thought. What if we all went into town together, and what if I could get the girls away? Would Stacie come? Would she understand the chance we had?

'You can take care of the girls, when we go,' he said. 'You'll do that, won't you? Let us have our little honey-moon?' There were still tears in his eyes, the tears over how Stacie wouldn't get out of bed, wouldn't look at him, didn't want him. But he believed he would marry her, and the truth was, he would, because she would have no choice. Unless she was beyond caring what threats he used. Unless she didn't care about me any more, or the kids. But even though she kept her face to the wall and cried and screamed, I thought there was still a part of her that cared. I couldn't believe that she was one hundred per cent gone. He would threaten us, and she would go.

What if we left while they were gone? What if we left Stacie with him? Would he kill her? Maybe he wouldn't realize what was happening until it was too late. Maybe we could get the cops here before they got back, and we could save her.

'I can watch the kids,' I said.

For the next two years, I waited for Stacie to turn eighteen. I thought about Kyle's plan. I realized that Stacie's name wasn't Stacie, and she couldn't prove who she was or that she was eighteen at all. Kyle celebrated Stacie's birthday every year as the day he took us, June 13. He didn't even know her real birthday. The judge in town probably wouldn't marry them. But Kyle didn't seem to think of that. He didn't tell Stacie what he was planning. But he would talk to me about it, any chance he got.

'You can fix this dress, can't you?' he said to me. Stacie was down by the river this time, and we were inside. Lola and Barbie were playing on the floor. Lola was using building blocks, and Barbie was basically just knocking down what Lola did. But Lola didn't get mad; instead, she would rebuild her block tower. Lola was a patient little girl, even-tempered, strong. If she could be that way, then so could I.

The dress was pink, of course. It was big enough for Stacie, but it belonged on someone Lola's age. It had frills and puff sleeves. Possibly it had once been a princess costume, before it ended up at a thrift store. He still saw her as a doll, even though she was a mother, and even though as soon as they got married, he was going to start raping her again. Did he think she would suddenly want him if he gave her a ring?

'Of course,' I said. 'It will look good as new.' I took the dress from him and looked it over. I would make it the most beautiful dress in the world, if it made him think his plan would work.

He bent over and kissed me on the cheek. It was over before I even realized what happened. He was up and out the door, whistling a little. Going down to the river to see the girl he claimed to love.

'Is that for me?' Lola asked.

'Silly,' I said. 'Would this fit you?' I held it up in front of her.

'Make it fit me!' she said.

'This one is for Mommy,' I said.

'Me! Me!' Barbie added.

'Maybe we can find one for you and you,' I said, pointing at each of them. 'But not this one.'

'When can Mommy wear it?' Lola asked.

'As soon as I can get it done,' I said. I imagined how Stacie would react. She would either put it on in silence and brood, or she would scream and cry and throw things, and then she would put it on. She would sometimes fight, but she would always lose. Over and over, she had retreated from screams into silence. But this time, it would be different. This time, she would think she had lost, but she would win. I couldn't tell her, risk her freaking out, risk her giving us away. She couldn't handle it, but that was OK. I could handle it for both of us, and this time, we were all going to be free.

Thank God he thinks he loves her, I thought. Now we have a real chance.

And then he told her.

And she hurt them.

And I was able to grab the lamp.

25.

'Holy shit!' Vinnie cries. 'Everyone into the car.' He grabs my arm and pulls me up.

I stand, but I'm a little dizzy. Maybe I'm not as OK as I thought.

Vinnie reaches down for Barbie.

'No! Chel!' Barbie cries.

'I'm OK,' I say. I lift her, and I'm not used to it. I've got weaker this past month. But I carry her to the back seat of the car and put her in. I'm aware that little kids are supposed to have car seats; I used to see that on TV. But we don't have any. She'll be all right in there for this one trip, won't she? I don't really know. I don't know anything about taking care of them outside our tiny little world.

Lee is holding Lola's hand, rushing her over to the car.

'Come on, Amy, get in,' Vinnie says. 'You can hold the kid on your lap.'

I'm watching Kyle's car come across the intersection. He's going to get here before we can leave. And there are no cops in sight. After all this talk of calling them, they aren't here.

'Amy, come *on*,' Lee says. She's putting Lola in the back seat on the other side of the car.

'We can't run away from him,' I say.

'Fuck yes, we can,' Vinnie says. 'Get in.'

'No, he's already here.'

'Get *in*,' Vinnie says.

Kyle is in the parking lot now. We don't have car seats. We can't race him. We can't get away.

'Shit. Does he have a gun?' Vinnie asks.

Kyle steps out of the car. He flows out of it, his big body seeming to materialize out of the metal. He stands with his head lowered, so his crazy self-cut hair falls over his face.

'No,' I say. He doesn't have a gun. He never had more than a pocketknife. He had his hands and his fists and his size and his threats. How did he do this to us, with nothing but himself? When he lowers his head like that, it means he's sad. It means that he's realized for a few minutes that Stacie doesn't love him back, before he returns to his delusion. It means that he wants something that he doesn't think he can have.

If he doesn't think he can have us, then he will never get us.

I close the door to the back seat, leaving Barbie inside.

As I turn, I see that Lee is on the phone again. She must be trying to get the cops here. But I know they won't get here in time. I have to handle this myself.

Vinnie steps out of the car.

'No, get back in,' I say.

'Amy, come on!'

'I know him,' I say.

Vinnie doesn't get back in the car, but he doesn't say anything else either.

I walk forward.

Kyle walks forward.

I don't know what Vinnie does. I can't see anything but Kyle. Kyle's feet shuffle but still manage to land hard and strong. I feel them on the pavement as they land. But I keep walking. I'm not going to run away this time. This time I'm going to stand up to him. But as we come closer, I look down, too. We're both looking down, and we both realize we're doing it, and we both look up, and our eyes meet.

I brace myself for the blow. But it doesn't come. He reaches his arms out and encircles me, and pulls me in. He holds me against him. My face is pressed against his chest. He is sweating through his long-sleeve T-shirt, but he doesn't stink. He smells familiar, like someone who has been in my life for years, like the familiarity of a father.

I can't pull away. He's too strong. But he can't take me away. Everyone knows where he is now. They all know about the girls. The police are coming. All he can do is kill me. But he won't get to them unless he goes through me. So if he wants to hug me, it's all right. He can hug me for as long as he wants to. He can do anything he wants to me, as long as he doesn't get past me and go to them.

'You can't have them,' he says. His arms pull me even closer, so I can't move at all. I can't speak. 'You thought you could have them if you killed her, but you can't.'

I turn my head, pushing against his chest, just enough to get out a few words. 'I didn't mean to,' I say.

He releases me from the hug but grabs my arm and pulls me towards the car. I brace myself to fight, to not let him pull me in. When you get in the car, you die. I'm sure that this time it's true. But he doesn't try. Instead, he opens the back door and reaches in, still gripping me with one hand. He pulls out the dress, the princess dress that he thought Stacie would marry him in.

'You want it,' he says. He pushes it into my chest.

Instinctively, I catch it. I don't know what to do with it. She hated it from first sight. She saw it, and she hurt them. She saw it, and there was no hope. But it was for her. It was everything Stacie became. If I drop it, I'll drop everything that's left of her.

He lets my arm go, and I wrap both arms around the dress. But it's empty. My arms come together, and I'm only hugging myself.

'I don't want it,' I say. But I keep holding it.

'It's yours,' he says. 'Get them.'

I almost begin to shake my head. He thinks I'm going to get the girls and get in the car with him, and then we're going to go away, all of us. He thinks I'm going to do this voluntarily, even though he doesn't have them, and he doesn't have Stacie. He has no one any more, and I have no reason to go with him.

He stares at me. His shoulders tense. This is the look he gets before he hits me. But his head is also angled down. This is the look he gets before he cries.

'We'll tell them you're eighteen,' he says.

The dress slips from my arms. He wants me to marry him. He thinks I'm going to do this. I take a step back, keeping my eyes on him.

He takes a step forward.

Somebody takes my left hand. It's Vinnie. I can feel his height over me.

Barbie and Lola are both crying. Somebody says, *Daddy*. I can't tell which one. They're crying because he's out here and they're not allowed to go. Lee is holding them back. Lola knew enough to be quiet, and to run, but she still wants her daddy. That's why it's the mom who makes decisions, because the child doesn't know who is her friend and who is not. I'm the adult here. I'm not ready to be one, but I am.

We all hear the sirens at the same time.

Kyle stands up straight and looks behind him. The cars come around the curve in the road. There are three of them, speeding towards us, lights blaring. Kyle looks from them to me to Vinnie. He leaps forward and grabs my free arm and pulls. Vinnie pulls, too, but Kyle is too fast. He tears me away from Vinnie and jerks me close. He presses my back to him this time, and his arm is around my waist. He's almost lifting me off the ground, he's so tall.

'Tell them to go away,' he says.

'You can't get them,' I say. 'You can kill me, but they'll kill you. You'll never get them.'

'Chelsea,' he says. 'Chelsea.' The arm that is not crunching me touches my face.

'It's Amy,' I say. 'There never was any Chelsea. There never was any Stacie. You made us up.'

'Stay back!' Kyle yells. His voice booms out across the parking lot. There are people coming towards us, people in black uniforms, and lights everywhere. It's hard to see them, or Vinnie. I look for the car. I see Lee's face inside it, and the top of Lola's head. They are safe.

'Her name was Dee,' I say. 'And she was good. She was sweet and friendly and fun and smart and loyal.' Tears are rolling down my face. I'm seeing her the way she was, that day at the river, before. I'm seeing her smile and her blue eyes, those real blue eyes that a doll's eyes could never do justice to. 'She was my best friend, and you killed her. *You* did.'

He pulls me tighter. 'I said, *stay back!*' But he hears me; I know he does. His voice trembles. He's hearing me for the first time.

'You *raped* her,' I yell. 'You raped her a million times and she was supposed to have years, and she was supposed to choose, but she couldn't. You *hurt* her and that's why she was crazy, and that's why she's dead. You!'

Kyle drags me in a half circle until we're facing the car. He slams me into it, and he's behind me, completely shielding my body from the outside, crushing me against the metal.

I don't hear the gunshot. I only hear him scream and see him stumble backwards. But he grabs me as he falls, and I fall with him. I fall half on his body and half on the pavement. There's another gunshot, and this time I hear it. Kyle screams louder. He lets me go and screams and screams. I get to my hands and knees, and I crawl. I crawl towards a man who is wearing black, and the lights blind me, but I put one hand in front of the other.

26.

I'm so used to not talking that when they start to ask me questions, I don't say a word at first. I'm in the back seat of a police car, and they say it's for my protection, but I don't know what they're protecting me from. Kyle is in the ambulance. I saw them put him on a stretcher and wheel him in. He was still screaming while they did it. In the movies, when the cops shoot someone, he falls down dead, but Kyle didn't die. It took one hit on the head to kill Dee, but somehow Kyle survived being shot twice.

There is a puddle of blood on the ground where he fell. Some of his blood is on me. It's on my pants and on my arms and on my hands.

He can't kill anyone, I think. He can't kill me and he can't kill them. But instead of relief, I feel nothing. I stare at the

245

blood on my arms, and I can't believe it. I can't believe that after six years, after what seems like my whole life, they're taking him away. I don't know what to do if he goes to jail. Everything in my life has revolved around him. Fear of what he might do. Needing him to bring us food. Needing him to tell me when to stand and when to jump. And what not to say.

'Amy?' a woman cop says, gently.

'Yes, my name is Amy,' I say.

The kids are still in the car. I can't see them, but I did see Lee as they were putting me in here. She was trying to get in front of the girls, to make sure they didn't see. They'll be sad. They'll cry and cry, and they don't know any better. They'll blame me. I killed their mommy, and now their daddy will be going away. They may never see him again.

Vinnie is talking to one of the cops. He keeps looking over at me.

I feel like everything is far away.

'Amy, what is that man's name?' the woman asks. It's the third or fourth time she's asked that.

'Kyle,' I say.

She waits.

'That's it,' I say. 'Just Kyle.' But the cops have searched through Kyle's pockets. One of them is holding his wallet. I've seen that wallet a million times, but I've never looked inside it. I've never wondered what Kyle's last name is. 'His birthday is February seventh,' I say. We celebrated his birthday every year. I cooked a special meal with extra meat, and the dolls sat in my chair. It was the same way for

Stacie's made-up birthday. I never had a birthday, the whole six years. But I remember what day it is now. December 9th. This year I'm going to celebrate.

'Yep,' says a cop, leaning in the window. 'Says here February seventh, 1985. Kyle James Parsons.'

The name rolls around in my head. *Kyle James Parsons.* It doesn't sound like him at all. It sounds like a stranger, like a minister's son, like the kind of person who wears a crisp button-down shirt and gets a regular haircut.

'What happened tonight, Amy?' the woman asks.

'I went back for the kids,' I say. 'He said that if I ever told anyone, he would kill them, but I couldn't leave them alone. So I went back, and he was asleep, so I took them.' I've made it sound simple, as if I made a coherent plan.

'What kids, Amy?' the woman asks.

I look over at Vinnie's car. Lee and the kids are still inside it. Nobody has made them come out. Maybe no one even noticed they were in there. 'My cousin Dee had two kids,' I say. 'Because Kyle raped her. Lola is five and Barbie is three.'

The man with the wallet follows my gaze. The man and the woman both stare at me.

'What did you think would happen after six years?' I ask.

The woman swallows. There is no other sound.

'I didn't have any,' I say. 'He didn't rape me; he just hit me a lot.' I look up at the woman. 'But I'm their mom.'

The male cop walks over to the car. He knocks on the window.

Lee's head appears. She opens the door, and she steps

247

out. Behind her, I see Lola and Barbie. They look like they're crying, of course. But they're safe. They're going to be safe now. Lee helps them out of the car.

The cop kneels down and says something to Lola.

Lola says something back. She looks at me.

I give her a little wave and as much of a smile as I can manage. Everyone is looking at me now. The male cop, Lee, Vinnie, the woman cop, and Lola and Barbie. It's like they're waiting for me to do something. The ambulance is gone, I realize. I'm not sure when it left. My heart begins to pump fast. Did I lose time again? Or was I just not paying attention? I can't keep losing time. I'm their mom. I have to be here. Here. I take a deep breath and let it out. *Here. Here. Here,* I think.

Lee takes Lola by one hand and Barbie by the other. She comes towards us. I push down on the door handle, but it won't open. The woman cop does something from her seat. The door opens. Lola is there. I hug her. I pull her up into the car.

'Chel, are we going home now?' she asks.

I lift Barbie up, and I see Lee behind her, Lee crying. 'Yes, I say. But it's going to be a new home.'

'What about the dolls?' Lola asks.

'We'll see,' I say, because I can't tell her that I'm never going back there and that I hope they burn down the cabin with everything in it, dolls and all. Right this second, I vow to throw the Stacie doll away. She isn't my connection to Dee; she's something terrible that Kyle owned. I never want to see that doll again.

'I'm so glad we found you,' Lee says, wiping her eyes. Vinnie is behind her now.

'Thank you,' I say.

'Thank you, Uncle Vinnie!' Barbie pipes.

'Oh, I'm Uncle Vinnie now, am I?' Vinnie says, leaning down.

'Auntie Lee says so,' says Barbie.

'Well, Auntie Lee knows,' says Vinnie. He's trying to pretend he isn't crying, but he is.

'Is Daddy coming?' Lola asks.

I don't answer. I just put my arm around her. There will be a time to tell her, but it isn't now.

It takes a lot less time than the bus did, with its meanders and its many stops, but it takes longer than it took to get here; at least, it seems longer. Vinnie has driven his rented, possibly stolen car back to the sketchy guy at the mechanic's shop, and his car has to be towed away, so Lee ends up riding with us in the back of the cop car. It's illegal to ride this way, two adults and two kids with no car seats, but nobody says anything. I guess the cops don't want to ask any questions with the kids here, and I'm glad. I don't want to give any more answers. Even now, my throat is closed up, choking on what's left of the truth.

Even now, there are things no one can know.

Aunt Hannah is going to want them. She's Dee's mom, but I'm only her cousin, and I'm only sixteen. It doesn't matter how old I feel or how long I've been their mother. No one is going to care about that. But at least I can see them. I will still be their cousin. But what if Aunt Hannah finds out what I did? She won't want to hear the reason why. Who Stacie became – that's something I can never tell her.

I'm standing in the middle of the cabin.

Dee is screaming.

Kyle has the girls. He has one hand on each, pushing them behind him. He's wearing a black shirt faded to grey and orangey work pants with a hammer loop. There's a rip in the left leg the length of my foot. He steps back, pushing the girls against the wall.

I open my eyes. I thought Kyle was behind Barbie. And he was holding Lola. That's how I remembered it, before. He had them, but they were exposed. The back of the seat in front of me is a dark brown. There are holes in the vinyl, like someone else who was back here ripped it with claws. I don't like being back here, even if I'm not in handcuffs, even if they're doing us a favour driving us home.

If Kyle was in front of the girls, then why did I pick up the lamp? He's so big, he could have stopped her from hurting them. But I was only going to stop her. She wasn't supposed to die. She wasn't even supposed to be badly hurt. He was . . . I try to remember how he was standing, but I can't. That part of the picture goes blank in my head. Then I'm shoving clothes into the Safeway bag. I'm outside the cabin.

Dr Kayla said, when something traumatic happens, you remember too much, so often that it hurts you. She said that was my problem– remembering. But now I can't remember. It's slipping away from me. I need to remember that they were in front of him and he wasn't protecting them, because then I had to do it.

'I had to,' I say out loud.

Nobody answers. Lee looks at me like she wants to ask what I mean, but she won't.

'I didn't want anyone to die,' I say.

Lee looks down at Lola, who is asleep under her arm. I am bursting with something, some need to tell everyone the truth, as far as I can remember it. I need to tell someone before it all flows away. Lee thinks I'm talking about Kyle, but I'm sure he won't die. I can't tell them what I really mean. Kyle is going to jail and I still can't tell them.

Tears leak from my eyes. I still don't feel like we're safe. I feel like he's still here. He is still leaning over me with those big ears and that floppy hair and big grin that turns into a grimace and the voice that coos at dolls and snaps before the fist follows. I can hear him through the bathroom door, his breathing when Stacie was silent. *She's mine,* I hear him say. But he took two bullets and didn't die. She's dead and he isn't and it's not fair.

The tears flow now. I didn't run. I didn't tell anyone, but it still happened. She died.

The woman cop stares at me. Her eyes squint; her mouth twists. She thinks I'm crying for Kyle. She thinks I care that he's hurt. I look up at her.

'I'm not crying for him,' I say.

She keeps staring, like she doesn't believe me. Lee stares at me, too. Lola shifts. I pray she can't hear us. But she's heard so much. This is just one more terrible night in a life of nights that should never have happened.

'I'm crying for Dee,' I say. And what about Dee I'm crying for is impossible to say because there's so much. If only I could really go back in time. But I feel Barbie leaning against me, and I feel guilty just for thinking it. There are two beautiful lives here because of Kyle. Were they worth losing one? If I could go back, I would.

If I could not get in the car. Just not get in the car. Run and tell somebody. Send the cops after her.

If I could not have picked up the lamp.

'At least she's going to have justice,' Lee says softly.

I just cry. And the woman cop keeps staring at me, even though she turns back in her seat. I can feel the corners of her eyes, still judging my tears, still believing I was sorry to feel Kyle's blood on me, to hear his screams as he slipped towards the pavement. But I'm not sorry about that.

Aunt Hannah is at our house when the cop car pulls up. She runs out of the door, and my parents run out behind her, and then Aunt Hannah stops, and my mom almost runs into her, and my dad almost runs into my mom, and he stops himself with two hands on her shoulders, and Mom grabs one of his hands in both of hers, and the car comes to a full stop in the driveway. The male cop turns the engine off, and the silence washes over us.

I'm glad that I can't get out of the back seat because I'm in a locked police car. I don't want to face this. Now I'm their mom, but once we get out of the car, I'll be their cousin. Aunt Hannah will tell them that I'm not their mom, and I'm not even Chel. And they'll tell her . . . It hits me for the first time. I'm not the only one who knows my secret – Lola and Barbie were there, too. Maybe I should tell everyone now, since the rest of the truth is out. But even if my parents understand, Aunt Hannah won't. She's been through enough, and she doesn't need to know what happened to Stacie, what she did. I tell myself that I'm keeping this secret for Aunt Hannah's sake, but I know that's only partly true. I can't face what I did, and I can't face her. If I tell the truth, I'll never be able to face anyone.

'Barbie,' I whisper. 'Barbie, honey, wake up.'

Barbie stirs.

'Daddy?' Lola sits up.

'Lee, can I talk to them alone for a minute?' I ask. 'This is going to be so strange for them.' I look up at the female cop.

She still doesn't look as if she trusts me, but she nods. Lee's door opens.

'I'll hold them off,' Lee says. She walks towards our parents. I turn away. I can't watch what they're doing, or I'll break down again. There is still a secret I have to keep, and I have to keep my mind on that.

The cops both get out of the car. They stand outside; whether they're protecting us or keeping us inside, I'm not sure.

'Lola, Barbie,' I say. How do I say this? What will

253

make them understand? 'What I did to Mommy, it was an accident. A terrible accident.'

'I know,' Lola says.

'You are about to meet Mommy's mommy,' I say. 'She's your grandma.'

'Mommy had a mommy?' Barbie asks.

'Yes, and she loves you very much,' I say.

'Like an auntie?' Lola asks.

'Yes, just like that.'

'Why?' Barbie asks.

'She loves you because you're special,' I say. 'Both of you. But if Grandma learns what happened to Mommy, she'll be sad. So I don't want to tell her. I'm going to tell her that Mommy fell into the river, and that's why she isn't here.' I've come up with this lie right this second. I hope it's a good one, because there's no going back.

'Mommy is by the river,' says Barbie.

'Yes, that's right!' I say.

'If Mommy didn't fall into the river, you have to stay here in the police car,' says Lola.

Where on earth did she get that from? 'No, baby,' I say. 'Nobody is going to keep me in the police car.' At least, I don't think they would. The police would understand that I had to do it, wouldn't they? That I didn't mean for her to die?

'It's OK,' says Lola. 'Don't be sad.' She crawls across the back seat and hugs me. I have both girls in my arms now. My girls. I don't want to let them go. I don't want to give them away to Aunt Hannah and let them forget that I'm their mom. I never wanted this before, but I want it now. I squeeze them.

The door next to me opens.

'Are you ready?' the male cop asks.

I climb out of the car and pick up Barbie.

Lola crawls out on her own. I set Barbie down and take their hands. We walk like this down the driveway. I expect Aunt Hannah to come running towards us, but she doesn't. She stands there holding my mom's hand, staring. Her face is white, and she almost shrinks back into my dad.

Lee comes around on my right side. She steps ahead of us. 'Mom,' she says. 'This is Lola, and this is Barbie.'

Aunt Hannah's hand shakes as she pulls away from my mom. She takes a step forward.

'This is your grandma,' I say.

'Mommy is by the river!' Barbie pipes.

Aunt Hannah shakes as she kneels down to be on Barbie's level. 'Oh, is she?' she asks. She reaches out and runs a hand through Barbie's hair.

'Yes, and there are two sticks like this.' She makes a little cross symbol with her hand. 'Because Daddy said this makes her go there.' She points up to the sky.

Aunt Hannah swallows. She pulls Barbie into a hug. She's still shaking – not just her hand, but all over.

'I'm so sorry,' I say. 'I had to protect them. That was why I couldn't tell you. I wanted to tell you, every day.' I hear myself speaking, but it's not me. I don't know where me is. I don't even feel like I'm here. I'm watching Aunt Hannah hold on to Barbie, and she reaches out for Lola, and now

I'm holding on to no one. Now it's just me, standing in a dark driveway in front of a police car. Dee is dead and Kyle is gone and Lola and Barbie are with their grandma, and it's all over. But *it* was everything I ever knew.

Stacie flips a card over.

'Miss!' I cry.

I take my turn and flip my cards. First one, then two. I didn't get a match either.

Stacie smiles. 'Miss!'

She was pregnant already then, but none of us knew. She was still in there.

If we had only run then.

If we had tried again, together.

If . . .

I'm in my twin bed in my room in my mom's house. I wake up with the sun streaming in the window. I remember standing in the driveway, but that's all. What happened next, how I got inside, is all a loss. But I'm not the only one in the room. Lola and Barbie are here, too. They're lying on sleeping bags on the air bed.

Lola is awake and watching me.

'What happened last night, baby?' I ask.

She looks at me solemnly. 'I knew you wouldn't remember,' she says.

'I got lost again,' I say.

She nods. 'The grandma lady said she wanted us to come home with her, but she said she bet we wanted to stay with you. And we said yes. And she didn't ask about Mommy, so that's OK.'

'Oh. Thank you, baby,' I say.

Lola begins to cry. 'I don't want you to stay in the police car.'

That wakes up Barbie. She doesn't know why we're crying, but she starts up, too.

I crawl out of bed and on to the air mattress. There's a hole somewhere, slowly letting all the air out. It settles and wheezes. 'That's not going to happen,' I say. I hold them both. 'Please don't worry. I'm here. Please don't cry.' I should never have said what I said in the car. Maybe they never would have said anything. Or maybe it's better that I told them, so now we can talk about it in the open and they won't worry in silence. I really don't know what's best for them. I don't know anything about being a mom. I don't know if I should tell them about how their dad will go to jail. Maybe it would be better to tell them now and let them be sad than to let them begin to feel better and then drop it on them. Maybe it's better to be very sad and then recover. Maybe I should ask Dr Kayla. I'm their mom, though, no matter what. I do know, somewhere inside. I know that I will never let Kyle see them again, and waiting to tell them won't make it any better.

'There's something I need to tell you,' I say.

'Not going with grandma lady!' Barbie says.

That almost makes me smile. In fact, it almost makes me laugh. But instead, it pushes a fresh burst of tears out of my eyes. 'It's not about Grandma,' I say. 'It's about Daddy.'

They look up at me.

'Daddy is . . .' I almost say he's like Mommy now. That

257

would be easier to explain, but it wouldn't be true. If I lie to them, they'll learn the truth sooner or later. 'Daddy has to go away to jail,' I say instead. 'He's done some bad things, and now he has to be punished. And he will get help, too. They will patch him up and make him feel better.' I hope that's not true. I hope he's in pain every single second of every day.

'How long does he have to stay there?' Barbie asks. 'A long time,' I say. 'A very, very, very long time.'

The girls cry quietly. I thought it would be worse than this. But maybe they don't quite understand yet.

'How would you like some breakfast?' I ask. 'There are these things called pancakes. You'll love them.' My heart begins to race as I stand up. Pancakes are not good for you. But I can have them. I can smother them in syrup, and not even the real kind. I can cover them in Aunt Jemima corn syrup and wash it all down with chocolate milk. As I step out of the bedroom, the girls right behind me, I smile, and the smile grows as I head for the kitchen. I feel like I'm floating. My feet are barely touching the ground.

As we pass through the living room, Lola runs up to the TV and turns it on. Voices escape, pictures and lights. She turns it off again, then on.

'Let me!' Barbie says.

My mom is already in the kitchen.

I can't remember if I spoke to her last night. I can't remember what she said to me. My smile fades. My bare feet are cold against the kitchen floor.

Kyle is still out of our lives. Her look can't change that.

The TV goes on and off, on and off. The girls giggle as they play with it.

Mom looks at me. Her deep brown eyes stare from underneath her plucked eyebrows. She's wearing a dark blue bathrobe and has a cup of coffee and a bowl of cereal, but it doesn't look like she's eaten any of it.

'I'm sorry,' I say.

She *looks*.

'I had to.'

'You were going to stay,' she says.

I look away. I look at the window over the sink, but it's dirty, and the glare from the morning sun flashes in my eyes. There's nowhere outside of this room to go to. Even my memories fail me.

'Do you know what I went through?' she asks. 'Do you *know*?' She slams her fist down on the table. Milk and bran flakes fly. The bowl goes skittering across the table and comes to a stop in the uneven gap where the two sides meet.

'Yes,' I say.

'No,' she says. 'You knew where they were. You knew they were safe.'

'I didn't know they were safe,' I say.

She turns her back on me and wraps her arms around her chest. She's shaking the way Aunt Hannah did.

'Mom, I'm sorry.'

'You could have told me,' she says. Her voice is barely a whisper now. 'Did you think I wouldn't love them, too?'

'He said he'd kill them. If I ever told anyone. He was

obsessed with these dolls, and he thought of Lola and Barbie and Dee like they were his . . . stuff.' But that doesn't explain it. It doesn't make any sense because it's crazy, but I have to make her understand. 'He threatened Lola once. Someone came to the cabin, and they might have found us, but . . .' I see the look in his eyes through the window, the hand over Lola's precious throat. 'You wouldn't risk it if it was me,' I say. 'You would have gone back, too, to save me.'

Mom turns around to face me. Tears roll down her face, and her jaw is set like she's so angry she wants to scream, but she grabs me and pulls me into a hug. It's so tight that she's squeezing the breath out. 'Yes,' she says. 'Yes. Yes. Yes. I would have done anything to save you.'

'Chel! Are we having panties?' Lola asks from the doorway. Barbie pushes in next to her.

'It's pancakes, honey,' I say. Mom is still squeezing me so tightly that it's hard to talk. 'And yes, we are. Mom, do you want to help me make pancakes for the girls?'

She only eases up a little. 'Yes,' she says. She keeps holding on.

'Mom, it's over,' I say. 'There's nowhere else for me to go.'

She releases me, finally, and pulls out the cookbook with her pancakes-from-scratch recipe. A minute later, Dad gets up, and a minute after that, so does Jay.

They both hug me. Dad goes first. He wraps me in his arms, and as my face presses into his chest, I realize that he feels like Dad, even though he's gained weight, even though things have changed. The arms are familiar, the aftershave, even his breath.

'I'm so sorry,' Jay says as he hugs me, too. His arms are bony, the opposite of Dad's, but it still feels right to have them around me.

'*I'm* sorry,' I say.

'Amy, you have nothing to be sorry for,' Dad says. He puts a hand on my shoulder, while Jay only half releases me.

'Let me help!' Lola says.

'*I* want to,' Barbie puts in.

'Well, of course,' Mom says. I hear the clatter of a bowl, the plop of a bag of flour on the counter.

'Thank you, Grandma Patty,' says Lola.

'Grandma Patty, well, that's very nice. I like that,' Mom says.

'That's what you call a mommy's mommy, right?'

Dad grips my shoulder tighter, and I need him and Jay both, because Lola just said she knows that I'm her mommy, too, and I was so afraid they'd forget that. I was so afraid they'd realize I wasn't.

'Yes, and this is your Grandpa Lon,' I say, wiping my eyes. 'And your Uncle Jay.'

Jay lets me go and kneels down in front of both girls, who somehow are already covered in flour. 'A lot was going on last night,' he says. 'I didn't get to give you a hug. Can I give you a hug now?'

Lola reaches her arms out, and then Barbie scoots past her, and Jay envelopes them.

'Thank you,' he says. 'I'm very glad you've come home.'

He looks up at me, and I know he means me, too, and I nod. I never had the courage to dream that this day would happen, and now that it's here, I'm overwhelmed. I have to sit down and let the others make the pancakes and absorb their voices, the girls and my mom and my dad and Jay all together – this perfect, amazing, impossible day.

We eat pancakes, and I pour as much syrup on them as I want, and Lola and Barbie love them. I close my eyes and savour the taste of Aunt Jemima's corn syrup and the feeling of my family around me, and I stay *here* and feel it.

27.

'It's not easy to keep all that inside,' Dr Kayla says, a few days later. Her long, dark hair is pulled back, and it makes her look younger. 'I wish I had been able to help you.'

'I'm sorry,' I say. These are the two words I know now.

'There's no need to apologize,' she says. 'I only hope that now you can tell me everything that happened so I can help you.'

Everything that happened. She has no idea what she's asking. There's a lump in my throat and a rock in my stomach. If I can tell anyone the whole truth, it's her. She's been on my side this whole time. She wants to help me, and she may be the only one who really can. But it seems like she likes me, and how will she ever keep liking me if she knows?

'A lot of things happened,' I say.

'I can tell that something's bothering you,' she says. 'Some specific thing that you've been wanting to say. Amy, this man is in jail. He will never be able to hurt you again.'

But as long as I remember, he gets to hurt me. As long as I remember, I have to hurt her. I think about what Dr Kayla told me before, about memory. How I'm hurting because I remember too much. If I don't tell her, this will never stop.

I jump in front of them. I grab the lamp.

Crunch.

Pieces of the lamp are falling. Dee is falling.

'I'm having trouble with my memory,' I say. 'This one thing.' But that makes it sound like nothing, and it's everything. I can't look at her while I say it, while I try to somehow start to explain. 'Something I remember two different ways.'

Kyle is behind Barbie, holding Lola.

Or he's in front, and they're behind him.

Kyle's dark orange cargo pants.

'What is that?' she asks.

'You can't tell anyone what I say here, right?' I ask. 'Not my mom or the police or anyone?' I know she can't, but I need to hear it from her mouth right now. Because I'm not ready to tell my family, and I don't know if I ever will be.

'That's right,' she says. 'I will never tell anyone what you tell me, and I have told you the exceptions.'

'I don't want to hurt myself or anyone else,' I say.

'OK,' she says. And now it's time. Now we'll see if she

264

hates me.

'It's what I already did.'

She waits.

'I killed Dee,' I say. 'I mean, he killed Dee. I killed Stacie.'

She waits.

'No, it was Dee. She was only one person. I killed her.'

Dr Kayla sits back in her seat. Her mouth drops open a little ways. She did not expect me to say that.

'You can't tell anyone,' I say. I shouldn't have said it, but I did. I said the words, and now I want to say everything.

She recovers a little bit, but she stumbles over her words. 'What happened, Amy?'

I look away from her, because I don't want to see it, when her shock and confusion turn to hate. 'That's what I'm not sure I remember right. I know that Kyle finally told Dee he wanted to marry her, and he showed her the dress, and she went crazy. And she hurt Barbie. She pulled a big clump of her hair out. She hurt Lola, too. And she was so mad. She was coming for us.' I stop. I'm looking at the corner of her wooden desk, the dust-filled indent on the top.

'By *us* you mean you and the girls?'

'Yes, but Kyle might have been in front of them.'

'Why does that matter?' Dr Kayla asks.

'Because . . .' Here is what I haven't said even to myself. Here is where I think about those times when Kyle played with the babies, when he took care of them, when he smiled, when it almost felt like things were normal. Those times when I forget to be angry and sad. 'What if I wanted to protect *him*?'

'Do you think that's what you wanted?'

'No.' I know that. With my heart and my soul and my mind, I know I never did anything to help Kyle unless it was to help them. But . . . 'I didn't *want* to protect him, but what if I *did*?'

'You acted to protect Lola and Barbie,' Dr Kayla says. 'I can see that.'

'You can?' I look up at her, and I try to find the hate in her face, but it isn't there. Her eyes are wet, and she grabs a tissue from her desk.

'Amy, now that you've told me about the girls, I can see why you did everything. You were faced with the most difficult choices, and you always did what you thought would protect them.'

'I did.' It's true. It really is.

'You will have to learn to forgive yourself,' she says. 'You acted solely out of love.'

I reach out and take a tissue from the box and watch Dr Kayla dab her eyes. This is the first time she's cried in front of me. I'm pretty sure she's not supposed to. She's supposed to be objective and distant. But now I can tell she doesn't hate me, not just from her words. I can tell that she cares about me as a person.

'There's one very important thing that you haven't recognized, Amy,' Dr Kayla says. 'You told me that Dee was coming for *you and the girls*. You have a right to protect yourself, too.'

I stare at her. Never in all this time did I once think of that.

'When we're in danger, we act to protect ourselves,' she says, 'and that's OK. It is OK to survive.'

'I don't know if that's true,' I say.

'It is true,' she says. 'It's not just OK, it's good. Amy, it's good that you're here today, that you're alive, and that you will be able to live a long, full life.'

I let the tears fill my eyes. It's *good* that I'm here. It doesn't feel good.

'It's good that you're here because you deserve a life like anyone else,' she says. 'But also, there are many people who love you and are very glad that you came back.'

'I keep thinking about it,' I say. 'I want to stop thinking about it. But I don't want to forget her. Even the bad times, I don't want to forget, because sometimes they were all we had.' Even when she was screaming, even when she was drinking soap, even that last minute, when she was pulling out Barbie's hair. That was all Dee, and I'll never be able to see her again.

'We'll work on helping you deal with this,' Dr Kayla says. 'We'll keep working until we have a solution.'

I swallow and wipe my eyes and blow my nose, and then I stare out the window and watch the people walking across the parking lot and the trees across the street swaying in the wind and a man walking his dog down the sidewalk. And then I tell Dr Kayla all the details – about the dress, and about the wedding, and about what happened when Kyle told her. I tell her more about the girls, more about Stacie, everything I've been afraid to tell. I know that here in this room alone with Dr Kayla, I'm safe. He can't hurt me, and neither can anybody else.

There is a street in Grey Wood that separates the town from the country. On one side of the street, there are blocks divided into neat squares, and houses all lined up in rows, and spots at regular intervals for parks and schools. On the other side of the street, grass grows long, and buildings look like they were dropped there, and there's a sign to the freeway and then a two-lane road that goes into the trees, where there are houses with land attached and sheep and cows.

Kyle James Parsons grew up out there, past the edges of the neat squares, in a small house with a lot of land attached. This is what the police tell me, and what I learn from the paper as the days go by. When his parents were alive, he lived fifteen minutes from where we lived. He grew up here and went to Grey Wood High School, home of the Otters. But after ninth grade, he dropped out. He worked at the Toy Castle in Portland until seven years ago, when they fired him, and that's the last job he ever had. They tell me that he spent time in foster care because his parents are dead, and I just nod. That was one thing he told me.

The newspaper says his sister, Felicity, died of the flu at age seven, when Kyle was nine. And when Kyle was ten, his parents died of accidental poisoning. The paper doesn't say what they were poisoned with or how exactly it happened.

It doesn't say that Kyle was suspected. It doesn't give me any clues about how Kyle the doll-loving parent murderer came to be Kyle the kidnapper and rapist and father and man-child. But what can a reporter tell *me*? I'm the person who knows Kyle best in the world, and I can't explain how he came to be. All I can explain is that it's good for him to be in jail, and it would be better if the police had killed him.

The fact that Kyle is in jail and I came back with two children is all over the papers and the TV, too. There are pictures of me getting out of the car in our driveway, but the newspaper has blocked out the kids' faces. I suppose I should be grateful that someone is trying to protect the girls, but when I see their little bodies without faces, I think of dolls. That's why, when Aunt Hannah comes over with papers to apply for birth certificates for the girls, I tell her to put down Barbie's name as Barbara. Aunt Hannah says that Lola is short for Dolores, so we put that down for her. Dolores and Barbara Springfield, because that was Dee's last name.

'We don't have to put these names down at all,' Aunt Hannah says.

'I don't want to confuse them,' I say. In front of me is a lined sheet of paper with space for me to write out my affidavit, since I'm the only person besides Kyle who knows when they were born and who their parents are. Whatever I write here will be the truth as far as the world knows. All the things Kyle did to make them and the pain they caused Dee and the moments when I washed the blood off of them and they first cried and looked up at me, all boil down to this little piece of paper. And I'm about to tell the world they aren't mine, that they're more related to Aunt Hannah than me. But I write the truth. I'm not sure of the exact dates, but I write what I remember. And how I know who the parents are. Then I push the paper back across the table.

'We have to take it to a notary,' Aunt Hannah says.

'OK.'

'Amy . . .' She sets her hands on the papers. It's as if her hands want to ball into fists and crumple the papers up, but the papers are too important, so she smoothes them and smoothes them.

'You want them,' I say. Right now, the girls are with my mom and dad. They are at the park a few blocks from our house, playing on the slide and the jungle gym. They went for the first time a few days ago, and they loved it. It was an amazing new thing. Life is a series of amazing new things for them now. Maybe it won't be so bad for them. Maybe they'll enjoy new things and not miss the old things.

'I want what's best for them,' she says. She smoothes and smoothes. 'I know what it takes to raise children. I have a stable home to give them. You need to go to high school and then to college. You deserve to have your own life.'

'I know what it takes, too,' I say. 'After five years, I know.'

She nods.

'Teenagers have kids all the time,' I say.

'There's another way we could do it,' she says.

I wait.

'You could come live with us. That way, the kids would

still have you, but I would be their legal guardian.'

'What about my mom and Jay?' I ask. I don't know if I can leave my mom again, after what I did, trying to go back. But what Aunt Hannah is offering is the best thing I could imagine. She's not going to take them away from me. I can't process this fully. She's giving me a way to be with them.

'We live in the same town,' she says. 'You and the girls could come over whenever you want. Even stay here some nights.'

'Yes,' I say. All of a sudden, the tension breaks. I burst into a smile and into tears. 'Yes yes yes yes.'

Aunt Hannah reaches one hand out and takes one of mine. Our hands lay clasped on the cold table. 'I'm sorry for how I treated you when I didn't know,' she says.

'It's OK,' I say. 'I'm sorry I couldn't tell you. I wanted to.'

'I know. They are precious. They're lucky to have you.'

I guess they're lucky to have Aunt Hannah, too. She's changed since I came back with the girls. It seems like she's gained weight in just a few days, and her cheeks are a better colour, and the way she sits – even though she's nervous, she's sitting taller. The girls have given her something to live for in place of Dee. They've given her a new hope. And now that I know I'm going to live with them, I have hope, too.

'I'm going to work through my issues,' I say. 'I'm working with Dr Kayla.'

'I know. I'm seeing somebody, too,' she says. 'When you lose a child . . . but I guess you understand that now.' She looks up, right into my eyes. 'Please, tell me what happened to my baby.'

'Dee fell and hit her head,' I say. I've thought about this every minute since I came back from seeing Dr Kayla, about whether I should tell Aunt Hannah the truth. But I'm not ready, and she's not ready. I just can't.

I realize that my story is a little different now than what I told the girls. In the car, I didn't think of the fact that someone may actually look at her body, that there's a way to tell whether she really drowned. So she was at the river, a place that even as Stacie she sometimes liked. Sometimes she got a chance to wade in it and feel the cold water on her feet, and if she was like me, she thought about our river, and Grey Wood, and maybe she remembered all the people who loved her. And she slipped while she was wading and hit her head.

'She was wading in the river,' I say, 'like we used to do all the time, and she slipped and fell. She hit her head on a rock, and then she went under the water. We pulled her out, but it was too late.' I imagine this. She is falling, and I am screaming, and Kyle is running down the bank. He jumps in to save her. He swims to the middle of the river, and the water is rushing all around him, and he pulls her out and carries her back to shore. He gives her mouth-to-mouth, he compresses her chest, he does everything, but nothing works. Dee lies there, her hair matted to her face, her blue eyes open to the sky.

In this version, Dee never did anything wrong. In this version, she never would have hurt her precious girls. The second before she fell, maybe she was even happy.

'You're not telling me everything,' Aunt Hannah says.

'It was an accident,' I say. 'Nobody killed her. It just happened.' There are so many problems with this story. I didn't think of them until it was too late. If she died in the river, then why did I leave? I'm sure Aunt Hannah is going to call me on it, but she doesn't. Instead, she gets up from the table and grabs her papers. I'm afraid she's going to take back her offer. She's going to tell me that she's taking the girls and I can't see them.

But she wraps her arms around my shoulders. 'It's all right, Amy,' she says. 'I can wait. I have two beautiful girls to focus on now. That's what Dee would want from us.' She leaves the house, and for a few minutes, I'm alone. I'm alone, and I am home. Kyle is in jail, and the girls are safe.

I don't know what to do with myself. I don't know what's right and what's wrong or who I am or what will happen. All I know is that it's over. I feel like bursting into tears, and I do, but also, I smile. It is actually, for real, finally over.

28.

It's a clear, warm night in June, warmer than average. I'm standing on the porch in the back of Ben's house, leaning on the cracked wooden railing. Empty and half-empty beer bottles litter the cheap outdoor furniture. I'm staring out at the overgrown backyard and up at the clusters of yellow stars. I'm remembering how I used to look up at those stars with Lola and Barbie, and how we made up our own names for the constellations. I see one we called the silly snake, one we called the donkey's ear. Even now, I don't know their real names. I don't need to know them because our names are just fine.

I take a long swig of my beer. It's a little warm, but it still tastes good. It tastes like freedom.

'Woooooooooooo!' Kara slaps me on the back. One of

her giant *pumpkins* knocks into me, too, pressing me against the railing. She's completely wasted.

'Graduates!' Christina is even worse. She wraps one arm around me. 'We're gradutates!' She bursts out laughing.

'We thought it would never happen,' Kara says. She lifts her beer. 'To miracles!'

'To miracles!' Christina and I say together. We raise our beers, and then we drink.

There's a crash behind us, and laughter. Marco is coming through the sliding glass door, carrying Lee in his arms. One of the plastic end tables has overturned, sending beer bottles every which way. Marco spins Lee around.

'Stop!' she squeals.

He puts her down clumsily, and she falls into his arms. Her hair is flying around her face, which is flush with the activity and probably with the beer, and with love, too. In the last two years, she and Marco have broken up and got back together about ten million times. But this year, they got back together just in time for senior prom, and they've been together ever since. This time, it seems like it just might last. Behind them, more kids from our school are hanging around in Ben's living room. They're listening to the music, or dancing, or lying on the couches. Ben disappeared a while ago with some sophomore girl. It's basically just another party. But this one is special because we're celebrating the end of an era. In a couple months, we'll all be going off to college. We'll be moving on from Grey Wood and the Fighting Turkeys and each other.

Even me. I'm only going to Portland, but still. For the

first time, I'll be living on my own. I'll be coming back every weekend to see the girls, but Monday through Friday, I'll be living like a regular eighteen-year-old college freshman. A college freshman who only went to two years of high school and still hasn't caught up to ninth grade math, but still . . . I'll be out there, past the edge of our little town. I don't know how I feel about it yet. I know that if Dee were here, she would be ready to jump into life. If she had had the life she deserved, she would be ready now to break away from her parents, to stay up late, to go to parties, to meet boys. In another life, she's already out there doing that. But I have a feeling the other me, the one who never was kidnapped, would still be a little different. I think she would miss our little town the way I will.

Kara climbs up on the railing and sits there, swinging her legs. Christina climbs up next to her. The whole thing creaks like it's ready to come down.

'Bail!' Christina yells, and they jump, rolling on the grass together. Whatever they were fighting about when I first got back, they got over it a long time ago.

I take one more drink of my beer, and that's the last of it, so I set the bottle down on the plastic end table that's still standing. I turn and brush past Lee and Marco, who are now making out on a lawn chair. Inside, I look for Vinnie and find him sitting on the floor, leaning up against his boyfriend's legs. Connor is passed-out in a full upright sitting position, his head lolling back over the top of the headrest. Vinnie is playing a game on his phone.

'Hey,' he says. 'You ready to go?'

'Yeah,' I say. 'I've got a long day tomorrow. Need to get a good night's sleep.'

Vinnie gets up and hits Connor on the arm. 'Connor. Hey! Wake up, dude.'

Connor opens his eyes.

'Time to go.' Vinnie helps Connor off the couch, but pretty soon it's clear he wasn't really passed-out, just asleep. He lopes along next to us as we head for Vinnie's car. My dad bought it for him after I stole and wrecked his old one. He says I did him a favour, because the Kia my dad got him is actually big enough for him to fit into, but I'm pretty sure he's just being nice. He's never got angry at me in all this time. Not once.

I get in the back seat, and as we head towards my house, the silence stretches.

'So you're really going to do this?' Vinnie finally asks.

'Yep,' I say.

'Dr Kayla—'

'I know what Dr Kayla said.' I keep my voice calm. I will not let anyone sway me from my goal, and I will not give anyone an excuse to call me crazy. I'm doing this because I know it's what I need, for me. Not for Dr Kayla or for Vinnie or Lee or Mom or Dad or Aunt Hannah or Barbie or Lola or anyone else. They don't have to understand.

Vinnie brings the car to a screeching stop in front of my house. I get out of the car and hover next to his window. Maybe I do need him to understand, a little.

'You sure you don't want me to drive you?' he asks.

'She wants to visit a man in prison, not risk death,

Vins,' Connor says.

'Ha ha,' Vinnie says.

'Good point, Connor,' I say. I lean on the window frame. 'This is something I have to do myself. Every thing that I do by myself, every choice I make, that's freedom. I don't want to be free just because they locked him up. I want to be free because I can face him, and then I can walk away again. I could have walked away all those years, but I didn't know it. I know it now. I'm going to go, and then I'm going to come back.' I slap my hands on the window frame.

'Amy, he'll say things,' Vinnie says. 'Whatever he said to you before, stuff you haven't even told us. All that shit he made up about you killing Dee. He'll do anything to hurt you.'

'But he can't hurt me,' I say. 'I know it's true, but I need to prove it to myself. By myself.'

'We're all here for you,' he says. 'Me, Connor, Lee, Kara, Christina, your family.'

'I know,' I say. 'That's why I know I can do it alone.'

Vinnie sighs. 'Not gonna change the lady's mind.' He turns to Connor. 'She rejected all this. Mistake after mistake.'

'Total idiot,' Connor whispers, and then he gives Vinnie a big, sloppy wet kiss.

'See you later!' I call, stepping away from the car.

'Good luck!' Vinnie yells after me.

I wave back at him as I head for the front door. I meant it when I said that my friends and family are the reason I know I can handle this. They have been with me every step of the way for the last two years. There were so many times when things were hard. I had so many breakdowns and so many issues and so much to learn. My dad went back to Colorado, but we talk almost every day now, and we visit each other. I even brought the girls to Colorado to meet Beth and Liam and Beatrice, and it was so much better than I hoped. The kids had a great time together, and that sealed us as one family. Mom is always over at Aunt Hannah's and we're always at Mom's. Things are even good with Jay. He's still frosty with Dad and refuses to even meet Beth, but with me, he's the brother I hoped and prayed I'd have again.

Aunt Hannah has been best of all, though. The change that came over her when she first met the girls stuck. There was a hole in her heart after Dee disappeared, and Lola and Barbie have mostly filled it. I say mostly because I know that one child can never replace another. But now she has two little girls to focus on, girls who aren't about to be grown up and out of the house like Lee.

'Hey,' she says as I walk in the door. She's sitting in the recliner next to the fireplace under a tall lamp, holding a book but not reading it. Her blonde hair is even longer, and you can still barely see the grey.

'Vinnie drove,' I say. 'He wasn't drinking.'

'It's all right,' she says. 'It's graduation. Time to let loose a little.'

'But you had to wait up,' I say. I haven't told her what I plan to do tomorrow. I wonder if Lee let it slip, or maybe she overheard us arguing about it last night. Lee feels the same way as Vinnie. She thinks I should listen to my therapist and all my friends who say it's a bad idea. Like *she* would do what everyone else said.

'I just have a bad feeling, Amy,' Aunt Hannah says. She stays in her chair, and I walk over. 'We've got our lives together over the past two years, and now things are going to change. I'm not good with change any more.' She wipes a tear off her face. I can see that she's been crying for a while now.

'Hey.' I walk behind her and wrap my arms around her neck. 'Nothing's really changing. We have the whole summer. And then I'll be back every weekend.' I turn my face away while I talk, making a futile attempt to hide the beer breath. But she doesn't notice.

'I know,' she says. 'Look at me. I'm being crazy again.'

'No C-word in this house,' I say.

'Lee will be all right, won't she?' Aunt Hannah asks. 'I know you will. You've made it through so much, Amy. But Lee. She's been the rock for me for so long, for all of us these past two years. I worry that when she doesn't have us leaning on her, she'll crack.'

'Lee won't crack,' I say. *She's not like Dee,* I think. *They look alike, and sometimes they talk alike, but they aren't.* 'Lee's strong and she'll always be that way. Trust me.' I kiss Aunt Hannah on the cheek. 'I need to get some sleep. Wake me for breakfast?'

'OK,' she says. 'Love you.'

'Love you, too.'

I lie in bed awake, thinking about what Aunt Hannah

said about Lee. I realize that's what happened to me. When I was with Kyle, I had to be the strong one. I had to be the mom, to take care of the girls and Dee and even Kyle. But once I got home and I was safe, I cracked. I started falling back into my memories, losing time, hiding from life. Back in the cabin, I could never afford to do those things, but when I got away, the dam of crazy just let loose. *No C-word in this house.* But I can't take my own advice. I was crazy. And now I'm finally living in the real world. I hardly ever go back there. It's been half a year since I lost any time. When I see Kyle, will I still be the person I am today, or will I go back to being crazy Amy, or will I go back to being Chelsea? Chelsea was strong, I think. It wasn't so bad to be Chelsea, in the scheme of things. Not when the alternative was being Stacie and cracking with the first blow.

I threw the Stacie doll away. It took a few months to get up the courage, but I did it. One night I went out to the corner where the trash can was waiting for pickup, and I stuffed her in. Not her, it. The doll that Dee had nothing to do with.

These thoughts used to send me back, make me fall into a memory and not come out until the sunrise. But instead, I stare up at the ceiling in my bedroom in Aunt Hannah's house. I don't need to see Kyle to be OK. I know he's behind bars. He pleaded guilty to kidnapping us and raping Dee. I guess it was hard for him to deny when we had two samples of their DNA. He even pleaded guilty to murder, because since Dee died while he was holding her prisoner, it legally doesn't matter how it happened. At first Aunt

Hannah wanted a trial so he would get the death penalty, but finally she agreed not to object to letting him plead. Otherwise he would have claimed he was insane, and I would have had to testify. Maybe even the girls would have had to come to court. I roll over on my side. He still got thirty years to life in prison. If he ever gets out, we'll both be old.

He told everyone who would listen that I murdered her. He said that I picked up that lamp and hit her over the head with it in cold blood, all because I was jealous that he was going to marry her and not me. He even talked to a TV reporter, and it was all over the national news. But nobody who mattered believed him. The autopsy proved she died from hitting her head on something, but they couldn't tell what. Officially, it was a rock in the river, and she died instantly.

I don't need to give him a chance to throw the truth back in my face. But at the same time, the truth is all I have to cling to. Dr Kayla says I have to face it, even if it's only between her and me. Facing the truth is one of the ways I stay here and now. I know that I killed Dee, but I also know that I was protecting myself and the girls, and I never meant to kill her. Dr Kayla says that what you mean matters.

I am strong enough to do this. I have to face him if I want to be truly free.

There are a few other people in the room, sitting at the tables. The tables are grey, the chairs plastic. I expected shouting and crying, but the people mostly talk quietly. This is a medium-security prison. I guess they don't think Kyle is much of a threat to anyone else. He's no criminal mastermind who might plan a daring escape. The people he hurt were only little girls. These bars, these walls are enough to contain him.

One of the guards stands behind me, a short, stocky man wearing a grey uniform with a black tie. There are no guards with any other visitors, but then, I'm special. As a victim, I had to go through a huge process just to get this visit. They acted like no other victim had ever asked, and maybe it's true. Maybe no one is as crazy as me.

'I have to do this,' I say.

'He's not worth it, ma'am,' the guard says.

'No, but she is.' I pull the picture of Dee out of my pocket and hand it to him. It's of her the spring before he took us, eight years ago now. It was the day she got her braces off, and she's smiling big. Her blonde hair floats around her face, and her big blue eyes are shining.

'This is the girl that died?' he asks.

'Yes,' I say.

'This guy doesn't care. Let him rot here, and you go on with your life.' He hands the photo back to me.

Another guard walks through the visiting room door with Kyle. Kyle is thinner. He's finally lost the flabby gut that used to bother him so much. His hair is almost half grey, but it's short. I've never seen him with such short hair before. It makes his tiny head look even smaller, a pinhead on bony but wide shoulders. He's wearing jeans that are too big for him and a grey sweatshirt. He sees me, but he doesn't react. He just stands next to the table.

'Sit down, Parsons,' the guard behind me says.

Kyle sits in the chair. He looks down for a few seconds, and then he looks up. He isn't smiling, and his eyes say nothing. They are brown, but at the same time, they seem grey. Everything about Kyle right now is grey.

I know I look different, too. I've let my hair grow out, and it's down to my shoulders. I've gained a little bit of weight, the result of eating like a normal teenager in a house full of people who love you and never throw away your food. I'm not wearing even a single piece of purple.

'Hi, I'm Amy,' I say.

'I know who you are,' he says. His voice is scratchy, like he needs a drink of water.

'How are you?' I ask. *Why am I asking that?* I think. It just seems like something that you say. As if we're two normal people who ran into each other on the street.

'They took away my dolls,' he says. 'I had to make them myself out of my socks, but they took them.' His eyes are wet.

'Oh.' I don't know where my voice went. There were so many things I wanted to say. About Dee, about me, about the girls, about who we are without him. But this person in front of me is worried about dolls made of socks. After so many years with him, his obsession had almost stopped being bizarre. Now I'm not sure what to do with it.

Someone on the far side of the room raises his voice. His female visitor yells something back about him not paying his child support. She tells him she needs money and she knows he has it. But I don't expect Kyle to provide for his children. There's nothing I actually have to ask of him.

'How are the girls?' Kyle asks. His eyes sharpen. His hands are handcuffed together, but he lifts them and sets them on the table. He leans in.

'They're doing really well,' I say. 'Lola just finished second grade. All As, every report card. She's doing soccer this summer. You should see her run. And Barbie was in kindergarten. She's a real little artist. She likes trees, and water. Most kids like to draw people and animals, but not Barbie. She likes plants.' The words spill out of me. I shouldn't give him anything, but I can't stop. I talk about them whenever anyone asks. I'm so proud.

'Do they know where I am?' he asks.

'Yes.' I look into his eyes. 'I told them you hurt their mommy, and so you had to go away. I don't know if they quite understand everything.'

'They will,' he says. He meets my gaze.

'When it's time, we'll have that conversation,' I say. They already understand more than he knows. Neither of them has said a word about the night Dee died, not since we had that talk in the back of the police car almost two years ago. I know they haven't forgotten, though. Seeing your mother get beaten to death is not something you forget. But they know that what you mean matters, just like Dr Kayla says.

'You can't change the truth,' he says. 'You may be the

285

perfect pretty little girl, the one who looks good in pictures that everyone can sob over, but you did it.' He leans over the table. 'You killed her.'

'Keep back,' the guard says.

Kyle pulls away, just a little.

I pull Dee's picture out of my pocket and set it on the table between us. 'This is Dee,' I say. 'You never met her. The second you grabbed her arm that day by the river, she was gone. But this was my cousin, my best friend. This is the girl you raped and killed. You didn't know her.'

'I loved her,' Kyle says. Tears sparkle in his eyes. 'I never killed her. I never would have.'

'But you did,' I say.

'*You* did,' he says. He picks up the picture in one hand and lifts both his shackled hands up to his face. 'She was beautiful, wasn't she? So perfect.'

'No, she wasn't. She was too quick to laugh. She talked too much. She didn't understand people. She could be jealous and petty. But she was a lot of fun. She liked to go out in nature and ride her bike and roller-skate and play games and be silly. She liked to eat Red Vines in bed and stay up all night talking. She didn't like to read books. She was always pulling me away, making me go down to the river with her. She wanted six children someday, but that was supposed to happen when she was grown up. That girl cried when she got her period for the first time.'

Kyle sets the picture down.

'Dee was not a doll,' I say. 'She was Dee. You saw how scared she was that first day, and you saw how she changed

286

after you raped her. You saw her break down and die inside, long before she attacked us. If you had never kidnapped us, she would still be alive. Her.' I push the picture back towards him.

'I wish I had killed you the first night,' he says. 'I never wanted two girls. If you hadn't been there, she would be alive. We'd be married now. The girls would have their parents. You're the reason the whole thing went wrong.'

'I'm glad I was there to save the girls,' I say. 'They're what matter now. They'll live long, happy lives with people who love them. People who treat them like precious children and not dolls. You will never see them again.'

Kyle pulls the picture of Dee towards him. 'I'm keeping this,' he says.

'Nope.' The guard comes around the table and holds out his hand.

Kyle shakes his head, but then drops the picture. The guard hands it back to me. I put it in my pocket. I have this picture on my computer. This one little print doesn't matter at all. But it's physical, a real thing to hold on to. It's something I have that Kyle doesn't.

I stand up. 'You're right,' I say. 'I'm the reason everything went wrong for you. I'm the one who got us out and sent you to prison. I hope you remember that, every minute of every day.' I turn around and head for the door. I move so quickly that I have to wait for the guard to catch up to let me through. I don't look behind me at Kyle. I don't want to know what he's doing back there, if he's upset, if he's angry, if he's just grey.

But his voice carries through the air. 'I have a right to my possessions,' I hear him say. 'They were my socks.'

As I walk out of the dark, gloomy prison into the blissfully sunny parking lot, I realize that I never saw Kyle smile. That clown face that used to scare me so much was gone. It's not until I've been driving for an hour that I realize the biggest thing. I am still in the here and now. Seeing Kyle didn't change that. He didn't send me back in time or make me crazy. My visit didn't change Kyle's mind. It didn't make him suddenly realize that Dee's death is his fault or make him sorry or turn him into a man worthy of being the dad to two brilliant, perfect little girls. But it proved that he no longer has power over me, and that is exactly what it was supposed to prove.

I let a couple of tears fall, but only a couple. They are mostly tears of happiness, and relief. I, Amy MacArthur, am still here. There's only one more thing I have to do.

29.

I park at the closed up old gas station, where the sign still reads $1.56. I'm there a little bit early, so I sit on the hood of Aunt Hannah's old Honda station wagon and watch the cars going by. Nobody stops or even seems to look my way. I wonder what would have happened to me if that lady hadn't decided to stop, if she hadn't agreed to drive me to the bus station and given me money. How far down the road would I have walked? Would I have given up at some point and decided that my only choice was to walk back up the hill again? Would he have let me come back? Would he have killed me?

What if I hadn't cut our adventure on the river short that day, and we had waded back the way we came? Would we have got on our bikes and ridden off? Would Kyle have kept following Dee, or would he eventually have given up, or found another little girl to be obsessed with?

What if I had hit Dee on the shoulders and not on the head? She might be alive, and we all might be up there to this day. Or I might have got the girls away, and the police might have caught Kyle, and Dee might be standing here right now. Or Dee might have got to one of the girls, and then . . . I think about my last session with Dr Kayla.

'We do things the best we can, Amy. Nobody's life turns out perfect, and nobody gets to do it over. I don't know if you made any mistakes or not, but if you did, all you can do is learn from them.'

'Don't hit somebody on the head when you could hit them on the shoulders, or on the stomach.'

'I don't know, Amy. I wasn't there. But you are here, and so are Lola and Barbie. All three of you are here because you took action. You have to give yourself credit for that.'

I didn't answer her. I will never give myself credit. I will never believe that I did the right thing by killing Dee, but I know that Dr Kayla is right about one thing: the girls are here. Nobody will ever hit them or pull their hair or hurt them in any way as long as I can take action. As long as I'm *here*.

After a few more minutes, I see Vinnie's car coming down the road. As he gets closer, I see that he has Lee in the front seat with him. That's exactly what I expected. But they also have Jay in the back seat, and behind them, Mom is driving her car with Aunt Hannah in the passenger seat and Lola and Barbie in the back.

As they all get out of their respective cars, I wait for Mom and Aunt Hannah to let me have it, but they don't. Instead, Mom gives me a big hug.

'Are you all right?' she asks.

'I'm fine,' I say.

She shakes her head but says nothing, just pulls me in tighter.

They all look at each other, and at the girls, and I know that I'm safe for now. No one is going to ask me for the details with them standing there. Instead, we all climb into the cars and begin the drive up the paved road.

We stand on the riverbank. I stand the closest to Dee's grave, to the cross made of two flat sticks that thrusts crookedly from the ground. Dee's body isn't there any more. There are rules and regulations, and Aunt Hannah had her moved to a family plot. But the cross is still there, and there's also a plaque. It doesn't say anything except her name: Dee Alicia Springfield. I hold the girls close to me, and they fidget. They're like she was – they'd rather be running around or wading in the river than standing here in silence.

Aunt Hannah stares into the water, and Lee leans on her shoulder. Mom and Jay stand a little way away. I guess they're all thinking about Dee, the way they knew her. Aunt Hannah and Lee must be thinking about how she would talk and talk, and about the way she laughed when she was happy and cried when she was sad and was all about experiencing everything.

Now that so much time has passed, she is more often the Dee that I think of, too.

Vinnie, who's been standing alone on the other side of Dee's grave, walks over to me. He reaches out a hand, and I take it.

'There's still a lot you haven't told us, isn't there?' he asks.

'All that matters is that we're here,' I say. I pull the girls close.

'Uncle Vinnie, can you swim?' Lola asks.

'Sure, kid,' he says. 'I swim like a dolphin.'

'What's a dolphin?'

'It's a . . . an animal that swims,' he says.

'So it's a fish?' Lola asks.

'Not exactly. How about we go to the library, and I show you a picture? And we can read all about them?'

'OK,' Lola says. 'I want to learn how to swim.'

'Me too!' says Barbie.

'Swimming lessons for everyone,' I say. 'Your mom and I took lessons together when we were your age.'

'Mommy Chel, is she still up there?' Barbie asks.

'She's at peace,' I say.

'She doesn't have to yell any more,' Lola says. 'Right? She's not sad?' She looks up at me with the big blue eyes that are copies of Dee's, those eyes that are so full of understanding beyond her years.

'That's right,' I say. 'She's happy now.' I look over at Vinnie. I hope he doesn't repeat what he just heard. I've never told anyone what Stacie was like, and I don't think the girls have talked about it before. There are some things that are only for the three of us.

Vinnie is tearing up, but I can see that he understands.

'Dee would be so proud of you girls,' he says. 'I mean Stacie, your mom.'

Barbie is crying.

'It's OK,' Lola says. She takes her little sister's hand. 'She's not sad any more.'

Vinnie wipes a tear away and puts his arm around me.

I hug both the girls at once. They know what happened, but it doesn't matter any more. All that matters is how we live our lives now.

The water rushes by, on and on the same today as yesterday, and the same yesterday as before we ever came here. I picture Kyle on the riverbank, wet and crying over Dee's dead body, her blue eyes open to the sky. I picture Dee sitting on the sandbar, telling me about how she got her period. I go back before that, to another day, when we waded in the river and talked and laughed and then went home again and slept in our own beds. Any of these things could have happened, or not.

Someday, I will tell them all the truth. They have supported me through everything, and they will probably support me in this. But for now, I want them to remember Dee the way she was. I want them to think of this girl in the picture, the one who is smiling, with her blonde hair floating around her face and her bright blue eyes shining. She was our cousin, our sister, our daughter, our friend.

She was a good person, full of love and full of life. She became the mother to two precious, brilliant, beautiful children. She was loved.

MARY G. THOMPSON was raised in Cottage Grove and Eugene, Oregon. She was a practising attorney for more than seven years, including almost five years in the US Navy, and is now a law librarian in Washington, DC. She received her BA from Boston University, her JD from the University of Oregon, and her MFA in writing for children from The New School.